JD Kirk is a multi-million-copy bestselling author and the pen name of award-winning writer Barry Hutchison.

He has authored over 150 books for children and adults, and is now thoroughly enjoying murdering people as JD Kirk. He resides in the Scottish Highlands with his wife and two children. He has no idea what the JD stands for.

JD KIRK

THE WOMAN DOWNSTAIRS

bookouture

BOOKOUTURE

First published in 2025 by Bookouture, an imprint of Storyfire Ltd.
This paperback edition published in 2026

1

Copyright © JD Kirk 2025

A CIP catalogue record for this book
is available from the British Library.

PB ISBN 978-1-83618-764-6
EB ISBN 978-1-83618-783-7

Printed and bound in Great Britain by
Clays Ltd, Elcograf S.p.A.

Papers used by Bookouture are from well-managed forests
and other responsible sources.

Bookouture
An imprint of Storyfire Ltd.
Carmelite House
50 Victoria Embankment
London EC4Y 0DZ

An Hachette UK Company

The authorised representative in the EEA is Hachette Ireland
8 Castlecourt Centre
Dublin 15 D15 XTP3
Ireland
(email: info@hbgi.ie)

www.hachette.co.uk
www.bookouture.com

For Chrissie Parker, without whom I'd never get any work done.

PROLOGUE

I should get the hell out of here. I should leave. This is…

This is…

I don't know what this is. It isn't something I was prepared for. How could I have been?

I need to regroup, rethink. But my curiosity has other ideas. Rather than head for the exit, I inch on through to the living room. I'm braced for it this time, but the shock of it still hits me like a cold hand on my suddenly too-warm back.

The walls, the flooring, the throws on the couches. They're all the same as mine. Identical. It's more than that, though. It's worse.

In my flat, there's a picture on the wall across from the door. It's a stupid illustration of a Highland cow I picked up at a shop on Princes Street, just to make the flat feel a bit more homely.

It's here, too. Same picture. Same frame. Same spot on the wall.

My eyes creep to the other pictures. Cheap prints picked up around Edinburgh. They're all the same as mine. I remember buying all of them.

A few of them are slightly blurry and less defined, and I realise that she's taken photographs of my artwork and printed them out on sheets of plain paper.

I feel as if I'm looking at a work in progress of someone taking over my life. Becoming me.

It's all too much. It's too messed up. I am suddenly filled with the sense that I should not be in this place. I need to leave. I need to get out of here, get back to my flat, figure out what the hell all this means.

And I'm about to. I really am.

But that's when I see it.

That's when I see the knife.

It sits on the draining board in the small kitchen tucked away off the living room. The kitchen cabinets are the same as mine, too, but then I think they always were.

Weren't they? Surely, she wouldn't have gone that far?

I creep closer to the sink. The blinds are closed on the window behind it, but I can see a little gap between two of them, one side slightly raised where she's been peeking out. Watching me.

The knife is a standard kitchen knife. Six inches long, maybe, with a straight back and a curved blade.

There's blood. It beads on the polished steel. Clings to the curve. Dots the scuffed metal of the draining board below it.

What is this?

What has she done?

And just what the hell is she actually capable of?

I thought I knew her. I thought I had a handle on all of this. But I suddenly get the sense that I am floundering, far out of my depth, miles and miles from shore.

I shouldn't have come here.

I should have stayed away.

CHAPTER 1

Diane

The blade moves through the skin and the flesh with sickening ease. A smooth, sharp slice, so quick I don't even notice it until the line of blood appears a half second later.

'Ooh, ow, ow, ow!' I yelp, dropping the knife and sticking the tip of my injured finger in my mouth.

I dance around the kitchen, not daring to look at the wound yet. The pain has started to rear its head, though. Damage has definitely been done.

The carrot I was chopping sits there on the cutting board, like it's taunting me. Mocking me. This is diet attempt number… what are we on now? Seventeen? Eighteen? I've lost count, much like I've lost the same stone and a half about twelve times over.

'Come on, Diane,' I mutter around a mouthful of finger. 'Get a grip.'

I steel myself, pull the digit out and take a look. My natural pessimism means I fully expected the whole tip to be hanging off, but it's not too bad. Still bleeding, but not enough to need stitches.

Sure enough, it stops when I wrap a bit of kitchen towel around it and press down. Just as well, given that I've got no idea where the first aid kit is. Or, for that matter, if I even have one.

Just because the bleeding has stopped, though, it doesn't mean I'm ready to forgive the carrot. These things are meant to be better for me than my usual microwave meals and takeaways, and yet I've never come to physical harm eating a bucket of chicken nuggets.

My arteries might beg to differ, of course.

Speaking of health matters…

I check my medicine box. Sure enough, Wednesday's container is still full. I swill a glass under the kitchen tap, then wash down half a dozen vitamins and tablets with several big gulps of water.

The pills used to be easier to swallow, but they stick in my throat more and more.

I'm thinking about skipping dinner altogether and just having a large glass of 'sod the diet' instead, when something catches my eye through the window.

It's a girl. Well, a young woman, with blonde hair and a tight crop top that shows off a stomach so flat I catch myself sucking in my own podgy belly to avoid immediately sinking into depression.

It's after six on a mid-October evening in Scotland, and the streetlights have already flickered on. They cast her in a sort of hazy orange spotlight, revealing denim shorts cut so high that the curve of her bum cheeks peeks out beneath the frayed edges. I stare at them, marvel at them. It's been a long time since I've paid attention to my own arse, but it's a safe bet that it never looked like that.

It's also far too bloody cold to be dressed like that at this time of night. She's a good ten to fifteen years younger than me, which puts her at early to mid-twenties. Old enough to know about jackets, certainly.

I watch her strutting up and down the pavement outside my flat like it's a catwalk in Milan. She's not supermodel stunning, though, more Instagram pretty. The sort of girl who'd get a million followers on TikTok just by wearing an oversized shirt and biting her lip for the camera.

There's probably a hundred thousand young men falling in love with her somewhere right now.

Probably a few of the dirty buggers doing other things, too.

I lean closer to the window and mutter out a couple of colourful expletives as my hip collides with the corner of the counter.

The woman is still pacing back and forth, checking her phone every few seconds, then glancing up and down the street. She's waiting for someone. Looking for someone.

'Oh my God!' I eject.

I know what this is! I suddenly realise what she's up to. I'm not daft. I've watched enough *NCIS* and *CSI* to know exactly what's going on here.

Well, she can forget it. Not on my street. Not right outside my windows.

I live a relatively quiet life and keep myself to myself. I get up, go to my job in the call centre, then come home and watch telly. Nice and simple. Maybe the occasional takeaway to spice things up a bit, but I can't be doing with too much excitement.

And I definitely can't be doing with the comings and goings of Edinburgh's working girls and their clients, thank you very much!

My mum and dad come round to visit every month. My mum's quite religious these days, and my dad's heart isn't what it used to be. If this whole street turns into a hotbed of hookers and drug dealers, there's no saying what it'd do to him.

No. This isn't happening. Not on my street. Not on my watch!

I should phone the police. That would be the sensible thing to do. But considering it took them two days to come see Carol at work after she was mugged on the walk home, I doubt they'll come rushing over to deal with this.

No, if this is getting sorted, I need to deal with it myself.

I hurry along my short, cluttered hallway, unfasten the security chain, and step out of my flat and onto the cold stone of the tenement close.

When I heave open the heavy communal front door and step outside, the girl turns to face me, backlit by the street lamp, her silhouette a slender hourglass against the deepening blue of the evening sky.

'Um, excuse me,' I say, summoning my most authoritative tone. Even I can hear that it falls some way short, though.

The woman blinks her big blue eyes. A flicker of surprise. She has a bruise on her cheek that is blooming in blacks and purples across her left eye socket. My first thought is that some client must've lost his temper. Or her pimp, maybe, if *CSI: Miami* is to be believed about such things.

My second thought is *poor lassie*.

She can't be much older than twenty. How the hell did she end up here, doing this?

'Yeah? Hello! Hi.' Her accent isn't what I expected. It's local. Soft. Educated. Not as perky as her... other assets, but not far off.

I'd come up with a speech on my way from the kitchen, but now that I'm face to face with her, I find it evaporating like an Edinburgh morning mist on those rare days that the sun shows its face.

How exactly are you meant to politely suggest to someone that they might want to go tout for punters somewhere else? What if she refuses? What if she freaks out and stabs me in the neck? I've already had one knife injury today, I could do without a second.

I'll give you that she doesn't look like the murdering sort, but then you don't know, do you? People can surprise you. Or disappoint you, I suppose.

I'm encouraged by the fact that, given the skimpiness of her outfit, she doesn't have a lot of places to conceal a blade. At least, nowhere with easy access.

'I, um, I don't think... that is... this isn't really the sort of area where people, you know... wait for... business opportunities.'

It's largely a word salad, but I nod and fold my arms, like I've successfully made my point.

Her eyebrows draw together in confusion. She really is very pretty.

'Sorry?' she says. There's a puzzled little smile on her pink-tinted lips that shows off a shiny canine tooth. It's a little too large. A tiny imperfection that somehow only serves to heighten all the good bits.

'You know. *Clients*,' I whisper, giving her a meaningful look. 'You might have more luck up near Leith Walk. Or, you know, somewhere less' – I gesture vaguely around at the leafy street, searching for a descriptor that doesn't make me sound too much like a judgemental snob. I settle on – 'residential.'

For a moment, she stares at me blankly. Then her eyes widen, and her mouth forms a perfect 'O'.

'Oh my God,' she says. 'You think I'm a…?' She glances down at her outfit, comprehension dawning.

The laugh that escapes her seems genuine enough to make me doubt my conclusion. Heat creeps up the back of my neck, spreading across my cheeks in what I'm sure is a rather fetching shade of mortified crimson.

'I'm just waiting for my delivery,' she explains, holding up her phone screen to show me a tracking app. 'Removal van. It was supposed to be here twenty minutes ago.'

'Delivery?' I repeat dumbly.

'Yeah. For my stuff.'

'Your… stuff?'

I turn and shoot a look at the basement flat directly beneath mine. It's in darkness. But then, of course it is. It has been ever since the last tenant moved out last month.

Suddenly, that creeping heat becomes burning embarrassment. I quietly pray for the ground to open up beneath me and swallow me whole, but if there are any gods listening, they're clearly enjoying my humiliation too much to intervene.

The sound of a diesel engine rounds the corner. A white van pulls up, panel sides emblazoned with *Speedy Movers: We'll Get There Before You Do*.

I hope, for their sake, that's not a money-back guarantee.

A lanky man in his forties jumps out of the driver's side, clipboard in hand. 'Sorry we're late, love. Traffic was a bastard on the bridges.'

'No worries,' the girl says, shooting me a smile that's far less smug than it has a right to be. 'This nice lady's been keeping me company.'

'Oh, right.' The man nods at me. 'You here to help with the heavy lifting, aye?'

Given how things have gone so far, it's a miracle I don't blurt out, 'No, I actually thought she was a prostitute.' Instead, I just smile vacantly at the driver as he heads to the back of the van and opens the doors.

From the corner of my eye, I catch the young woman staring down at the darkened basement flat. She shivers. I don't think it's because of the cold.

She brightens when she clocks me watching, her smile returning like she's flicked a switch. Even with the bruise staining her skin, she's depressingly radiant.

'I'm Chloe,' she announces, thrusting out a hand for me to shake. 'I'm your new downstairs neighbour.'

CHAPTER 2

Diane

The basement flat smells riddled with damp and misery. It's bloody freezing in here, too. The sort of cold that seeps into your bones and makes them ache. I exhale, trying to see if my breath makes clouds, while Chloe fumbles with the light switch.

'Sorry,' she says when the bulb finally splutters into life. 'Sarah said it might be a bit chilly. The heating's been off for a couple of weeks.'

The light doesn't reveal any breath clouds. I'm oddly disappointed.

'Sarah?'

'My friend. It's her flat,' Chloe explains. She runs her hands vigorously up and down her arms, smoothing away the goosebumps. 'She's letting me use it.'

'Ah, right,' I say.

The owner of the basement flat has always been a bit of a mystery to the rest of us. It's been rented out to a succession of tenants – at least four or five different ones over the three years I've lived in the ground-floor apartment – most of whom have been varying degrees of unpleasant.

Sarah, though. Never heard of her.

Chloe's feet crunch on the pile of mail that's accumulated behind the door. She scoops it up, scanning through it with a slightly anxious expression, like she's dreading what she might find.

'Looking for something?' I ask.

She shakes her head. 'Just seeing if there's anything for me.'

'You live here before?'

'What? No,' she says, confused by the question. 'First time.'

I'm about to point out it'd be pretty quick to have received post already, but Chloe has disappeared into the kitchen with the bundle of letters. She returns a moment later, rubbing her hands together and blowing on them.

The removal guy scoots past us, a large cardboard box in his arms. 'Where d'you want this one?'

'Um...' Chloe peers into the empty living room. I know it's the living room because, beyond the position of the front door, the layout is exactly the same as my flat directly above. The only difference is, mine has furniture in it, and doesn't look like it was decorated during a period of post-war austerity. 'Just stick it down anywhere for now. I'll sort it all later.'

I could easily slip back up to my flat. I desperately want to, in fact, but it feels rude to just leave her without a good reason, especially given how I'd earlier mistaken her for a lady of the night. My face heats up at the memory. It's the only source of warmth in the place.

'Let me help,' I suggest, following the delivery man up the half-dozen steps to the pavement and collecting one of the smaller boxes from the back of the van.

There's no weight to it. I almost scream when I see the eye staring up at me through a gap in the top. It's blank and glassy, the eye of a porcelain doll. It's a creepy-looking thing. I'm relieved I didn't drop it in fright. I've had enough mortifying moments in front of Chloe for one night.

It only takes about twenty minutes for the removal guys to get everything inside. There's not a lot. A few boxes, two holdalls, and a collection of furniture that wouldn't look out of place in one of those pokey little Stockbridge antique shops, where the staff watch you like hawks and the window displays haven't been changed in a decade.

The sofa's a particularly dire specimen, all dark stains and fraying fabric. The black metal frame of the bed looks like it belongs in a Soviet prison, and the dining chairs don't match the table. Or each other, for that matter.

'Home sweet home,' Chloe says with a smile that doesn't quite reach her eyes.

I could have called Ronan to come help with the move. He only lives across town, and he tends to come racing over when I text him.

He'd think it was for a booty call, though, which is why I didn't. The last thing I need is him getting an eyeful of Chloe in her short shorts and crop top. He'd be immediately smitten. I wouldn't get a look in. And I probably wouldn't even blame him.

The removal guys wrap up the job, lingering longer than strictly necessary, as if hoping Chloe might offer a tip. When none is forthcoming, they troop out, leaving us alone in the grimy flat.

'Thanks so much for your help,' Chloe says. 'I appreciate it.'

There's a sincerity in the way she says it that makes me think she genuinely does.

'No problem,' I tell her. I open my mouth to start making an excuse to leave, but she jumps in before I get a chance.

'Do you want a drink?'

I should really head back upstairs. I've got literal *months* of reality TV shows stacked up that aren't going to watch themselves.

It's not a great excuse, though, so I grab desperately for another one.

'I can't. I need to feed my cat.'

'Oh.' She looks disappointed, but then her spirits lift. 'You've got a cat? That's cool! What's she called?'

'He,' I correct. 'His name's Cowboy Meowboy.'

She laughs at that. It's not the delicate series of musical notes I'd expected. It's a good, proper laugh, with a snort somewhere in the middle.

'Quality name,' she tells me.

'I thank you,' I say, bowing my head, and I'm pleased with myself for having come up with it.

She reaches into a box and pulls out two bottles of wine, one red, one white.

My eyes creep up to the ceiling, linger there for a moment, and then drop back to the Malbec.

'Ah, bugger it,' I say. 'He can wait.'

While Chloe hunts through the boxes for glasses, I sink down onto the sofa, trying not to wince at the sound of springs creaking beneath me. The fabric feels rough and slightly damp against the back of my legs. I'm already regretting my decision to stay, but it's too late to change my mind now without looking unfriendly.

I try some small talk to take my mind off all the tiny organisms that might be writhing in the cushion beneath me.

'So,' I begin. 'What brings you here? To the flat, I mean? You a student, or…?'

I can't think of a natural ending to the question, so I just leave it hanging.

Chloe pauses in her search, her shoulders tensing. She takes a breath before answering.

'No. I just… I needed to get away.'

'Oh. Right. Aye.' I can't stop myself from asking the next question, even though it makes me sound like a right nosy cow. 'From what?'

She hesitates again before answering. Even longer this time.

'My ex.'

She gives up searching for wine glasses and settles on a couple of chipped mugs, which she brings over along with the bottle. The corkscrew is much easier for her to find. She pulls it out of a small handbag, and I'm slightly concerned by how long her gaze lingers on the pointy bit.

All her focus goes on the ritual of inserting the point into the cork, as if postponing the moment that she has to elaborate on her last remark.

I almost tell her that she doesn't have to say any more. That it's none of my business.

But I don't. My enquiring nose would never forgive me.

'He wasn't a nice person,' she finally adds, her voice smaller than before.

The penny drops. That black eye. The nervous glances she's making at the window whenever a car comes past. The way she seems to startle at every sound.

'Got a bit handsy, did he?' I ask. I'm trying for casual, but the question sounds clumsy as it tumbles out of my mouth.

She nods, pouring the wine with slightly shaky hands. 'You could say that.'

'I'm sorry.'

There's no hesitation now. If she was holding back before, she isn't any longer.

'He's into all that Andrew Tate bullshit,' she continues, handing me a mug of wine that's filled almost to the brim. 'Thinks women should "know their place". Wants to control everything – what I wear, who I talk to, where I go. He'd go through my phone, check my messages. That sort of stuff.'

She takes a hefty gulp of her own wine. 'When I told him I was leaving him, he said I was his property and I'd leave when he said I could.'

'Christ,' I mutter. 'He sounds like an arsehole.'

She smiles at that, but it's a fleeting thing, there one moment, gone the next.

'I left while he was at work. Just grabbed what I could and ran.'

I look around at the furniture. Did she grab that? It was one thing to shove her stuff in a few boxes and bags and flee into the night, but I'd imagine he'd have something to say about his couch being taken.

Then again, after sitting on it for a few minutes, I'd be happy to see the back of the bloody thing.

I steal a glance at her face. The bruise seems darker in this light, spreading out from her eye like an ink stain on wet paper.

'Did he do that to your face?'

Her hand flutters up to touch the bruise. 'Yeah,' she confirms in a voice so quiet I barely hear it. 'That's when I knew I had to get out.'

'You've reported him to the police, right?'

She lets out a bitter laugh. 'What's the point? They never do anything. Besides, he's... connected.'

The way she says 'connected' makes me think she doesn't mean he's been working to grow his following on LinkedIn.

'And your friend said you could stay here?' I ask, raising the mug to my lips. The wine is surprisingly good. Much better than the cheap plonk I usually buy for myself.

'Sarah. Yeah. She owns this place. We've known each other online for a while. She lives in London now. When I told her what was happening, she said I could stay here for a bit, rent free.'

My eyes go wide at that, and I almost choke on my wine. 'Rent free? In Edinburgh? You've struck it lucky there!'

Once again, I want the world to open up beneath me.

'You know, apart from the whole fleeing an abusive relationship thing,' I add. 'Obviously.'

The smile she shoots me is sympathetic. Kindly. She knows I put my foot in it, but she's not holding a grudge.

'I told her I'd decorate,' she explains, as if keen to impress on me that she's not a freeloader. As if my opinion matters to her. 'The place could do with brightening up.'

Her eyes dart to the window, her whole body tensing as a car pulls up at the junction outside. We sit there, breath held, listening to the engine. Then the headlights cast long, shifting shadows across the living room wall as the car pulls away again.

'He doesn't know where you are, right?' I ask.

She shakes her head, but doesn't look convinced. 'I don't think so. But he's…'

'Connected,' I say when she doesn't finish.

She nods. 'And persistent.'

We sip our wine in silence. The cold is starting to seep through my clothes, and I suppress a shiver. I can't imagine spending the night in here without the heating.

'Are you staying here tonight?' I ask.

'Yeah. I'll be fine. Just need to unpack my duvet and stuff.'

'And sort the heating?'

She nods, glancing around the flat. 'I'm sure it'll warm up once I figure out the boiler.'

She suddenly stands, moving to the door and checking the locks. She twists the deadbolt, then tugs the handle as if testing its security.

Or locking me in.

'You can always come up to mine if it gets too cold,' I offer. 'The sofa pulls out. It's not much, but it's warm. Warmer than this, anyway.'

Chloe gives me a grateful smile. Her eyes fix on me, shimmering, like she's staring into my soul and seeing something in there more beautiful than I have ever given myself credit for.

Or maybe she's just trying to think of a way to say no.

'Wow. Thanks. That's *so unbelievably* kind of you, but I'll be fine,' she says, and I get the impression she's fighting back tears. 'I can't believe how nice you've been. Nobody's ever that nice to me.'

I stop short of pointing out that she's been given free access to a flat that would reach at least fifteen hundred quid on the open market, and instead just drain my mug and swallow back the urge to belch.

'Shall we swap numbers, at least?' I suggest. 'In case you need anything?'

I'm only fifteen years or so her senior, but she seems so young, so perky, so *alive* that I half expect a, 'Nah, you're alright, grandma.' Instead, she seems positively giddy at the idea.

We exchange phones, and I tap my number into hers. As I hand it back, a notification flashes up on her screen. Her face drains of colour, and her hands start to tremble.

'Everything OK?' I ask.

'Yeah, fine,' she says quickly, sliding the phone into her pocket without looking at the message. 'Just spam.'

She doesn't meet my eyes. Right then, I'm not sure she could, even if she wanted to.

I finish my wine and get to my feet. 'I should get back upstairs. Let you get settled in.'

'Of course,' she says, following me to the door. 'Thanks again for your help. And the company.'

'Anytime. Just give me a shout if you need anything. Even if it's just to borrow a cup of sugar, or whatever.'

'Or to see your pussy,' she says.

I make a noise. I've got no idea how to describe it other than that. It's not a noise I'm particularly proud of, but it brings a smile to her face.

'Cowboy Meowboy,' she says, and I let out a breath that got trapped in my chest.

'Right! Yes! The cat!' I say a little too loudly.

Unlike mine, her front door opens straight into the fresh air. I step out onto the tiny square of patio. It somehow feels warmer than the flat, although that might just be my latest flush of embarrassment talking.

Chloe leans against the doorframe, her slender form looking oddly vulnerable in the dim evening light.

'Uh, so… See you around, then,' I say.

She grabs for my wrist. Grips it, her fingers locking together, holding me in place. She's stronger than she looks.

'I've got a feeling we're going to be great friends, Diane,' she tells me.

Something about the breathless way she says it makes the hairs on the back of my neck stand up. But before I can respond, she releases her grip, closes the door, and I hear the deadbolt slide firmly into place.

It's only when I'm back up the stairs and in my own flat that I'm able to shake the feeling that she's somehow still watching me.

CHAPTER 3

Diane

I shouldn't text Ronan. Not at this time of night. Not on a weekday. I should just sprawl here on the sofa, shovelling junk food into my face and watching shite telly. It's a routine that's become so common I've come to think of it simply as 'Weeknights'.

My thumbs ignore all that and type out a message. It's short and simple.

Hey! U up?

It whooshes off into the digital ether. I'm not proud of the message, or of sending it. It's only recently, following some merciless ribbing from a few people at work, that I've given in to 'text speak'. Shortening full words into single letters is painful, but I'm getting the hang of it.

If they want to take away my punctuation, though, they'll have to prise it from my cold, dead fingers.

I lie there, slouched on the couch, phone in hand, staring at the screen. The notification under the message says it has been delivered but not yet read. If he sees it, he'll know what I'm hinting at and be round here in fifteen minutes flat.

There's no response, though. The message remains unread. I'm not worried, not really. It's late, and he's probably asleep. Or out.

Or with someone else. Our situation is more of an arrangement than a relationship these days, so I shouldn't care either way.

But I do, just a bit.

With a sigh, I toss the phone onto the cushion beside me and reach for the remote. The telly flickers to life, bathing the living room in its blue glow. It's getting late, and I should probably go to bed, but going to bed means I'm one step closer to having to get up for work in the morning, and I'm keen to put that off for as long as possible.

And so I shuffle to the kitchen and rummage in the freezer until I find a French bread pizza. I have to dust off the ice crystals that have formed between the clumps of grated cheese, and I daren't check the date in case it's well past it. If I know it's out of date, I won't eat it. If I don't look, though, it'll be fine.

I stick it in the microwave and close the door with a plasticky *bang*. There are a dozen buttons on the display, offering a plethora of cooking, reheating and defrosting options, which I have never bothered to investigate.

Instead, I blast it on full power for four minutes, while I take a plate from the dishwasher and give it a wipe with a mostly clean tea towel.

When the microwave pings, I take out the pizza and recoil when I see how soggy and unappetising it looks. The bread base is slightly mushy at the ends, and the whole thing sags in the middle like an old mattress with burst springs.

I convince myself it'll taste better than it looks, and while it does, it's a close-run thing. The base is soggy, the sauce is bland, and the cheese appears to be fashioned from some sort of inedible plastic.

I eat it anyway. Food is food, after all, and this diet attempt has already bitten the dust.

Monday. I'll start again on Monday.

I settle back on the sofa and scroll through some of the trashier telly channels, before settling on *Dr Pimple Popper*, which is exactly as disgusting as it sounds. More so, if anything.

I've seen this episode before, but it's strangely comforting in its familiarity. As I watch, and despite my best efforts to keep them open, my eyelids grow heavy.

'No, no,' I say out loud, shuffling into a more upright position. Suddenly, I'm ten years old, and it's Sunday night, just after bathtime, with school looming like some cancerous growth on the horizon.

I'm not going to sleep.

Not yet.

I refuse.

'Waaargh?'

A noise jolts me awake. The uneaten half of my pizza leaps up from my lap and lands, face down, on my thigh. I can feel it through my thin pyjama bottoms.

Cold.

For a moment, I lie there, disorientated, trying to figure out just what the hell is going on. I have my suspicions, of course. The string of drool on my chin certainly points to one obvious conclusion.

'Damn it,' I whisper.

The telly's still on, but it's a different show now, the little Johnstons having given way to an *I Am Jazz* marathon I would normally be one hundred per cent on board for.

The flat is dark, save for the TV's flickering light.

I was asleep. I must've nodded off, despite my best efforts.

So, what woke me up?

I hear it again then. Shouting. Hammering. Coming from outside, from down below.

I fumble for my phone. The screen says 2:07 a.m.

'What the hell?' I mutter, dragging myself off the sofa and moving to the window.

Down in the tiny stone garden of the basement flat, a man is pounding on Chloe's door. Even from here, I can see he's built like a brick shithouse, muscles straining against the fabric of his T-shirt despite the October chill.

'Open the fucking door, Chloe!' he yells, each word punctuated by another blow to the wood. 'I know you're in there!'

This has to be the ex. The one who's 'connected'. The one who gave Chloe that bruise that's blooming across her face like a crop of deadly nightshade.

'Get out here, now!' he roars. 'I want to talk to you!'

His voice is like a punch to the chest. I've heard a voice just like it before – that barely contained rage that threatens to bubble over into explosive violence.

I think of my new neighbour's black eye. I think of bruises I've had myself over the years. Open-hand slaps. Tightly clenched fists.

There's an old cigarette burn on my back that I can only see in the mirror. Not that I look.

It took a real effort for me to go out there and confront Chloe earlier. There's no way I'm challenging this guy, though. I can't imagine it would end with us laughing over a bottle of Sauvignon Blanc.

I pull out my phone and dial 999.

'Emergency. Which service?' asks the operator.

'Police,' I say, keeping my voice low, though I doubt the man outside can hear me over the sound of his own bellowing.

When I'm connected to the police, I quickly explain the situation. A woman being harassed by her violent ex. Potential domestic abuse. He's trying to break down her door.

'We'll send someone as soon as we can, madam,' the woman on the other end assures me.

'And how long will that be?' I demand, watching as the ex kicks the door hard enough to make the whole frame shudder. The whole flat, in fact, mine included.

'We'll send someone as soon as we can,' she repeats, her tone clipped. I can almost hear her rolling her eyes at me.

'Right. Great. Thanks,' I snap and hang up.

The ex is still down there, alternating between hammering on the door and shouting Chloe's name. An image of her flashes into my mind – cowering, huddled on the floor, terrified.

She's only a young woman. Barely out of her teens. This isn't fair. It's not right.

'Fuck this,' I say, and the determination in my voice catches me by surprise.

I stomp to the kitchen and grab the knife I accidentally cut myself with earlier. I'm well aware of how sharp it is, and the edge glints in the dim light from the hall.

I grip it for a moment, feeling the weight of it in my hand, imagining myself confronting the man downstairs with it.

Thankfully, common sense kicks in. What am I going to do? Wave it around? Stab him? I couldn't successfully chop up a carrot with the bloody thing, let alone wield it as a weapon.

I set the knife down and look around for something else. My eyes land on the bucket over in the corner. The one I use for mopping the floors.

Perfect.

I stuff it under the mixer tap and open up the cold, letting the water rush in until it's full almost to the top. It's heavy but, thankfully, the sink is only a few inches away from the window, so I don't have to carry it far. I slide the window open as quietly as I can and peer down.

He's still there, his face a red knot of rage as he pounds on Chloe's door.

'You can't hide from me forever!' he shouts. 'This is madness, Chloe! You need to come out. Now!'

He's right below me. Without giving myself a chance to reconsider, I tip the bucket, sending a cascade of icy water down onto his head.

The howl he lets out is immensely satisfying.

He leaps back, looking around wildly, water dripping from his hair and clothes. He's soaked to the skin, his eyes wide with outrage and shock, already shivering in the October chill.

'What the fuck?' he bellows. His brain catches up with events, and he finally looks up, his eyes finding me at the window.

'I've called the police,' I call down to him. 'So, you'd better piss off!'

'Trust me, sweetheart, you're going to want to stay out of this!' he snarls. He takes a threatening step forward, as if he's about to climb straight up the wall and in through my window. 'This is between me and her!'

'Not when you're waking up the whole bloody street at two in the morning, it isn't!' I shoot back. 'The police are on their way. I mean it. I'd get going, if I were you.'

As if on cue, a siren wails in the distance. It's probably nothing to do with us – Edinburgh's never short of emergency vehicles rushing around – but the man downstairs doesn't know that.

He hesitates, glancing in the direction of the sound, then back at Chloe's door. For a moment, I think he might ignore me. Then he looks straight up at me, meeting my eye.

'You have no idea how much you just messed up.' He stabs a finger at me. 'You'd better watch your back!'

Then muttering a string of expletives, he stomps back to his car – a flashy BMW that's probably compensating for something – and slams the door.

The engine roars to life, and he guns it, tyres squealing as he speeds away down the street.

I watch until his tail lights disappear around the corner, then slump against the window frame, my heart hammering in my chest. I've never stood up to anyone like that before. Clumsily accusing someone of being a prostitute was about as far as I'd got until right this moment.

It felt good. Terrifying, but good.

When my pulse slows to something approaching normal, I throw on my dressing gown and slip out of my flat. The ground feels cold through my slippers as I pad down to the door of the basement flat.

'Chloe?' I call, knocking softly. 'It's Diane. From upstairs,' I add, as if it might be some other random woman with the same name. 'He's gone now. Are you OK?'

There's a shuffling sound from inside, then the click of a lock. The door opens a crack, and Chloe peers out just above the security chain, her face tear-streaked and pale.

'He's gone? He's really gone?' she whispers.

'Yeah, he took off when he heard a siren,' I tell her. 'I don't think he'll be back tonight.'

I've got absolutely nothing to base that on, of course, but it feels like the right thing to say. It works, too, because she unfastens the security chain and the door opens wider. Chloe practically falls into my arms, her body heaving with sobs.

'I was so scared,' she chokes out. 'I thought he was going to break the door down.'

'It's OK,' I say, awkwardly patting her back. 'You're safe now. I dumped a bucket of cold water on him.'

She pulls back, her delicate features and smooth forehead marked by her confusion. She looks down at the puddle on the ground and the wet marks where the water sprayed in all directions.

I think she's about to laugh, but then she bites her bottom lip. She looks worried, and I feel a sudden rush of regret that makes me wonder if I should have kept out of it.

But she's so young. So vulnerable. So afraid.

'Is there someone I can call for you?' I ask. 'Family, or…?'

She shakes her head. 'No.'

'Nobody at all?'

She shifts uncomfortably and shoots me a worried look. 'Just my sister. But she's… sleeping.'

'Sleeping?'

She's looking intently at me now, her lips barely moving as she mumbles an explanation. 'There was an accident. A few years ago. A car hit her. She hasn't woken up.'

I hesitate. What do I say to that? What can I say?

The poor kid's had it rough.

'Do you want to come up and stay with me tonight?' I ask. 'That sofa bed is still up for grabs, if you fancy it.'

For a moment, it looks like she's going to jump at the chance, but something stops her. She shrinks back and shakes her head.

'I'll be fine. Thanks, though. Like you say, Marcus probably won't come back. I think you scared him off.'

Marcus. So that's his name.

I remind her that the police are on their way, and ask if she wants to talk to them. There's a flash of panic at that, and she tells me that she'd rather not. She just wants to go to sleep and forget it all happened.

'You can't just run away from it,' I tell her. 'He's clearly unhinged. I know it's tempting to run away and hide, but do you really think he'll let you? I've known guys like that. I know what they're like.'

She shrugs. It's a small, furtive movement. Mouse-like. I can't imagine her standing up to him. I can't imagine her standing up to anyone.

'Listen, at least give me his address,' I say. 'Maybe the police can go around and put the wind up him a bit.'

'I don't know if that's a good idea,' she says, but I persevere, telling her he'll only come back, again and again, until he gets what he wants from her.

It takes a bit of convincing, but she finally gives in. I stand, shivering in the cold, as she slowly types the address into her phone. She hesitates, like she's having second thoughts, but then she sends it to me. Upstairs, through the open window of the kitchen, I hear the *ping* of the message arriving.

'Thank you again,' she mutters.

She's stepped inside and closed the door almost all the way now. All I can see is the bruised eye, which is now red and puffy from crying. 'I don't know what I'd do without you.'

It strikes me as an odd thing to say, given that I only met her that evening, but I smile and shake my head.

'Anyone would have done the same thing,' I say.

'No,' she whispers through the crack in the door. 'They wouldn't.'

I head upstairs, the cold biting at me until I'm back in my flat, back on the couch, huddling under the fleecy throw that hides the stains and spills.

It's a few minutes later, when I've stopped shaking, that I realise how desperate I am for a pee. I rush through to the bathroom. Then, when I'm done, I resist the urge to return to the living room.

I close my bedroom door behind me and sink onto my bed, suddenly exhausted. It's been a hell of a day. First meeting Chloe, then all that business with her crazy ex. I should be asleep the moment my head hits the pillow.

But as I lie there in the darkness, I can't help but listen to the sounds of Chloe moving around downstairs. The creaking of floorboards. The sound of her TV. The almost imperceptible sound of kitchen drawers being opened and closed.

I find myself holding my breath, straining to hear what she's doing down there, hoping that her ex doesn't decide to come back.

It's a long time before I finally drift off to sleep.

CHAPTER 4

Diane

It's not even 8 a.m., but I'm standing in my dressing gown, shaking my kitchen bin over the big shared dumpster out the back of the flats. As usual, I've overfilled it and all the jammed-in rubbish is refusing to fall out.

'Come on, you stupid thing!'

This is all I need after last night. I'm still shaking a bit, and there's a headache from lack of sleep that I know is going to hang around all day. Is there such a thing as an adrenaline hangover? If so, I'm pretty sure that's what I can feel kicking in.

And this bloody bin isn't helping matters.

'Come on!'

I shake it. I smack the plastic bottom like it's a drum. The open dumpster stinks, so I'm trying to do it all while breathing as little as possible, but the effort of shoogling the heavy bin is starting to take its toll.

'Oh, for God's sake, why won't you just—'

'Morning!'

The voice comes from right behind me, right up close. It's perky and high-pitched, like the *ding-dong* of a doorbell. It startles me so badly that I drop the whole bin into the dumpster, and it thumps against the metal bottom, well beyond my reach.

Chloe is dressed in a pair of silky jogging bottoms and a tight

T-shirt. I can't quite tell if it's running gear or pyjamas, but the trainers on her feet suggest the former. Of course, she exercises. You don't get to look like that without putting in the effort.

I am suddenly mortified by the shapeless shabbiness of my floor-length dressing gown.

'You dropped your bin,' she tells me, like I could have somehow failed to notice. She's smiling as she says it. 'You dropped your wee bin in the big bin.'

'Aye, I know,' I tell her, and I laugh about it because what's the alternative?

She stretches up on her tiptoes to look into the dumpster, like she needs to see the situation for herself, but the smell wafts her away again, her face crumpling up in disgust.

'Oof. That's not pleasant,' she says.

'No,' I agree, joining in the small talk while waiting for the big talk to start.

It's only when she starts asking about breakfast and talking about the weather that I realise she has no intention of discussing what happened last night.

'Frosties. And yeah, it'll probably rain,' I say, then I take the plunge that she's been avoiding. 'How are you doing? After last night?'

'Last night?' she asks.

I stare at her, half-smiling, like she's making a joke. She just looks blankly back at me, though, as if she has no idea what I'm talking about.

She can't have forgotten. Can she? That's not possible.

'Your ex. All the, you know?' I lower my voice to a whisper, like I'm worried he might be around here somewhere, listening in. 'All the drama. The hammering and shouting.'

'Oh, that, yes!' She laughs and gives herself a little bump on the side of the head. In other circumstances, it would be a cute, goofy little gesture. Here and now, though, there's something worrying about it.

Had she forgotten? Is that what she's implying?

'I'm fine. Honestly. Thanks for coming to my rescue,' she says. 'I was worried for a while, but I think you scared him off.'

I feel my concerns fading a little. She remembers. That's a relief.

'That water *was* pretty cold,' I say.

She lets out a giggle that makes me think of a mischievous schoolgirl, and it immediately brings a smile to my face.

The smile soon fades, though, when I think of how angry he looked. How violent. It looks like Chloe's made some attempt to cover her black eye with make-up, but it's still clear to see.

'What if he comes back, though?' I ask. 'Today, or tonight, or whenever? I don't want any drama. I don't... I don't handle stress well.'

She puts a hand on my shoulder and looks me in the eye. There's an invasive sort of sincerity to it, and I feel like I'm back in high school being told by Mr Gordon, my PE teacher, that I should probably just sit on the sidelines and catch up on my science homework.

'Don't worry, Diane,' she says. 'I'm going to take your advice.'

'Advice?' I wrack my brains, trying to remember what I said last night. 'What advice?'

'I'm going to confront the problem head-on. I'll talk to him. I'll sort it out.'

'Is that safe?' I ask.

'It's fine. He'll have calmed down,' she assures me. 'I'll smooth all this out, I promise.'

She sounds confident, and I allow myself to relax a little more. I was dreading days of drama and stress, but if she can sort it all out, maybe things will go back to normal.

'How's your cat?' she asks out of nowhere.

'What? Oh. He's fine,' I say.

'I can't wait to meet him!'

I smile, but it feels fake, even from where I'm standing. I jab a thumb over my shoulder at the dumpster. 'I should probably get my bin.'

She looks past me, and though she does her best to sound enthusiastic, I can tell her heart isn't in it. 'You want me to give you a hand?'

'No. No, it's fine,' I say.

The last thing I want is to endure the indignity of having her watch me clambering into a stinking old dumpster in my PJs and dressing gown.

'You go do your…' I look her up and down.

'Run,' she concludes.

'Yes! You go do that,' I say. I'd tell her to enjoy it, but having tried the Couch to 5k app half a dozen times now, I'm honestly not sure such a thing is even possible. 'And good luck with your ex.'

'Good luck with your bin,' she says.

And, with a smile and a wave, she turns and goes jogging off along the path.

It's only when she rounds the corner, out of sight, that I let out a breath I've been subconsciously holding in.

She seems nice. She does. A bit young, naïve and vulnerable, but nice.

I hope she's OK. I hope her talk with her ex goes well. I hope things work out for her. I do.

So, why are my hands shaking even worse than they were before I bumped into her?

Adrenaline hangover. It must be a thing.

And, right now, I've got bigger things to worry about.

'Right, then,' I declare to nobody in particular. I put one foot on the side of the dumpster and grab the rim at the top. The smell, even from here, is overwhelming. 'Here goes nothing.'

CHAPTER 5

Diane

'So when you've got a customer who's angry about their bill, or roaming charges, or just the service they've received, what's the first thing you say to them?'

Three blank faces stare back at me. Two boys and a girl, barely out of school, sitting in a row of identical office chairs. The girl is picking at her nail polish. One of the boys is trying, and failing, to discreetly check his phone under the desk. The other one just looks like he'd rather be anywhere else than here in this call centre training room.

Him and me both.

'Anyone?' I prompt, stifling a yawn that threatens to dislocate my jaw. 'No suggestions?'

The boy who isn't on his phone – Jamie, I think his name is – shrugs. 'Tell them it's not our fault?'

I blink at him slowly, composing myself. We've already been over this very subject this morning. Twice!

'No, Jamie,' I sigh. 'Telling an angry customer that it's not our fault is actually the opposite of what we want to do.'

'But if it isn't our fault, then—'

'It doesn't matter whose fault it is,' I cut in. 'The customer just wants to feel heard. They want validation. When someone's shouting at you about their experience, the last thing they want to hear is excuses. They want to know you care.'

'What if we don't care, though, miss?' the girl asks, like I'm a high school teacher rather than a workplace trainer.

'Well, I mean, *of course* you don't actually care,' I say. I've completely blanked on her name. Sonia, or Sophie, or Sarah-Louise. An S name, I'm sure. 'Nobody *actually* cares,' I tell her, and the absurdity of the idea almost makes me smile for the first time today.

Sindy, or whatever her name is, tuts loudly and goes back to picking her nails. Jamie has sunk lower in his chair and is now barely keeping his eyes open.

Again, I know exactly how he feels. I'm running on about three hours' sleep. Every time I closed my eyes last night, I kept hearing things from downstairs. Creaking floorboards. Bumps. Voices. That last one was probably just the telly, but still.

I never did hear back from the police. No blue lights, no follow-up call, nothing. Part of me is relieved – I wasn't in the mood to be interviewed at 3 a.m. – but mostly I'm annoyed. What if Marcus had come back? What if he'd broken in? He could've smashed the door down and murdered everyone in the block, for all they know. For all they care.

I'm pretty sure I still smell of bin juice, too, even after my shower.

'Miss?'

The girl – Shona, maybe – is looking at me with her elaborately chunky eyebrows raised. Her eyebrows were the first thing I'd noticed about her when she arrived. That was hardly a surprise, given that they were so thick they'd entered the room a half second before the rest of her.

'Sorry,' I say, blinking myself back to the present. 'What?'

Shannon, possibly, looks at the two lads flanking her. Her brows come together in confusion above her nose, which must take a real effort on her forehead's part.

'You just totally zoned out, miss,' she says.

'You alright, miss?' Jamie asks.

The lad who's been fiddling with his phone under his desk doesn't so much as look up. At least, I hope it's his phone he's fiddling with.

'I'm fine. And don't call me "miss". I'm not your teacher.'

'Aye, you are, though, miss,' Jamie points out.

'OK, yes, technically…' I sigh, pulling myself together and trying to marshal my thoughts.

I indicate the name badge on the lapel of the dowdy grey suit jacket I'm wearing. That and the matching pencil skirt looked great on the mannequin in store, but it's doing me no favours. Or maybe I'm the one that's letting the outfit down.

'Diane Shelley,' I say, reading the name on the badge out loud.

Jamie's hand shoots up.

'It's not school. You don't have to raise your hand,' I tell him.

He keeps it up while he asks his question. 'Do we call you Mrs Shelley, then?'

'No. I'm not married.'

'How come you're not married, miss?' the girl asks.

The lad with the phone glances up at me, like he's sizing me up. His eyes quickly drop back again, though, clearly dismissing me as potential wife material.

'It doesn't matter,' I say. I tap the badge again. 'Diane. Just call me Diane. I'm not your boss. I get paid the same as you do.'

Even just saying that out loud depresses me. I'm twenty years older than these kids, and as soon as their two-week trial is over, we'll be on the same hourly rate.

'Anyway,' I say, pressing on. 'As we were discussing, the first thing you say to an angry customer is…' I pause, hoping one of them will jump in with the answer.

None of them do. They continue staring at me like goldfish who've just been asked to solve a complex mathematical equation.

'You *apologise*,' I tell them. 'Alright? You say "I'm sorry you're having this problem". You take ownership of it. Simple as that.'

'But if it's not our—'

'Jamie, I swear to God, if you say "not our fault" one more time, I'm going to stick your pal's phone somewhere the sun doesn't shine.'

The words come out sharper than I intend, and all three of them look momentarily startled. Then Selma giggles, setting off the other two. I don't blame them. I'm hardly the image of professional authority today, with my unwashed hair scraped back in a ponytail and dark circles under my eyes that not even my emergency concealer could hide.

'Look,' I say, softening my tone. 'The point is you need to make the customer feel valued. Like their problem matters to you. People respond to empathy. It's amazing what happens when you're nice to someone.'

They're barely listening. I might as well be teaching customer service techniques to the potted plant in the corner. At least it wouldn't answer back.

I glance at the clock on the wall. Only an hour until lunch. I can make it that long without running screaming out the door. Hopefully.

'Let's try a role play,' I announce, which earns some puzzled looks from the three of them.

'What, like sex stuff?' the boy with the phone asks. I can't even begin to guess at the first letter of his name, much less the rest of it.

I feel my cheeks stinging slightly as they all giggle again.

'What? No! Of course not… Why would it be…?' I pinch the bridge of my nose, take a deep breath, and try not to regret every one of the life choices that led me to this point. 'Customer service role play. Jamie, you be the staff member, and…' I look hopefully at the girl.

She just stares back at me, offering me nothing to work with.

'You,' I say, skipping over her myriad possible names. 'You can be the person making a complaint.'

'What will I do?' asks the boy with the phone.

I want to tell him that I don't care, but instead I tell him just to observe the conversation. He takes that as his cue to go back to scrolling beneath the desk.

Shannon – is it Shannon? That feels close – sits up straighter, getting into character with surprising enthusiasm. She mimes dialling a number, then brings an invisible phone to her ear and says, 'Ring ring ring.'

Jamie looks up at me for guidance. I just nod, encouraging him to go for it. He stares down at the desk in front of him, like he's actually searching for the phone, then mimes pressing a button.

'Hello?' he says, all that work we did earlier on call answering techniques having already gone right out the window.

'Your company's shite!' maybe-Shannon barks down the invisible phone line.

Jamie nods solemnly. 'Aye. I know. Sorry. We're total shite.'

'Wait, hang on. What are you doing?' I ask.

'You said to agree with them and say sorry.'

'No, that's not... Not like that,' I say, struggling to stop myself raising my voice. 'Try it again.'

'Ring ring ring!'

Jamie reaches for the button. I start telling him he doesn't need to do that bit, but then I decide it's not worth the bother.

'Hello?'

'Your company's shite!'

'Is it fuck!' Jamie shoots back.

I bury my head in my hands as the conversation becomes an argument. It escalates quickly, until it's eventually interrupted by the loud *ting* of a phone notification.

'Right, phone away,' I say, pointing to the nameless lad playing with his mobile under the desk.

'It's not me, miss.'

'Don't call me "miss",' I remind him. There's another *ting*. Then a third. Three messages, one after the other. 'I mean it, put the phone away.'

'It's not his phone, miss,' Jamie says. He nods at my bag sitting on the table behind me. 'I think it's yours.'

I try very hard not to cringe. Usually, I put my phone on silent when I come to work. I guess I was just too exhausted this morning to remember.

'Right. OK. Yes,' I mumble because I'm not really sure what else to say. I take the phone from my bag, fully intending to switch it to silent.

Until I see the messages.

Three of them, all from Chloe. My stomach does a little flip as I read them.

PLS COME QUICK

I'm at Marcus house

No police

I stare at the phone, my mouth suddenly dry. What the hell…?

I look up to find all three trainees watching me with far more interest than they've shown in anything I've said all morning.

'Everything OK, miss?' the boy with the phone asks. There's a smug look on his face that makes me want to slap him.

'Uh, yes,' I say, tightening my grip on the mobile.

What's happened? Why is she sending me these messages? Is she OK? Why is she mentioning the police?

Maybe I should call her, or at least text her back to let her know I'm at work and can't talk right now. I definitely can't go racing over there to help her.

Can I?

Another message comes through. My heart is hammering against my ribs as my gaze is drawn back down to the screen.

It's just one word. Some part of me is pleased to see that she's at least taken the time to punctuate it, but the rest of me is curdling up in fear at what it might mean.

HELP!

I look at the three faces staring back at me, more interested in this than they've been in anything else I've said all morning. I should get on with it. Finish their training.

The messages are still there on the screen. Waiting. Pleading. Desperate.

Something must have happened.

Something bad.

I try to tell myself it's not my problem, that I should stay out of it, that I shouldn't get involved.

And yet…

'Ah, screw it,' I say. 'None of you'll bother coming back tomorrow, anyway.'

And, as they mumble their agreement, I grab my bag and hurry out the door.

CHAPTER 6

Diane

It rises like a tidal wave. Like magma rushing from deep beneath the Earth's crust. An inevitable force of nature that I'm powerless to stop.

Chloe darts clear, avoiding the backsplash as my stomach contents splatter onto what, until recently, would've been quite a nice carpet.

'Oh, God! What did you do that for?' Chloe squeals. 'You're making it worse.'

I stare up at her, still bent double, a string of vomity drool hanging from my bottom lip.

'Worse?' The word is a squeak. A squawk. A single shrieked syllable of disbelief.

I look around the living room of her ex-boyfriend's house. At the carnage. At the blood. At the body lying on the floor, eyes open, puncture wounds punctuating his flesh like emphatic full stops.

'How the hell can it be any worse?'

'You were *sick*!' Chloe says, as if this fact had somehow escaped my notice. 'On the floor. You were sick!'

'Can you blame me?' I shout at her.

She scuttles back, eyes wide in panic, like I'm going to attack her.

Which is ironic, really, given what she's presumably done to the man on the floor.

It occurs to me then that shouting at her probably isn't the best idea. I take a few deep breaths, trying to quell the panic attack I can feel hovering around me, but the smell in the room – blood, sweat and Marcus's loosened bowels – immediately makes me heave again.

I turn away from the body and look out of the front window, composing myself as best as I can. It's a nice house, detached, out on Howden Hall Road just south of Liberton. A few minutes ago, my biggest concern had been the cost of the Uber fare to get out here.

That had slipped way down my list of worries the moment that Chloe had opened the door.

I should've run. As soon as I'd seen her, with her bloodied hand and T-shirt, I should have turned around and legged it. But she'd grabbed for me, hugged me, and now the front of my jacket and skirt are almost as caked with blood as she is.

Marcus lies spreadeagled on his nice carpet. It used to be cream. Now it's pink, in places, and a deep, dark crimson, still glistening wet in others. His T-shirt, the original colour of which I can't even guess at, is torn and soaked through with blood. I can see multiple puncture wounds in his chest, his stomach, all over his body. His mouth hangs open in what I can only imagine was his final scream.

My stomach twitches, and it takes everything I have not to be sick again.

Chloe stands above him. She's shaking, her eyes wide and unfocused, as if she's no longer really seeing me.

'Did you call the police?' she whispers.

I debate with myself, trying to work out what's the best thing to say. I could lie and say I phoned them and they're on their way, but what good would that do me? It might just make her angry.

And I want to avoid that at all costs.

'Good. Good,' she wheezes when I shake my head. 'They'll think I did it.'

'Didn't you?' The words are out of me before I can stop them. She looks hurt by them. Wounded.

'Of course not!' she whispers, her voice shaking. 'I came round to talk to him and just found him like this.'

I almost laugh. I almost call her a liar.

But I don't. I daren't. Instead, I try to stay cool and keep her calm.

'What happened, Chloe?' My voice doesn't sound like my own. It's high and strangled. I'm a ventriloquist's dummy being operated by fear. 'What the hell is this?'

'I don't know,' she says, and her voice is different, too. It's small. Childlike. 'I just… I came over to talk to him. To ask him to leave me alone. I didn't want to keep running from him, like you said. I had to face up to him.'

'I don't think that's quite what I said…' I mutter. I can't face the thought of being in any way responsible for this.

Chloe doesn't seem to hear me, though. She carries on, voice trembling, tears cutting tracks through the bloodstains on her cheeks. 'The door was open, and I found him like this.'

'And what did you do then? Fucking roll on him?' I cry, gesturing at her head-to-toe wash of dark, glossy red.

It's not the most appropriate thing to say, but I have a natural tendency to try and joke my way out of bad situations.

And this is up there with the worst ones I've ever found myself in.

It gets worse a moment later when I finally notice that Chloe is holding a knife. A kitchen knife, its long black handle now slick with blood.

I eye up the door that leads out to the hall, trying to remember how many other doors stand between me and the exit. There's a glass one that opens onto a little porch, I think, then the main door itself.

Could I make it, if I ran? Could I get out of here without her catching me?

Maybe, if I went like the clappers. But it's too risky to put to the test.

'Chloe,' I say, keeping my voice as soft and as level as I can. 'How about you put down the knife?'

She frowns, then looks at the knife as if seeing it for the first time. For a moment, she doesn't react, but then she ejects a panicky, 'Wah!', and chucks the knife into the air. It lands on the coffee table, point down, and *boings* back and forth when the point sticks in the wood.

'I wasn't… I didn't… It wasn't me!' she insists again. She's in floods of tears now. 'I just… I heard you at the door, and I thought maybe the killer had come back, so I-I grabbed it, and…'

She drops to her knees beside the body, her hands all over him like she's searching for a switch that might flick him back into life.

From the moment I walked in and saw him there, I've assumed that Chloe killed him. Now, though, watching as she frantically fusses over him, I feel my first flicker of doubt.

She's distracted. I should leave. I should turn around, make a run for it, and get the hell away from here. That's what any sane, reasonable person would do.

But I don't do any of that. I don't know why, but instead of fleeing, I step further into the room, closing the door behind me. My hands are trembling. My whole body is trembling, in fact.

'Chloe,' I say, trying to keep my voice steady. 'We need to call the police.'

She shakes her head violently, her blood-matted blonde hair whipping around her face. 'No! No police!'

'But—'

'I told you, they'll think it was me!' There's a desperate, wild look in her eyes. 'Look at me! I'm covered in his blood. He gave me a black eye. I ran away. And now he's dead. Don't you see? They'll lock me up and throw away the key!'

I want to argue. I want to reassure her and tell her none of that will happen.

But who would I be trying to kid? It all looks bad. Very bad.

'What were you doing here?' I ask. 'Why would you come to his house?'

'It was like you said. I couldn't keep running from him. It was your idea!' She swallows hard but continues again before I have a chance to object to that statement. 'I thought… I thought if I came to him, on my terms, I might… I don't know, make him see reason.'

'He was trying to batter your door down last night!' I remind her.

'I know, but—'

If there was an excuse, or an explanation, or some further reason she could offer for coming here, it dies in her throat.

As I watch her kneeling there, sobbing over the remains of a man who was undoubtedly violent towards her, I give up trying to make sense of it. I'm an outsider here. I don't know how abusive and coercive the relationship was, or how much control he had over her.

Maybe she really did think she could reason with him. Or maybe she'd even come to apologise, believing she was the one at fault.

I reach a hand for her skinny shoulder.

'Chloe, I—'

'You have to help me,' she pleads, grabbing my arm. Her fingers are tight again, locking in place. This time, I can feel the blood squidging between her skin and mine. Marcus's blood. 'Please, Diane. I can't go to prison for something I didn't do.'

'OK, well…' I swallow, not quite believing what I'm about to say. 'We could just go.'

She shakes her head again. 'What? No. We need to get rid of him.'

That panicky urge to laugh grips me again. 'Get rid of him?' I splutter. I look from her to the dead man and back again. I can feel my eyes trying to bulge all the way out of my head. 'You mean get rid of the body?'

'Yes.'

She says it with such certainty that a chill runs through me. She gets to her feet, still gripping my arm. This isn't the same frightened girl who was cowering from him last night. There's a steely resolve in the sparkling blue of her eyes now.

'We can't leave him here. They'll look for me first. I need time to think, to figure out who did this.'

'And how do you suppose we "get rid" of a body?' I ask, my voice rising with hysteria. 'Dig a hole? Throw him in the Firth of Forth?'

'I don't know!' she cries. 'Alright? I don't know yet!'

I look down at Marcus's lifeless face. His eyes are still open, but cloudy and unseeing. I've never seen a dead body before, not in real life. It looks both exactly like you'd expect and nothing like it. He's clearly dead, not sleeping. There's an absence there, a vacancy that even my shock-addled brain can recognise.

'We should call the police,' I say again, but even I don't sound convinced by the idea now. 'You can tell them what happened. That you found him like this.'

'And you think they'll believe me?' Chloe lets out a bitter laugh. 'Look at me, Diane! I'm covered in his blood! I was in his house! I've got his DNA all over me, and mine is probably all over him and this room now. They'll say I came here to kill him.'

I feel sick. This is wrong. All of it is wrong. But she's got a point. The police would have a hard time believing her story. I'm not sure I believe it myself.

'We can't go to jail for this,' she says.

And the world goes silent around us.

A moment ago, I could hear the cars passing on the street outside. The hissing of a bus's hydraulics. The roar of a motorbike.

Now, there's nothing. Just me, her and the dead man, floating in a vacuum.

'What do you mean *we*?' I ask.

She raises an arm and points to the little mound of vomit on the floor.

Oh, God. I might as well have left a calling card.

'Your DNA is here too now,' she says, but she sounds far away, drowned out by the screaming in my head. 'You'll be an accessory. We're in this together.'

She's right. If the police trace this back to her, they'll trace it back to me, too. DNA. Fingerprints? Did I touch the doorknob? Have I touched anything?

Not that it matters, given that the contents of my stomach are currently seeping into the living room carpet.

'Shit, shit, shit,' I whisper, wrenching myself free of her grip. I run my fingers through my hair, tangling them in it, grabbing and pulling until tears spring to my eyes.

I should never have come here. How the hell did this even happen? I should be losing the will to live trying to train those three new-starts, not figuring out how to dispose of a dead man.

Because that's what I'm doing, I realise. My mind is already racing, whirring away, trying to solve the biggest problem of my life.

'I need to think,' I mutter, more to myself than to her.

Chloe doesn't reply. She just watches me, her eyes calculating. The blood on her face is drying now, turning from bright red to a dull rusty brown. She looks like something from a horror film. I just can't tell if she's the victim or the monster.

If it's the former, she's been dealt the world's worst possible hand. Escaped an abuser only to be framed for his murder.

That's if she's telling the truth.

The more cynical part of me wonders if this is all an elaborate act. She could have killed him. Plunged that knife into him over and over, years of rage and hurt finally boiling over.

But why invite me into it? Why drag me down with her?

Then again, look how quickly I came running when she texted. I've known her less than a day, and here I am, standing over a corpse, trying to figure out how to get rid of it.

Clearly, she's not the only one here with issues.

I look out of the window at the BMW sitting in the driveway. It's a 5 Series. Big car. Big boot.

'Is there a tarp or anything in the shed?' I ask finally.

Hope blooms on Chloe's face, cutting through the mask of blood. 'I don't know. Maybe? I can check.'

'Be quick,' I tell her, surprising myself with how steady my voice sounds.

It's afternoon now, tipping towards evening. The overcast skies will help add an extra few degrees of darkness, too. Still, can't be too careful.

'But don't let the neighbours see you,' I add.

She nods and hurries out of the room. I listen to her footsteps retreating down a hallway, then the sound of the back door opening and closing.

I'm alone with Marcus now.

'What the hell am I doing?' I whisper to him. He doesn't answer. Of course he doesn't. He's dead. Murdered. And I'm about to become an accessory after the fact.

I can still leave. I can still walk out the front door and call the police. Tell them everything. That Chloe texted me, that I found her here with the body, that she asked me to help her dispose of it. I can show them the messages.

But then I think of the black eye she was sporting when I first met her. I think of him pounding on her door in the middle of the night, threatening her. I think of her fear, her tears.

Murder wasn't the answer, of course. It's never the answer.

But what if she didn't do it? What if someone else did? And what if I abandon her now and she goes to prison for a crime she didn't commit?

I'm still wrestling with my conscience when Chloe returns, breathless and dragging a big roll of something behind her.

'I couldn't find any tarp,' she says, then she presents me with the roll. 'But I found a big load of bubble wrap.'

Bubble wrap.

Fucking *bubble wrap*!

'It'll have to do,' I tell her.

And we get to work.

CHAPTER 7

Diane

If I never hear another bit of bubble wrap popping, it'll be too bloody soon.

I've spent the last forty-five minutes rolling a dead man up in the stuff, and every few seconds there's another *pop* as one of the little air pockets bursts beneath the pressure. I flinch every time it happens, as if a gun's been fired.

Or a knife has been plunged into human flesh.

'Can we hurry this up?' I whisper, though I'm not sure why I'm keeping my voice down. The neighbours can't hear us. Marcus certainly can't.

'I'm trying,' Chloe says, frantically tearing off another length of bubble wrap. Her hands are still shaking, leaving smudges of dried blood on the clear plastic. 'It's harder than it looks.'

I don't doubt it. We're having to manhandle his heavy limbs, trying to arrange them so he'll be easier to transport, then wrapping him all up like he's a prized antique we're preparing to post to some high bidder on eBay. It doesn't feel dignified for anyone involved.

I still can't believe I'm doing this. That *we're* doing this. I keep thinking I'll wake up at any moment, back in my flat, shaking my head at the latest episode of *My 600-lb Life*.

But I don't wake up. And we keep wrapping.

Pop. Pop. Pop.

'We need to hurry,' I stress again. Or, at least, the words come out of my mouth. I'm not sure it's even me saying them now. Some bigger, older, wiser version of me has stepped in to take the reins, while the rest of me quietly has a meltdown in a dark room at the back of my brain. 'Someone might come looking for him.'

'Who?' Chloe asks, like the idea is absurd. 'He doesn't have any friends. He's an absolute wank—' She stops herself, as if suddenly feeling bad about speaking ill of the dead. Even when the dead was, from what I could gather, a monster.

'Work colleagues? Family?' I suggest.

'His family all live in Glasgow,' she says, with the certainty of someone who's been forced to memorise such details. 'And he's off work this week. He won't be missed until Monday, at the earliest.'

That's the best news I've had since I entered the house, although that's not exactly saying much.

I'm still not fully convinced, but there's nothing for it other than to keep wrapping, trying not to think about what – who – I'm touching beneath the layers of plastic.

Another pop, another flinch.

'What are we going to do with him once he's… you know… packaged up?' Chloe asks.

It's a question that's been on my mind since we started this, but I've been too afraid to dwell on it. Too afraid of the answer. Of what I might have to do.

Chloe's waiting for my response. The shrug I give doesn't fill her with confidence. She brushes a strand of matted hair away from her face, leaving another rust-coloured smear on her forehead.

'There's the crematorium just down the road,' she announces, like this is the solution to all our problems.

I stare at her, trying to work out if she's joking. The blank expression on her blood-spattered face suggests she isn't.

'I don't think they let you rock up and use it anytime you want!' I exclaim. 'You can't just bring your own body along and chuck it in!'

Her expression sinks. For a moment, she's a child who has been told that Santa isn't real. 'Oh. Right. Yeah.'

I push myself up from where I've been crouching beside the corpse, my knees popping almost as loudly as the bubble wrap. I pace the room, careful to avoid the patch of vomit that's still soaking into the carpet at one end and the puddle of blood in the middle.

'We need to get rid of him completely,' I say, thinking out loud. All those seasons of *NCIS* are coming in useful now. 'No body, no crime.'

My mind had initially gone to dumping him in the water somewhere, but it's too risky. There was something on the news the other day, in fact, about a school janitor who went missing from a school in Stockbridge a while back. Someone pulled him out of the canal. He'd been in there for over a year.

We need Marcus to be gone. Completely gone.

Destroyed.

I stop pacing, an idea forming. It's a terrible idea. A horrible idea. But it's the only one I've got.

'We burn him,' I say quietly. 'Fire destroys evidence. DNA. Everything.'

'That's what I said!' Chloe cries. 'The crema—'

'Not, not the fu—' I snap, then I remember the knife still sticking up from the coffee table, and how it made a colander of the man on the floor.

I take a steadying breath. I almost don't notice the smell now. The realisation of that makes me feel even more sick than the stench did.

'Not at the crematorium,' I say, keeping my voice level. I look out of the window at the gleaming BMW in the driveway. 'In his car.'

It takes another twenty minutes to finish wrapping the body, then we drag it towards the front door. It's heavier than I expected. I've heard the term 'dead weight' before, of course, but I didn't realise it was quite so literal.

Despite having lost all that blood, Marcus feels like his bones are made of lead, and I get a sharp twinge in my lower back when I hoist up my end and shuffle clumsily backwards towards the front door.

'Why have I got the head end?' I ask, but Chloe is too busy struggling with the weight of his feet to answer me. Her skinny arms shake with the effort and, despite our best efforts to fully lift him, his padded arse drags through the drying pile of sick by the door, smearing it across the carpet and into the hall.

I eject a string of expletives so loud and explicit that Chloe drops the feet end in shock. The sudden extra weight yanks the bubble wrap from my grip, and even through the layers of wrapping, I hear the sickening *thunk* of the dead man's head hitting the floor.

The panicky voice – the real me – rushes to the surface. I shake. I squeal. I feel another wave of nausea and a tensing in my gut.

But then it's all swept aside by the autopilot that's been steering me for the past hour and a half and is driven back down into the dark.

'Sorry,' Chloe says, grabbing for the feet again.

It's only then, as I look along the dead man at her, that a thought hits me. How could I have been this stupid?

'We can't go out like this,' I whisper. 'Look at us.'

Chloe looks down at herself, then at me. We're both covered in blood. It's dried now, flaking off in places, but still unmistakable.

'Oh, shit, yeah,' she says. She drops the feet again. *Thud.* 'Hang on.'

She darts upstairs, leaving me alone in the hallway with the body, the bubble wrap and a number of regrets.

A few minutes later she returns, dressed in clean jeans and a long-sleeved T-shirt, with a bundle of clothes under one arm.

'These are mine,' she says, handing me a top and a pair of jeans. 'I didn't have time to grab everything when I left him.'

I take the clothes, but the moment I hold the jeans up against myself, I know they won't fit. They're tiny, designed for someone half my size.

Someone like Chloe.

'Um, these aren't going to work,' I point out, trying to keep the note of embarrassment out of my voice.

Chloe glances at the jeans, then at my hips, then back at the jeans. 'No?' she asks, raising a carefully manicured eyebrow.

'What do you…? No. Definitely not,' I say, laying one of the legs against my thigh. 'Look at it.'

'Right. OK. Hang on.'

She disappears again, and I'm left standing there, feeling a hot flush creep up my neck. I can't believe, given everything else going on right in this moment, I'm embarrassed about my weight.

Still, all this might help. After seeing a murder victim so close up, I don't think I'll ever feel like eating again.

When Chloe returns this time, she's carrying men's clothing – a pair of grey jogging bottoms and a black hoodie.

'These are his,' she says. 'They should fit you.'

Somehow, wearing a dead man's clothes almost seems worse than being covered in his blood, but I don't have much choice. I don't really want to contaminate any of the other rooms with my DNA, so I tell Chloe to turn around while I hurriedly get changed there in the hall.

The joggies are loose around the waist but still snug on my thighs. The hoodie at least provides some anonymity, especially with the hood up.

Chloe fetches her bloody clothes from upstairs, and we bundle them all into a carrier bag to dispose of later. It's a supermarket Bag for Life. Which, given the circumstances, feels a bit ironic. She produces a packet of wet wipes that I think are meant for cleaning leather, but we use them to wipe the blood off our hands and faces, then stick the used wipes in the bag, too.

It's amazing how well she cleans up. She looks like she's just stepped out of a studio dressing room, ready for an Instagram photo shoot. You'd never know what she'd just done.

I wish I could say the same for myself. I just know I look a right state, but Chloe assures me that at least there's no obvious blood on my face.

'OK,' I say, once we're ready. 'Let's get him in the car.'

Chloe fetches the car keys from a bowl in the hallway, then rushes outside to back the BMW up to the front door, boot open. She parks so close to the house that she has to fold down the seats and clamber through the inside of the car to get back to me.

Between us, we heave Marcus's bubble-wrapped body into the boot. It's a good thing Chloe lowered the back seats, or he'd be too long to stuff inside.

'Right. Is that us?' Chloe asks.

I wish. I'm desperate to get the hell out of here, to get away, to put all this madness behind me.

But there's still the carpets to deal with, both in the living room and here in the hall.

'We need to take these too,' I say, pointing to them. 'Get a knife from the kitchen.'

She hurries off, and I stand there beside the car, looking up and down the darkening street, sure that at any moment I'll see a neighbour standing watching me, or the flashing lights of an approaching police SWAT team.

The street remains empty, but my heart refuses to slow down.

Chloe returns with a kitchen knife, and together we hack the carpets into manageable pieces, which we pile on top of Marcus in the car. Not only does it help dispose of evidence, but it also conceals the obvious outline of a body if anyone peeks in the window while we're stopped at traffic lights.

My arms are shaking by the time we're finished. It's probably the most strenuous workout I've had in years and, without doubt, the most stressful. I want to curl up and cry, but I can't. Not here. Not yet.

I clench my hands into fists to try and stop the tremors.

'Right,' I say, and my voice is surprisingly steady. 'Let's go. We need to find somewhere isolated.'

'Diane, wait,' Chloe says, and there's a flatness to her voice that sends a shiver down my spine.

I turn to find her staring at me, something clutched in her hand. My heart leaps into my throat when I see it's the knife. The murder weapon. We stand there in silence for what feels like forever before she turns the handle towards me.

'We forgot this,' she says.

I exhale, slowly, and indicate the open boot with a slow tilt of my head. She stuffs the knife under a square of carpet, then climbs back through the car, over the body of her ex-boyfriend this time. The engine purrs into life, and she pulls forward enough so that I can get out of the house.

Before I do, I pull the sleeve of Marcus's hoodie up over my hand and then wipe down any of the surfaces I might have touched. The door handles. The frames. The coffee table.

My heart thumps in my chest like it's trying to escape, to get away from here.

Is that all? Is there anything else I might've touched? Anywhere else I might have left a telltale fingerprint?

The blasting of the horn out front makes me jump. With the sleeve still over my hand, I pull the front door closed, racing round to the open door on the driver's side of the BMW.

'What the hell was that for?' I ask, looking left and right to see if anyone is watching.

There's a tall hedge at either side of the driveway, blocking the view. Up ahead, where the drive meets the pavement, a young woman goes striding past. She's got a set of headphones on, though, and if she heard the horn, she does nothing to show it, not so much as glancing in our direction.

'Sorry,' Chloe says. She smiles. There's something ice-cold about it. 'I just thought you should get a shifty on.'

I don't know how I've ended up being the one doing the driving, but I don't say anything about it. I barely say anything at all, in fact, as we head south to the bypass, then hang a left towards East Lothian.

Neither of us wants to talk about what we're doing. After about twenty-five minutes, as the sky starts to darken into a deep indigo, Chloe points out a narrow farm track that leads up into the hills. It's bumpy and poorly maintained, with dense woodland on either side.

I drive until the track peters out into nothing more than a grassy clearing surrounded by trees. It's the perfect spot – secluded, hard to reach, and with enough open space that the fire won't immediately spread to the surrounding forest.

'This will do,' I say as I cut the engine.

We sit for a moment, the silence pressing in on us. I can hear my heartbeat in my ears, like the sound of distant drumming. Of an ancient army approaching over the hills.

'Are you sure about this?' Chloe asks. Her voice is small. Scared. She's getting younger by the moment.

No. God no. Of course not. I'm not sure about any of it. I've never been less sure of anything in my life.

But what choice do we have?

'It's too late to back out now,' I say, opening the car door.

The cold October air hits me like a slap. I shiver, pulling Marcus's hoodie tighter around me. I make sure everything is there in the back – the clothes, the carpet, the knife.

The body, of course.

There's a petrol can in the boot. I clocked it while we were wrestling Marcus into the car and tucked it in beside his bubble-wrapped feet. It's good that he was the type to keep an emergency supply of fuel close to hand. Very considerate of him.

Chloe stands beside me as I splash petrol over the boot and back seats, making sure to saturate the areas around the body and the carpet pieces. I can't believe I'm doing this. I can't believe this is happening.

I pour the rest through the open windows onto the front seats and dashboard, until the can is empty and the chemical smell is making my eyes water.

It's only then that it occurs to me we don't have any way of actually lighting the thing. I'm hissing my way through the start of a panic attack when Chloe produces a box of matches.

I haven't seen her smoking at any point, so I've got no idea why she has them. I decide not to ask.

'Stand back,' I warn.

My hands are shaking so badly that it takes three attempts to light a match. When it finally catches, I hesitate for just a second, then toss it through the open driver's window. The petrol ignites with a *whoosh*, flames leaping up and lashing at me like the tongues of angry demons.

We both stumble backwards, the heat intense even from several metres away. The fire catches quickly, engulfing the interior of the car. I watch, mesmerised, as the flames dance across the leather seats and the bubble-wrapped bundle in the boot.

Pop. Pop-pop.

Chloe steps closer to the blaze, holding her hands out towards it. I shoot her a look, like I can't quite believe what she's doing.

'It's cold,' she says, rubbing her hands together, then warming her palms on the heat from the fire that's currently consuming her ex-boyfriend.

The sight is surreal. The burning car, the dancing flames, the young woman warming herself like it's a bonfire on Guy Fawkes Night. I feel disconnected from reality, like I'm watching all this happen to someone else.

I wish.

The smell brings me back. Burning plastic, melting upholstery, and something else underneath it all. Something earthy. Something worse.

'We should go,' I say, my voice hoarse. 'Before someone sees the smoke.'

Chloe nods, her face illuminated by the orange glow. We turn and hurry back down the track, away from the burning car and its grisly contents. The flames light our way for the first hundred yards or so, before the trees close in and we're left in near-darkness.

We've gone almost half a mile before I finally speak.

'I'm going to call Ronan,' I announce, pulling out my phone. 'He can pick us up.'

'Your boyfriend?' Chloe asks.

'He's not really my boyfriend,' I say automatically. It's my standard response whenever anyone refers to him that way. 'It's… complicated. But he'll come if I ask him.'

As I wait for the phone to connect, a thought that's been niggling away at me for a while suddenly makes it to the surface. I've been so preoccupied with everything else that there's only now room in my head for the thought to fully form.

The awful, terrible thought.

'Do you think his friends will come after us?' I ask, unable to keep the edge of panic from my voice.

'What friends?' she says, looking confused. 'I told you, he doesn't really have friends.'

'OK, his… connections, then. You said he was connected.'

She shakes her head and laughs. She actually *laughs*. The sound is absurd given what we've just done. Obscene. 'Oh, *that*! No, he didn't have those kinds of connections. I didn't mean he was a gangster or anything like that.'

I feel a wave of relief wash over me. At least we don't have to worry about being tortured to death by some violent Midlothian crime syndicate.

Chloe looks up at me, her face half in shadow. 'He was in the police.'

CHAPTER 8

Diane

'You alright, babe?'

Ronan's voice is softer than you'd expect from a man his size. Everything about him is solid – his square jaw, his thick neck, his broad shoulders that strain against the fabric of his work T-shirt. Even now, at gone eleven at night, he's still wearing his work boots, tracking little specks of dirt across my floorboards.

I'd normally complain about it, but honestly, a bit of mud feels like the least of my worries. He could spray liquid silage across the floor right now, and I'd barely bat an eyelid.

'Babe?' he prompts again, and I realise I've been standing in the middle of my living room for God knows how long, staring at nothing.

'Fine,' I say.

That's not remotely true, of course, but what else can I say? That I've just helped dispose of a dead policeman? That I set a car on fire with a man inside it? That I've committed crimes that will put me away for the rest of my life if anyone finds out about them?

'You don't look fine,' he says. There's not a lot of emotion to it. Showing concern has never really been Ronan's thing, though. It's not that kind of relationship. It's sexual, nothing more.

It used to be different. We were a proper item once, until I did something to drive him away. I thought he wanted nothing more to do with me until quite recently, so even if it's only for a few occasional late-night fumbles, I'm grateful to have him back in my life.

He awkwardly holds a hand out, as if he's going to pat me on the shoulder. I step back, suddenly unable to bear the thought of being touched. Not even by him. I'm contaminated somehow. The presence of death has seeped into my skin, and I'm afraid it might be contagious.

'I said I'm fine,' I snap, and immediately regret it when he recoils back a step.

I'm not being fair to him. He dropped everything to come and pick us up when I called. He didn't ask questions, even though he must have been bursting with them. He just jumped in that white van of his – *Ronan's Renovation's*, stray apostrophe and all – and drove out to the middle of nowhere to fetch us.

I can't stop thinking about the journey back to the flat. The three of us squashed up in the front of the van because, of course, Ronan wouldn't have anyone in the back, where all his tools were. Not that I'd have minded. I'd have happily clambered in with the drills and hammers if it meant getting safely back home.

Chloe is back downstairs in the basement flat now, leaving Ronan and me alone. I can't get my head around how chatty she was on the drive back. Barely twenty minutes after burning her ex-boyfriend's corpse, she was sitting there between us, filling the silence with cheerful small talk.

'So, what sort of things do you build?' she'd asked, turning those big blue eyes on him.

'Bit of everything,' he'd replied, shifting uncomfortably in his seat. 'Extensions, mostly. Some decking. The odd garage conversion.'

'Oh, I've always wanted to try my hand at DIY,' she'd gushed. 'I bet you're good with your hands.'

I'd stared out of the window, focused on the side mirror as I searched for any sign of the burning BMW in the distance, unable to summon the energy or the headspace to care about her blatant flirting. Maybe it was her way of coping. Maybe she was in shock.

Or maybe she's just a better actress than I'd given her credit for.

Ronan shifts his weight from one foot to the other, clearly uncomfortable with the silence that's fallen between us. The short sleeves of his T-shirt show off forearms corded with muscle from years of hauling bricks and timber. A small scar on his left wrist catches the light, the result of an accident a while back. He doesn't like to talk about it, but I know it still bothers him when the weather turns cold.

'So, uh, do you want me to…?' his voice trails off as he glances at the bedroom door, the question hanging in the air between us.

'No,' I say quickly, knowing exactly what he's asking.

Under normal circumstances, I'd be all too happy to drag him off to the bedroom and lose myself in the physical comfort that he offers. Not tonight, though. Maybe not ever. After tonight, I can't imagine I'll ever feel those sorts of urges again.

'I want to be on my own. It's been a long day. I just need to… process some stuff.'

He nods, and I get the sense that he's relieved. It's not the first time I've noticed that about him – how he sometimes seems a bit standoffish, almost reluctant. Like he's going through the motions out of obligation rather than desire.

Something's not right there, but I can't bring myself to care about that either. Not now. Not after everything.

'OK. Well, you know where I am,' he says, backing towards the door. 'I'm sure you'll call if you need me.'

'Ronan,' I say.

He stops at the door, gripping the handle, ready to leave.

'Yeah, babe?'

There's so much I want to say. So much I want to tell him.

'Thanks for the lift,' is all that comes out of my mouth.

He nods, just once, not turning. 'No bother,' he says, then he lets himself out.

I listen to his footsteps on the stone floor of the close, then the creak of the building's front door.

I deflate then. Every ounce of air leaves my lungs, collapsing me, shrinking me down into myself. My hands shake. My heart thumps in time with a stabbing headache that builds rapidly behind my eyes.

Oh, God.

Oh, God, what have I done?

I'm filled with an urge to shout, to wail, to scream the whole building down. The whole damn world. I stuff a hand in my mouth, biting down on it, stifling the sound until it becomes a series of silent staccato sobs that spasm inside my chest.

It's then, over the stifled sound of my sobbing, that I hear the voices. Low. Muttered. Secretive.

Coming from outside.

I sidle to the window and peer out. The streetlights cast an orange glow over the pavement just a few steps down, where Ronan and Chloe are standing close together, talking in low voices. She's got her hand on his arm, her face tilted up to his.

I can't hear what they're saying, but there's an intensity to their body language that makes my stomach clench. Ronan glances up, catching me watching, and immediately steps back from Chloe. The guilt on his face is as clear as day, even from this distance.

'So, eh, nice to meet you, anyway!' he says, much louder. Then he hurries to his van, jumps in, and drives off at speed. Chloe turns and heads down the steps to her flat, not once looking in my direction.

I let the curtain fall back into place, too numb to feel betrayed. Let her flirt with him. Let her have him, if that's what she wants. I've got bigger problems right now.

A police officer.

He was a fucking police officer!

The thought sends a fresh wave of panic through me. We didn't just kill some random guy. We killed a cop. And not just killed him – we wrapped him in bubble wrap and burned him in his own car.

Not to mention the mess we made of his flooring.

Wait. What am I saying? *I* didn't kill him. I didn't kill anyone! All I did was get rid of his body.

My legs give way, and I sink onto the sofa, burying my face in my hands. What have I done? What the hell have I done?

I thought Chloe was in trouble. I thought she was in danger and needed my help. But what if she is the danger, and I'm the one who needs help?

I don't know how long I sit there, trembling, but eventually I drag myself to the bathroom. I need to wash away the stench of petrol, smoke and death that I can feel clogging up my pores.

The shower hisses to life, steam quickly filling the small room. I strip off, avoiding looking at myself in the mirror. I already know what I'd see – a woman I barely recognise, with wild eyes and a face forever etched with the knowledge of what she's capable of.

And what she's done.

But then, that's what I see most days.

The water is scorching, just shy of unbearable, but I welcome the pain. I step under the spray and let it pound against my skin, turning it an angry red. It feels like penance, like punishment, although I know it's nowhere near enough.

I scrub at my skin until it's raw, trying to wash away the invisible stains of guilt, but it's no use. They're too deeply embedded. My legs give way again, and I sink to the floor of the shower, curling up as the water continues to rain down on me.

That's when they come again – great, heaving sobs that wrack my entire body, the sound of them drowned out by the rush of the water. I cry until I'm empty, until there's nothing left but a hollow ache in my scorched-red chest.

Eventually, the water begins to run cold, forcing me to move. I climb out of the shower on shaky legs, wrapping myself in a towel that feels too soft, too normal for this new, terrible reality.

I pull on my pyjamas and grab a bin bag from under the sink, filling it with Marcus's clothes – the joggies and hoodie I'd been wearing. I tie it up tightly, as if that could somehow contain the horror of what they represent, and then drop the bag on my armchair so I don't forget to dispose of it tomorrow, somewhere far away from here.

Yeah, like I could possibly forget.

My bed looks inviting, promising an escape from the nightmare my life has become, but I know sleep won't come easily, if ever. Still, I'm about to turn off the light when the intercom by the front door buzzes, making me jump out of my skin.

I freeze. Hold my breath. Try to shrink down and become too small to notice.

Who the hell would be calling at this time of night?

Chloe? Has something happened?

Has Ronan come back to apologise for his clandestine chat with her out front?

The buzzer goes again. Whoever it is, they're not going away.

I get up and approach the intercom, creeping towards it like it might leap from the wall and bite me. My fingers hover over the handset for a moment before I finally pick it up.

'Hello?' My voice sounds high and strained.
'Hello, is that Diane Shelley?' a man's voice asks.
It's a voice I don't recognise. Formal. Official.
Terrifyingly so.
'It's the police.'

CHAPTER 9

Diane

I'm screaming so loudly inside my head that I'm sure they must be able to hear it. The two uniformed officers are standing in my hallway now, and I'm struggling to control my expression, to look normal, to look innocent.

How can I possibly look innocent after everything I've done?

'Miss Shelley?' the taller policeman prompts. 'Can we come in?'

He's in his late twenties, I guess. Younger than me. He's puffed up, like he works out. Probably trying to compensate for something.

'What? Oh, yeah. Of course.' I step aside, pulling the door wider for them to enter.

My mind is racing, every possible scenario hurtling towards the others like competitors in a demolition derby about to smash into one another. They've found the car. BANG! They've traced it back to Marcus. CRASH! They've found traces of my DNA at his house. KABOOM!

Can they smell the smoke, I wonder? The petrol? The blood?

I am suddenly hyper-aware of the black bag sitting on my armchair. It's in direct view of the front door. With just a slight turning of their heads, they'd be looking straight at it right now.

Oh, God.

Why didn't I move it? Why didn't I hide it in the back of my wardrobe or something? They're going to go into the living room, open the bag, and declare me a cold-blooded killer.

I'm done. It's over. My whole life is over!

'Sorry for disturbing you so late,' says the shorter officer. He's younger still, barely into his twenties by the look of him, with a baby face that probably gets him ID'd every time he buys a beer. 'I'm PC Campbell and this is PC Watson.'

'We're following up on a call you made last night?' the taller one – Watson – adds, his statement rising at the end like a question.

'Call?' I mutter. My thoughts are a jumble. 'What call? I—' Oh.

Relief threatens to buckle my knees. They're talking about my call to 999 last night, when Marcus was hammering at Chloe's door.

'Yes! That's right!' I cry with far too much enthusiasm. I shrug and try to play it cool. Or cooler, at least. 'It was fine.'

PC Campbell raises an eyebrow. 'It was fine?'

'Yeah. It was nothing,' I say.

Watson checks his notes. 'You, eh, you called about a man causing a disturbance.'

'Outside the basement flat,' Campbell adds, glancing at his own notepad. 'You reported a man banging on the door, shouting threats?'

'Uh, yeah. I thought someone might come round,' I say, and though I don't put it there on purpose, there's a note of accusation in my voice that neither man likes.

'We did. We're here now,' Campbell says.

'I'm sure you appreciate how busy we are,' Watson says. 'We can't be everywhere at once, can we?'

They both stare at me, and I realise it isn't a rhetorical question.

'No. Suppose not,' I concede.

PC Watson, the taller one, looks along my hall and into my living room. Right at the chair. Right at the bag of the dead man's clothes. Even from here, I can smell the smoke from them. I'm sure of it. The men must be able to smell it, too.

I swallow hard, trying to get some moisture back into my mouth. 'It was just some drunk guy hammering on the door at two in the morning.'

It's Watson's turn to cock an eyebrow. 'Drunk? How'd you know?'

'Well, I mean, you can tell, can't you?' I say, fidgeting slightly. 'He was staggering about, slurring. And, I mean, why else would anyone be hammering on someone's door at that time of night?'

'Don't know,' Watson says.

'You tell us,' Campbell adds.

Again they wait for a response. Watching me. Studying me. There's something intimidating about them that goes beyond the possibility of them arresting me as an accessory to murder.

'Did you get a good look at him?' Campbell asks.

I shake my head. 'Not really. It was dark. I just saw a man. Quite big. Dark hair.'

I realise I'm describing Marcus. That's who they're asking me about. The same Marcus currently reduced to ash and melted bubble wrap in a burned-out car in East Lothian.

Scratching at my head, I frown like I'm trying to remember. 'Although, no, he might have been blonde, actually,' I say in a pathetic attempt to throw them off the trail. 'Older. Fifties or so. Sixties, maybe.'

Both men regard me in silence. Campbell writes something in his pad without looking at it.

'Right,' he says.

'And what happened then?' Watson prompts.

'I, um, I threw a bucket of water on him.'

That earns me a surprised look from both of them.

Watson turns an ear towards me, as if he has trouble hearing. 'Sorry, you…?'

'I dumped a bucket of water on him. From my window.' I gesture vaguely towards the kitchen. 'Filled up a bucket and emptied it over his head. Thought it might sober him up a bit.'

'Right,' Campbell says slowly, making a note of this. 'And then?'

'I told him I'd called the police,' I continue, the words feeling like they're being squeezed out through a too-narrow tube. 'He heard a siren and scarpered. Got in his car and drove off.'

'He was driving?' Watson asks, surprised. 'In that state?'

I suddenly worry about them checking cameras and running number plates for all the vehicles in the area last night. That would be bad.

'Might've been a taxi, actually,' I say. 'I think he flagged it down.'

A look passes between them. I have no idea what it means, but it makes me nervous. Even more so than I already was. Considering I've been hovering on the edge of a complete nervous breakdown for the past several hours, that's really saying something.

'So you didn't actually need police assistance in the end,' Watson says. It's a statement, not a question, and there's a hint of condescension in his tone.

I feel a flash of irritation cut through the fear. 'How was I supposed to know he'd run off? He was threatening to break the door down.'

'And the occupant of the basement flat?' Campbell interjects. 'How did they respond?'

Shit. *Shit!*

They're going to go downstairs. They're going to talk to Chloe. What if she contradicts what I've said? What if she blurts out everything that happened this afternoon?

'No, she slept through it all,' I say, tripping over the words in my rush to get them out. 'I checked on her this morning. She didn't hear a thing.'

They don't say anything, just keep watching me. Nerves make me keep talking.

'She just moved in yesterday, actually. Young girl. She reckons she must've slept right through it. I was awake.'

'She just moved in? But you think the man was specifically targeting that flat?' Campbell presses.

I shrug. 'Probably not. I think he just got the wrong place. Probably just too pissed to know where he was.'

It all sounds so flimsy, I'm sure they're going to call me out on my lies, but the officers just exchange a look. The taller one shrugs. The smaller one smirks.

'Overreacted a wee bit, did we?' Campbell says, still smirking.

He's patronising me. Laughing at me. All I dare do is nod and smile.

'Yeah. Wee bit,' I say, looking suitably embarrassed.

'Not your fault,' he says, though I can tell he doesn't believe that. 'Better safe than sorry.'

I manage to keep my smile fixed in place. 'Yeah, sorry to waste your time.'

'No, no, not a problem,' Campbell assures me, though his eyes tell a different story. 'Glad it all calmed down. If it happens again, or he comes back, maybe give us another call before you chuck water on him.'

I want to point out that I wouldn't have *had* to chuck water on him if they'd bothered their arse to turn up, but I just force a little laugh instead.

'Thank you,' I say. 'I'll keep that in mind.'

'Right then,' Watson says, snapping his notebook shut. 'That's all we needed. Sorry to disturb you so late.'

He heads out the door.

Campbell moves to follow him, then stops. Turns. I feel my heart dropping into my stomach as he sniffs the air.

'You have something burning in here?' he asks.

My throat goes dry. My mind goes blank. I stare. For however long, I stare.

'Toast,' I finally say. 'I, uh, I burned some toast.'

He looks at me with a slightly curious expression on his face, then nods. 'Hate it when that happens,' he says, before following his colleague into the hallway. 'Goodnight, Miss Shelley.'

'Goodnight,' I echo, watching as they head for the exit.

I close the door and lean against it, sliding down until I'm sitting on the floor, my legs no longer able to support me.

I press my forehead against the cool wood, breathing deeply, trying to slow my racing heart.

That was too close. Far, far too close.

And something tells me that it's only the beginning.

CHAPTER 10

Diane

Somehow, I sleep. Not easily, and not for long, but I manage a handful of hours before the alarm starts wailing at me to get up.

I slap my hand on top of it, pull the covers up around my chin and try to grab another five minutes.

It's then that I remember. The body. The blaze. The bubble wrap.

I latch onto that last one, trying to use it as a distraction. Why would a man have such a large quantity of bubble wrap in his shed? What was he doing with it all?

My efforts are in vain, though. A little editorial voice reminds me he wasn't just a man, he was a *police*man.

And now he's dead, his corpse incinerated in his own car, all alone and miles from anywhere.

I feel sick. I feel dirty. I feel that nothing in my life is ever going to be the same again.

The four-minute snooze period runs out, and the alarm goes off again. I'm suddenly gripped by a rage that makes me yank on the bloody thing until the cable rips from the socket. I launch it across the room like a shotput, and then wince when its plastic casing shatters against the wall.

At least that silenced it. If only I could say the same for the voices in my head, accusing me, condemning me, punishing me for what I've done.

As if that's not bad enough, I'm supposed to be at work in forty-five minutes.

It's Friday, which means a prompt start and an early finish. I'm tempted to phone in sick, but would that look suspicious? I'm already going to have to explain running out halfway through the day yesterday. I'd told Colin that it was a 'lady emergency', and he hadn't asked any more questions.

But Carol, the manager, will be back in today, and she's always *very* open about her own plumbing issues. Far too open, if you ask me. Nobody wants to know about what's going on in her downstairs department, but she's determined to let us all in on it, nonetheless.

She'll have questions – and plenty of them.

I get up, have a pee, then jump in the shower again. I don't really have time for it, but I can still smell the smoke lingering on my skin. I can't see the blood, but I know it's there, hidden in the creases and clogging up the pores.

This shower isn't nearly as scalding. I used up all the hot water last night, and it hasn't had a chance to build up in the tank again.

I'm shivering when I get out and wrap myself in a towel, then go hurrying through to the relative warmth of my bedroom.

I don't particularly like the skirt suit that I usually wear to the office. It's not exactly flattering, although, not much is these days. It's a sensible choice, though. A safe bet. I've got into the habit of wearing it all week and washing it at the weekends.

Of course, that was before it got drenched with blood and burned to ash.

I slide open the wardrobe, deliberately avoiding my eye in the mirrored door. Rummaging around, I find a pair of brown slacks and a cream shirt I reckon I can get away with. The trousers are flared at the bottom and look a bit more *Saturday Night Fever* than *Friday Morning Call Centre*, but they'll do the job.

I wrestle *the ladies* into an ill-fitting bra, pull on the rest of the clothes, then stuff my feet into a pair of brown boots I haven't worn in years. Yesterday's shoes are in the black bag along with the dead man's clothes. I need to destroy those today. I need to get rid of them ASAP.

It's only as I'm pulling on my jacket that the dread begins to gnaw at me. It's not the general panic that's been haunting me since last night, but something more specific. Something precise.

I know it isn't there. Of course I do. All the same, my hand goes to my left breast, my fingers tiptoeing anxiously across the front of my shirt.

The room spins.

Suddenly I'm back there, beside the burning BMW.

Beside the body.

Beside the bag with my bloodied clothes in it.

And my name badge pinned to the lapel.

I run to the bathroom, bouncing off the walls, the floor heaving below me like the deck of a ship. Even as I throw up, I'm trying to convince myself it's going to be OK, it's going to be fine, it's not the unmitigated fucking disaster it appears to be.

The badge is plastic. The letters are vinyl. It would have melted, curled up and been consumed by the heat and the flames.

But what if it didn't? What if some part of it survived? Maybe not my full name, but a letter or two. The company logo. It'll be enough for the police to narrow it down, honing their list of suspects until only one possibility remains.

Me.

Not Chloe.

Me.

There's a knock at my front door. Not the buzzer. A knock.

Someone is inside the block, standing right by my door. What if it's the police? What if they never really left? What if they've been waiting out there for me to mess up in some way, to give the game away, to let slip the awful, terrible things that I've done?

The letterbox opens. The voice that calls out to me isn't one of the officers from last night.

For some reason that I can't quite put my finger on, I almost wish it was.

'Hey, Diane! You there? It's me!' She's somehow whispering but shouting at the same time. 'It's Chloe.' She waits a few seconds, then adds, 'From downstairs,' in case I hadn't yet been able to place who she was. 'Yoo-hoo! You in?'

I flush the toilet, wipe my face and hands on the towel and dart to the front door. I pull it open just as she's about to knock again. She smiles when she sees me, visibly relieved.

'Oh, thank God!' she says. 'I was worried you might have run away, or, you know, killed yourself or something. After—'

I grab her by the arm and pull her inside, shooting a glance up the stairs in case the upstairs neighbours are standing there, listening in.

She looks confused when I slam the door closed, confused as to why I'm in such an obvious stinker of a mood.

'What the hell are you doing here?' I hiss.

Chloe looks hurt by the question. Her blue eyes shimmer, moist and questioning.

'What? I just thought—'

'You shouldn't be here. You shouldn't have come up here,' I tell her. 'We can't be seen together.'

'What? Why not? We're friends!' she says, and for a moment I think she might be about to laugh, like she thinks I'm winding her up.

'Friends? What? No. We're not friends, Chloe,' I say, spitting out the words. 'I mean, maybe we could've been, if you hadn't dragged me into… into…' I gesture wildly, agitated, searching for the words but not wanting to say them out loud. 'All that stuff!' I eventually declare.

She looks at me, her face impassive, her eyes wide with innocence.

'What stuff?' she asks, and I feel like the hallway constricts around me.

What stuff? What the hell does she mean *what stuff?*

I honestly don't know what to say to her. Did we agree to pretend it never happened? Is she going to gaslight me into thinking I've imagined the whole thing?

It's only when she cracks a smile that I realise the truth is even more far-fetched.

'Just kidding,' she says, and the way she looks at me is like she's inviting me to laugh. Urging me to.

Commanding me to, maybe.

I don't. I can't. My sense of humour burned up in a woodland clearing less than twelve hours ago.

'Did you kill him?'

The words arc out of me before I can stop them. For a split-second I panic, but then I double down.

'Did you kill Marcus?'

'What?' Chloe looks outraged. Betrayed. 'No! Of course not! I told you! I went to the house to talk to him, and I found him like that.' She shakes her head, and there are tears in her eyes. 'I wouldn't lie to you, Diane. Not to you.'

She stresses that – *not to you* – like I'm someone special. Someone important to her.

And to think, forty-eight hours ago, I had no idea this woman even existed. What I wouldn't give to go back to that.

'You believe me, don't you?' she asks.

There's no emotion on her face. None. It's like all her muscles have gone slack at the same time. Her eyes remain fixed on me, one ringed by her pale, freckled skin, the other circled by purple and black.

'I need you to believe me, Diane.'

I start to answer, but the words get snagged in the barren desert of my throat. I clear it and try again.

'I believe you,' I tell her.

I'm not sure that I do, but I don't think it matters. Not now. Not after what we did.

God help me, we're in this together now.

'Listen, I, um, I have to go to work,' I say.

She stands there in silence for a second. Two. Three.

Then her smile returns, and she nods. 'Of course! Where's your cat?'

There's no gap between the two sentences, and I'm still processing the first when the second filters through.

'Cat?' I say, then I look along the hall. 'Oh. He's… I don't know. I haven't seen him in ages. Probably out somewhere. He likes to roam about. He comes back when he's hungry.'

'Shame,' she says. 'I'd like to meet him. I'd love a cat.' Her smile fades a little, losing some of its lustre. 'But Sarah says no pets.'

'Uh, right. Fair enough. That's a shame,' I say, then I make a show of looking at my watch. I'm already too late to get the bus. It'll have to be an Uber. 'Listen, I really need to go.'

'Of course. You get going,' she tells me.

She takes a sudden big lunge closer like she's going to strangle me, and I instinctively draw back, cracking an elbow and the back of my head against the wall behind me.

I'm about to push her away when I note the lack of pressure on my throat, and lack of hands around my neck. Instead, she's fiddling with the lapel of my shirt. Her hands are fine and nimble, and I'm suddenly aware of how the shirt's stretched material tugs at the buttons.

'There we go,' she declares, stepping back.

I look down and see my missing work badge pinned in place, my name and the logo emblazoned across it. It's not in the car. It's not with the body.

So why am I no less afraid?

'I saved it for you,' Chloe says.

She looks me over, eyes darting left and right and up and down as she fully checks me out. It makes me feel naked and exposed, and I cover my belly with my arms even as she gives me a double thumbs-up.

'Well now,' she breathes. 'Don't you look positively *perfect*?'

CHAPTER 11

Diane

'What was it? Your period? You still get periods, yeah? At your age?' Carol points down to her crotch area and spins her finger around, lowering her voice to a conspiratorial whisper. 'It's all still going on down there, is it?'

'I'm thirty-seven!' I tell her, not quite able to hide my shock.

We're standing out the back of the building, at the smoker's hut. I don't smoke, but Carol very much does, and so many of her one-to-one meetings are held out here, surrounded by dog-ends and damp.

It's raining – a steady downpour that rattles off the plastic roof and makes me pull my jacket more tightly around myself.

'I wasn't much older than that when it all went to shit,' Carol announces. She takes a long, solemn draw on her cigarette. 'Tits went. Tubes. Got hair on my backside.'

Incredibly, that's only the second most distressing mental image to get inflicted upon me in the last twenty-four hours. I still can't shut my eyes without seeing the stab wounds in Marcus's throat and chest.

'You got anything like that going on?' she asks. This time, it's my crotch she shoots a look at. 'Downstairs?'

'It was just stomach cramps,' I say.

'Oh, well, make the most of them while you can, Diane,' Carol says. 'You'll miss them when they're gone.'

I sincerely doubt that, but just nod slowly, like I appreciate these offered words of wisdom.

'And also, wax. Get a treatment. Don't just shave it. The backside, I mean.' Carol takes another long draw. The smoke curls around her, a spectral entity enshrouding her. 'It's like sitting on a bloody hedgehog.'

I thank her for her time, apologise again for having to leave so suddenly, and then she waves me away with the yellowing fingertips of her free hand. Hurrying across the courtyard, I duck inside and shake off the worst of the raindrops before they have a chance to soak into my clothes and hair.

Two of the three new-starts from yesterday are waiting in the training room. Definitely Shannon (I checked) and Kyle, the guy with the phone, both returned for their second day. Jamie, the one I actually had the most hope for, didn't bother to turn up.

Still, no great loss.

I don't have the energy to deal with them, so I stick on a DVD about identifying inappropriate workplace behaviour, then head to the tearoom to make myself a coffee. Extra strong. Five sugars. It's barely gone half nine and I already need the energy.

The tearoom stinks of egg when I open the door, and I immediately know who the culprit will be. Sure enough, Colin, the assistant manager, sits huddled at a table for one in the corner, eating sandwiches from a Tupperware tub while scouring the sports pages of the daily paper.

I've got nothing against Colin, and I've got nothing against sandwiches.

But egg? In the confined space of a workplace tearoom? That's not right.

And, also, I do actually have quite a few things against Colin. He is, by and large, a knob.

'Jesus, Nora!'

The door, which just closed behind me, has flown open again. Emma, from HR, comes striding in, waving a hand in front of her face and scowling in Colin's direction.

'Not egg again, Colin? I thought we spoke about this?'

Emma is ten years younger than me but already has her life more together than I likely ever will. She strides through the call centre like she owns the place, in wide-shouldered jackets and impossibly skinny trousers.

She's short – five three, maybe – but makes up for it with towering heels and a general air of rock-solid confidence.

Colin is technically her boss, but this never seems to bother her, even though he can be a vindictive bastard when he wants to be. She might feel like she's protected by her encyclopaedic knowledge of employment law, or maybe her position just means she's been privy to a lot of his dirty laundry.

'You said no egg mayo,' Colin replies.

'And what's that?' Emma asks, nodding to the container like it's got something toxic lurking inside.

'Just egg,' Colin tells her. 'On its own.'

Emma sighs. She shoots me a look that's half scorn, half pity. 'That's the most depressing thing I've ever heard, Colin,' she tells him. 'Cover it up. There's been complaints.'

Colin looks from Emma to me, then back again. 'From who?'

'Never you mind. That's sensitive information. Pop the lid on it. Pronto.'

Muttering, Colin closes the lid, but in a final act of defiance, he shoves the bit of sandwich he was still holding into his mouth. It's made with thick Bloomer bread and a *lot* of egg, so it's a struggle for him to fit it all in.

I can tell from his eyes that he deeply regrets the decision, but he chews as best he can, pausing only to take short, panicky breaths through his hairy nostrils.

Eventually, he manages to clear enough space in his mouth to mumble, 'Happy now?' but Emma has turned to me, the assistant manager and his eggy onslaught apparently forgotten.

'Diane! Yes! Hello!' she says, as if only just spotting me. 'This afternoon? Yes? All good?'

I cock my head and narrow my eyes. 'This afternoon…?' I say, dragging it out to buy time while my brain frantically tries to remember whatever it is I've previously committed to.

Am I due an appraisal?

Have I been 'invited' to a disciplinary hearing and missed the email?

Wait. No. Friday.

'Drinkies,' Emma says, jumping in. 'Bibi's birthday. Cocktails and canapés. Remember?'

'Bibi's birthday,' I say, far too late to convince her that I hadn't forgotten. 'Yes. No. I remember.'

I'm trying to think of an excuse not to go beyond the obvious one that Bibi's an insufferable cow, but she's already headed for the door, shooting Colin a stern look as she goes.

'No egg,' she says, pointing at his Tupperware. 'Mayo or no mayo.'

I should chase after her and let her know I won't be coming. How can I possibly go out to celebrate after yesterday? I can't go to the pub, I should be…

What? Fleeing the country? Changing my identity?

At best, I'll go back and pace around the flat, just waiting for the police to come and arrest me. I've been scrolling the news apps on my phone all morning, but there's nothing about a missing police officer, or a body in a burned-out car.

Still, it's only a matter of time until they find him.

Only a matter of time until I'm caught, and my life is over.

'Might as well get shitfaced first, I suppose,' I mutter.

'What?'

I turn my back on the assistant manager and click on the kettle.

'Nothing, Colin,' I say, and some of Emma's bravado has clearly rubbed off on me. 'Just shut up and eat your egg.'

Yes, a night out might be good for me. One last evening of drinking and dancing before I'm carted away and slung in jail for the rest of my life.

One final hurrah.

I mean, what could possibly go wrong?

CHAPTER 12

Diane

'So, then I says to him, I says, "Brian, you're not getting back in these knickers for all the Prosecco in Tesco!"'

Bibi throws back her head and howls with laughter at her own story. The rest of us join in, but I'm only half present, my smile fixed in place like it's been nailed there. My mind keeps drifting back over the events of yesterday, spiralling down, focusing in on all the little details.

The body. The blood. The flames.

And the black bag that's now stashed at the back of my wardrobe.

I need to get rid of it. I should've tossed it in a bin far from home before coming out tonight, but I was already running late, and disposing of a bag of a dead man's clothes on the way to a birthday party seemed a bit... dark.

Even by my recent standards.

We're huddled around a high table in a private room at the Dirty Raven, a mock-Victorian gastropub where dinner costs more than I'd spend on a week's shopping. Emma knows someone – Emma knows everyone – so the canapés portion of the evening is on the house. The cocktails, sadly, are not.

'God, your ex is such a tosser,' Carol says, drawing deeply on a cigarette despite the smoking ban that's been in place for years now. Nobody seems to have the nerve to tell her to put it out, though. God help them if they tried.

The party is half birthday shindig, half celebration of Bibi's recent divorce. She's been legally separated from her ex-husband for all of three weeks. It was her third go at marriage, which is either impressive for a thirty-five-year-old, or… whatever the opposite of impressive is.

Still, say what you like about Bibi, she fully commits to her relationships. She just doesn't stay committed to them for all that long.

'He's an absolute twat,' Bibi agrees, swigging her gin. She's got her hair in bunches and is wearing way too much foundation and eyeliner. She looks like a five-year-old who just found her mum's make-up box. 'But let me tell you, girls, he was hung like Black Beauty. Eye-watering, so it was.'

There is more laughter at that, and a few whoops among the cackling.

'Jesus, Bibi,' Emma splutters into her mojito. 'Some of us are trying to eat.'

She gestures to the plate of fancy finger food in the middle of the table. There's not much left, and what remains looks like it landed on the platter after being kicked down the stairs. The canapés were served over an hour ago, and the room has only got louder and messier since.

Much like the women in it.

'What? I'm just saying I won't miss the man, but I'll miss what he's got between his legs!' Bibi replies. She'd be a picture of wide-eyed innocence, if six G&Ts hadn't started welding one of her eyes shut.

A young barman approaches with a fresh round of cocktails. His eyes are firmly fixed on the ceiling as he sets them down, clearly desperate to escape the conversation. He needn't have worried. Everyone's too sloshed to even acknowledge him.

'I think it's time to move on,' Emma declares, looking at her watch. 'I've booked us a booth at Hoon's.'

Carol groans. 'The nightclub? Can I smoke in there?'

'You can't smoke in *here*!' Emma says, but Carol just breathes out a perfect smoke ring, and everyone cheers again.

'Is that the one that's full of daft young lads in tight trousers?' Lucy, from reception, asks. She's only been with the company a few months, so is making the effort to be one of the girls.

'How tight are we talking?' Carol asks, suddenly interested.

She downs her drink and gathers up her handbag, now itching to go. The rest of us follow suit, and soon we're spilling out onto the pavement, a giggling gaggle of tipsy women. Six of us in total. A couple of the others are from different departments, and I don't know them well enough to remember their names, especially not when I'm focused on not thinking about human flesh melting in a German-made automobile.

I'm not as drunk as the rest of them. I've had a few sips, that's all, then ditched the rest when no one was looking. I need to stay clear-headed, and I'm not supposed to drink on the tablets I'm on.

It hasn't stopped me before, but I don't want to risk saying anything stupid. Not tonight.

We stumble along the street in a chaotic cluster, arms linked, the drizzling rain doing nothing to dampen the mood. Hoon's is only a few streets away, which is good because the mix of booze and adrenaline surging through my system means my legs aren't quite working the way they should.

It's alright this, though. All day I'd lurched between thinking that coming along was a great idea and a God-awful one. Now that I'm out, though, now that I'm here, I'm glad I came. They're work colleagues, not really friends, but they're not a bad bunch, all in all.

I fall behind a step or two as we turn onto George Street, rattling off a text to Ronan, telling him I want to see him tonight, and hinting at some of the things I'd quite like to do to him.

Might as well take the chance when I can.

'Wait for me!' I call when I realise the others are pulling ahead.

I lurch into an unsteady run, misjudge the stopping distance and barrel through the middle of them like they're a set of skittles.

Emma snorts with laughter. Bibi calls out, 'Easy!', while Carol stumbles clear, holding her cigarette up in the air and off to one side to protect it from damage.

My momentum slows. I stagger to a stop just in time to avoid crashing straight into a woman stepping out of a pub.

My subconscious must recognise her first. That's the only way I can explain the jolt of shock that travels through me, and the way my heart sinks into my stomach.

It's her.

It's Chloe.

She apologises, as if the near collision was her fault and goes to step past. For a brief, blissful moment, I think she won't properly notice me, that she'll just walk on by and disappear into the night.

No such luck.

'Diane?' she says. Her face lights up with a grin. 'Oh my God! What are you doing here?'

Before I can respond, or better yet, pretend I don't know her, Carol's voice booms out beside me.

'Who's this then? Friend of yours?'

'Uh… She's my neighbour,' I mutter. The words feel thick in my mouth. 'She just moved in. Downstairs.'

'Ooh, cheeky!' Lucy, from reception, says, but if it's an innuendo, it's a bit of a stretch, and everyone just ignores her for trying too hard.

'Your neighbour!' Bibi squeals, as if this is the most exciting news she's heard all evening. 'That's so cool! Come with us, we're going to Hoon's! You heard of it?'

Chloe glances at me, then back to Bibi. 'Um, no. Is it nice?'

'God, no. Shitehole,' Bibi tells her. She puts an arm around Chloe's shoulders. 'But that's the whole point!'

The alcohol seems to evaporate from my bloodstream – boiled away, leaving me cold and horribly sober. Chloe looks back over her shoulder, her smile now a smirk, as my colleagues cluster around her, absorbing her into the group.

And into another part of my life.

'Another round!' Bibi shouts the words like they're a war cry, before slamming her empty glass onto the table. 'Same again for everyone!'

We've been at Hoon's for over an hour now, crammed into a booth just off the dance floor that's really meant for four people, not seven. The music is too loud for proper conversation, but that hasn't stopped anyone from trying.

Everyone except me, that is. I've been nursing the same vodka and Coke since we arrived, watching with mounting horror as Chloe continues to ingratiate herself with my colleagues.

She and Emma have been up dancing twice. A few lads gravitated towards them at various points, but they pretended not to notice, and then collapsed into laughter when one of the bolder ones tried to slide in between them.

Chloe is amazing. Chloe is brilliant. Chloe is *hilarious*.

So they all keep telling me.

But there's one thing I can't help but suspect that Chloe is *not*. She's not here by coincidence.

Edinburgh's not the biggest city in the world, but it's big enough that I can go months without accidentally bumping into anyone I know. Years, even.

So, what are the chances of me almost walking straight into Chloe?

Did she somehow know where I was going to be? Did she follow me? It's an absurd thought. But at the same time... is it?

'How long have you two known each other?' Emma asks Chloe, having to lean in close to be heard over the thumping bass. Chloe is sitting directly across the booth from me, squashed in between Bibi and Lucy.

Carol's gone out for her fifth cigarette, following a very vocal and almost violent confrontation with a bouncer when she tried to light up at the table.

'Only a couple of days, actually,' Chloe replies, her words slurring slightly. She's had at least three cocktails since we got here and shows no signs of slowing down. 'But we bonded yesterday. Had a real... adventure together, didn't we, Diane?'

'Oh yeah? What was that?' Emma asks.

She's smiling, and the question is friendly, but I can practically see her HR hat being pulled on. She knows I left early yesterday. I'd given her the same stomach cramps story I gave Carol. She seemed to buy it.

And Chloe's about to blow the whole thing.

'Nothing really,' I say before Chloe has a chance to respond. 'I just helped her with some boxes.'

'No.' Chloe frowns as she laughs. 'You helped me get rid of my ex, remember?'

I feel my stomach thudding through the floor.

Oh, God.

Oh, shit.

'What? No, I…'

I look around, searching for… something. An exit, maybe. An approaching SWAT team. But all I see are pulsing lights, and smoky swirls of dry ice, and sweaty bodies, twisting and writhing on the dance floor.

Is this Hell? I briefly wonder as the pounding dance track matches the beat of my hammering heart. *Have I died?*

'Chloe, I don't think—'

Chloe waves her hand, shushing me. 'He was hammering on the door. Shouting. Swearing. Telling me I had no right to leave him. He's the one who gave me this, by the way.'

She points to her now slightly more faded black eye, and the other women all mutter and coo and curse.

Chloe leans in closer, like she's sharing a secret. My whole body is tense. Body parts I didn't even know I had have puckered up. She smiles at me across the table, her hand snaking between the empty glasses until it rests on top of mine.

'Then, just as he's trying to kick in the door, Diane opens her window upstairs and chucks a full bucket of cold water on him,' she says.

The table erupts. It's the greatest thing they've ever heard. The funniest. The most well-deserved. I'm slapped on the back. I'm called a hero, a legend, a bucket-wielding champion of the downtrodden.

And all the while, Chloe keeps her hand in place and her eyes fixed on mine.

'I think it's safe to say I've *burned my bridges* with him,' she adds, drawing more laughter.

'Chloe,' I say, my voice tight with panic. 'Could I have a quick word? In private?'

Her expression goes momentarily blank before the smile returns. 'Sure thing, buddy!'

I practically drag her out of the booth and towards the toilets, away from my still-cackling workmates. Carol's just come back in, and I can hear them filling her in on Chloe's story, already embellishing the details.

'Nearly drowned him, so she did!'

'Serves him right!'

'She should've used boiling oil on the bastard!'

The narrow corridor leading to the loos is mercifully quieter than the main dance-floor area, although the bass still thrums through the floorboards.

'What the hell are you doing?' I hiss, keeping my voice down despite the noise.

'Having fun?' she offers, tilting her head like a confused puppy. 'Your friends are nice. I like them.'

'They're not my friends, they're my colleagues,' I snap, though I don't know why I feel the need to explain this to her. 'And you need to be careful what you say to them. What were you thinking, bringing up yesterday?'

'Relax,' she says, placing a hand on my arm. 'I didn't say anything specific. It's just small talk.'

'Small talk?' I repeat, incredulous. 'Small talk is chatting about the weather, or what you watched on TV, not hinting at… at…'

I can't say it out loud, even here, even now.

Chloe sighs, rolling her eyes like I'm being ridiculous. 'You worry too much,' she says, patting my cheek with a cool hand. 'No one suspects anything. We're just two friends having a night out.'

I grab her wrist, harder than I mean to, pulling her hand away from my face. 'This isn't a game,' I whisper fiercely.

'I know that,' she says, and for a moment her mask slips. There's something cold and dark behind her eyes, something that makes me instinctively loosen my grip on her wrist. Then the moment passes, and she's smiling again. 'But we might as well enjoy ourselves, right? What's the point of being alive if you're not living?'

The question hits me like a slap. What *is* the point? I've spent the last twenty-four hours in a state of terror, waiting for the other shoe to drop, waiting for the police to knock on my door. And here's Chloe, drinking and laughing like she doesn't have a care in the world.

Either she's an exceptional actress, or she really doesn't feel any guilt at all about what we did.

I'm not sure which possibility frightens me more.

'We're leaving,' I announce, straightening up and squaring my shoulders. 'Right now.'

'But the party's just getting started,' she protests.

'I don't care,' I say, my voice leaving no room for argument. 'We're going home.'

I march back to the table, Chloe trailing behind me like a reluctant child. 'Sorry, everyone,' I announce, grabbing my coat from the back of the seat. 'We have to go. Chloe's not feeling well.'

There's a chorus of disappointed *boos* and a few concerned questions, but I ignore them all, making vague promises to catch up at work next week. Chloe, to her credit, plays along, holding her stomach and looking appropriately queasy.

'Thanks so much for including me, everyone,' she says, and it sounds cloyingly genuine. 'It was really nice to meet you all.'

'Take care of her, Diane,' Emma calls as we make our way to the exit. 'Text me when you get home safe!'

I nod, not trusting myself to speak, and practically shove Chloe out of the door and into the night air.

We walk home in silence, the night having turned cold and clear, stars prickling the sky above us. I'm sure the alcohol I consumed earlier is still swimming through my system, but the fear and anger keep me sharp, my senses hyper-attuned to every sound, every shadow.

Chloe seems content to trail along beside me, occasionally humming a tune I don't recognise. She doesn't seem bothered by my mood, or by the fact that I've dragged her away from what was clearly an enjoyable evening for her.

When we finally reach our building, I stop at the top of Chloe's steps. The light is on in the hallway of the basement flat. I can just make out a couple of tubs of paint and a long-handled roller through the dimpled glass of the door.

'Right. Goodnight,' I say, pointing down the steps.

I don't wait for her to respond. Instead, I turn towards the front door to the rest of the block, fishing in my bag for my keys.

I'm in such a rush to get inside that I almost don't notice the shape on the front step. I almost stand on it, in fact. As I peer down at it, I realise with a sick jolt what it is.

A bird. A sparrow or something similar. Small. Brown. Dead. Headless.

'Oh! Someone left you a present,' Chloe says, appearing behind me.

I stare at her.

'Looks like someone loves you,' she says, curling the fingers of one hand in front of me, rippling them like they're claws. 'Meow!' The noise is strangely childlike coming from her adult mouth.

A chill crawls up my spine that has nothing to do with the night air.

Then she turns and descends her stairs, whistling quietly, leaving me with nothing but a headless bird and a growing sense of dread for company.

CHAPTER 13

Diane

The headless bird feels like an omen. A foretelling. A rotten wee message from the universe letting me know that this is only the beginning of the horrors that are headed my way.

Great.

I stare down at the tiny corpse while I try to slide my key into the lock. The severed neck is ragged, not clean. Whatever killed it tore rather than sliced – teeth and claws rather than the sharp edge of a blade.

I need to get rid of it. I don't want to touch the thing – the thought of picking up its stiff little body makes me gag – but I can't just leave it there.

I finally manage to unlock the door to the tenement and hurry across the close to my flat like something is chasing me. I don't feel safe until my own door is closed and bolted behind me.

I don't feel safe, even then.

I lean against the door for a moment, my heart racing. I can hear my breath rasping in the tight confines of the hall.

Calm down, Diane.

I force myself into problem-solving mode. I need a carrier bag for the bird. Two bags, preferably, one for each hand.

I set my handbag down and march with a false determination towards the kitchen, which takes me through the living room.

That's where it hits me. It's so sudden and visceral that I actually stop mid-stride and almost trip onto the coffee table.

Something is different.

Someone has been here.

I can't say how I know. Nothing is obviously disturbed. The cushions on the sofa are still arranged in the same haphazard pile I left them in. The empty coffee mug from this morning still sits on the side table. The TV remote is wedged between the arm of the couch and the cushion.

And yet…

Something feels different. Wrong.

The air itself seems strange. Not like my flat. Not like me.

It's as if the entire place has been moved an inch to the left, and now nothing quite lines up the way it should.

'Hello?' I call out, instantly regretting it. What do I do if someone answers? Soil myself and pass out, probably, and that's hardly going to help matters.

I stand frozen, straining to hear, but there's only silence. Slowly, quietly, I edge into the kitchen. I find the knife block on the worktop. It's mostly empty, but I pull on the one remaining handle.

It's the bread knife.

'Shit,' I whisper, and I carefully lower the door of the dishwasher and remove the biggest knife I have from the top rack.

It's dirty. Slimy bits of raw chicken still cling to the blade. I'm about to run it under the tap when I realise how ridiculous that is. If I'm stabbing some intruder to death with it, I doubt they'll be too concerned about the possibility of salmonella poisoning.

The weight of it is reassuring in my hand. I hold it out in front of me like I'm warding off a vampire, and begin to creep through the flat.

The bathroom door is ajar. I nudge it open with my foot. The hinges creak, just slightly, but in the silence, the sound is like an out-of-tune orchestra.

There are wet towels strewn across the floor. Blobs of toothpaste in the sink. Clothes abandoned in the corner.

All normal.

I head along the hall to the spare room, although that's a generous description of what's essentially a large cupboard you could maybe fit a single bed in, if you didn't mind it touching the walls on at least three sides.

I fling the door open and step back, knife raised in my sweaty hands, pulse machine-gunning up through my neck and into the base of my skull.

Nothing. Just boxes of Christmas decorations, a clothes horse I hang stuff on to dry and some random bags of junk I keep meaning to take to the charity shop.

That leaves only one more place to check. My bedroom.

I approach it slowly, heart thudding so hard I can feel it in my throat. The door is closed, just as I left it this morning. I press my ear against the wood. Listening. Trying to detect any sound of movement.

Silence.

I take a moment to compose myself, to tighten my grip on the knife. The flat is still in darkness, but the blade reflects the dim light coming in from the small window above the door.

I hold my breath. I count to three, then five, then ten, just to be on the safe side.

I grip the door handle, turn it slowly, and push my way into the room in one quick movement, brandishing the knife.

There's someone there. Standing *right there*, clutching a knife, poised to strike.

I scream something that's like a word but not one. It's something more primal than that. Something from before language.

I'm stumbling backwards, waving my knife, even as my brain finishes processing what it's just seen.

My reflection in the mirrored door of the wardrobe. Just me. Only me.

'Holy shit,' I mutter, dropping my arm. I let out a shaky laugh, feeling like a complete idiot.

Then my blood runs cold in my veins.

The wardrobe door is open. Just a little. Just a crack. A couple of inches at most. But I'm certain, absolutely certain, that I closed it properly this morning. I always do. And this morning especially, because inside that wardrobe…

Oh, God.

The bag.

I throw the bedroom door wide open, flick on the light, and rush to the wardrobe, yanking open the mirrored door with such force that it bounces against the wall. I toss the knife onto the bed and begin frantically pawing through the wardrobe's contents, shoving aside coats and jackets, digging past shoes and boots.

Where is it? *Where is it?*

Panic rises in my chest, threatening to choke me. It's not here. *It's not here.*

Someone's been in. Someone's taken it. Why? Who? Was it Chloe? How would she have got into my flat? Surely I'd have noticed signs of a break-in? Does she have a key?

My fingers dig into soft plastic at the very back of the wardrobe, tucked away behind a pair of winter boots I haven't worn in years. I grab it and drag it out. Please, please let it be the right one.

I peer inside.

The clothes.

I buckle forwards, sobbing with relief. Marcus's hoodie and jogging bottoms are still there, stuffed inside the bin bag, just as I left them. My hands shake as I close the wardrobe door, and when I catch another glimpse of my reflection, there's something monstrous in the wildness of her eyes.

I need to get rid of these clothes. Now. Tonight. I can't risk keeping them in the flat a moment longer.

But how? I can't exactly start a bonfire in the middle of Edinburgh. Even if I had a garden, which I don't, a fire at this time of night would attract attention.

I spy a possible solution through the open bathroom door. It's not ideal, but it's better than nothing. If I can't burn the evidence, maybe I can destroy it another way.

I grab the bag and rush into the bathroom, dumping the contents into the tub. The hoodie and joggies land with a soft thud on the bottom. My bloodied shoes clatter against the plastic.

The sight of the clothes, and the lingering smell of smoke, make my head spin and my mouth fill with bitter saliva. I swallow it down. Steady myself. I need to focus.

I run through the house, yanking open cupboards, rummaging through the bottles and sprays below the sink, grabbing anything that looks caustic enough to do damage.

Bleach. Yes. Definitely bleach.

I unscrew the cap as I run back to the bathroom, and pour the whole bottle over the clothes, watching as the dark fabric absorbs the liquid, the sharp chlorine smell making my eyes water.

What else? What else?

Drain cleaner. That's basically acid, isn't it?

I add that to the mix, then remember something about vinegar and bicarbonate of soda creating a reaction. I've got both under the sink. I rush to get them, return to the bathroom, and dump them in as well. The mixture starts to fizz and bubble, emitting a noxious cloud that makes me step back, coughing.

Oven cleaner. That's good for breaking down organic matter, right?

I spray it over the sodden clothes, then use a toilet brush to poke and prod at them, making sure every inch is saturated with chemicals. The stench is overwhelming, a toxic miasma that makes my head spin. Even with the window open, I have to step out of the bathroom every few minutes just to catch my breath.

After about twenty minutes of manic chemical warfare, I stand back to survey my work. The clothes are a soggy, discoloured mess, the original black fabric now mottled with patches of grey and brown. The smell is indescribable, a poisonous cocktail that no crime scene investigator could possibly extract DNA from.

Or at least, that's what I tell myself.

I can't leave them here, though. I need to dispose of them, ideally spreading them out so they can't be easily found.

I grab more bags from under the sink and use the toilet brush to scoop the sopping garments out of the bath. The jogging bottoms go into one bag, the hoodie into another. My shoes into a third. I tie them up tightly, then double-bag each one for good measure.

The bath is a mess, stained with streaks of chemicals, but I can't worry about that now. I'll clean it when I get back.

I grab my keys and head for the door, the three bags clutched in my hands. The cold of the tenement gnaws hungrily at my skin. It's fine. I'll cope.

As I step outside, there's a sickening crunch beneath my foot, and I know immediately what it is.

The headless bird. I'd completely forgotten about it.

I look down to see it flattened beneath my boot, a smear of feathers and flesh against the concrete step.

Somehow, it seems entirely appropriate.

. . .

It takes me an hour to get rid of all three bags. I eventually dump them in different bins about half a mile apart, after dodging down side streets and back alleys, avoiding the places where CCTV cameras are likely to be.

I should have got changed before I came out. I should have dressed differently. Covered my face, at least. I might have kept off the main roads and stuck to the shadows, but there are hundreds of cameras around the city centre. Thousands, probably. What are the chances I managed to avoid all of them?

Damn.

Damn.

What an idiot. I was so desperate to get rid of the evidence that I've probably made myself look even more suspicious.

Stupid, stupid, stu—

'Alright there, gorgeous?'

The voice comes at me through the haze of panic I'm surrounded by. I shoot it a sideways look and see two young lads in their late teens falling into step beside me, one on either side. They're wearing tracksuits and cheap aftershave. Carrying cans of lager that, judging by how they're swilling the contents around, are nearly empty.

I can smell the booze on their breath, the pungent scent of cannabis that trails in their wake.

'Had a rough night, sweetheart?' the one on my left asks.

'Looking for a wee bit of fun?' adds the one on my right.

They sound drunk, or wasted, or just plain thick. Their words are slow, as if they're having to wade through treacle to reach my ears.

They might be idiots, but they're both taller than I am. Stronger. Faster.

'How're you no' saying nothing?' Lefty drawls.

'You no' like us or something?' Righty demands. He burps, and the air becomes even more foul.

'You a total stuck-up bitch or something?'

'I just… I'm just going home,' I say, picking up the pace and hoping they take the hint.

'Want us to come wi' ye?' Righty asks. There's a leer in his voice that makes the hair on the back of my neck stand up.

'We'll give ye a good night,' Lefty adds, and both lads snigger as they meet each other's eye above my head. 'Proper night to remember.'

I want to run. I want to cry. I want to be back home, on my own, far away from these two, far away from everything.

I keep calm. I've learned how to over the years. Don't wind them up. Don't antagonise. Don't risk it.

Be nice, be gentle, play along,

But then Righty burps again, almost directly in my face. I see the yellow scum on his teeth as his mouth twists and he laughs at me.

It's like a wave, rising up inside me. Something swelling. Something rushing from the deep.

My knee comes up between his legs. Fast. Hard. I see his eyes bulging and his face contorting and watch as he crumples backwards, downward, crashing into a bollard before sinking to the ground.

Lefty draws back in fright as I round on him, shoving him, screeching at him to 'Piss off and leave me alone!'

And then, as suddenly as it started, this burst of bravery splutters away, and I'm left with the cold, gnawing fear of all the possible terrible futures that lie ahead in the next few minutes.

I do run then. As fast as I can, down the alleyways and side streets, winding my way back in the direction of my flat.

I expect to hear their footsteps chasing me, hunting me down. But no. Nothing. Just a few shouted insults about my weight and my face and how they wouldn't have touched me if I'd paid them.

I'm back to walking by the time I reach the flat, my chest painful and heaving, tears cutting tracks down my cheeks. My fingers shake as I tap out a text to Ronan, telling him I need to see him, to come quick, to please hurry.

The lights are on downstairs in the basement flat. It's late, but through the window I can see Chloe moving a paint roller up and down a living room wall.

She doesn't notice me. Thank God.

I enter the tenement, enter my flat, and spend a good five minutes just leaning against the door and crying.

It's an hour later, after I've cleaned out the bath and got ready for bed, that I notice Ronan hasn't read my message.

And it's a few hours after that before I realise that the dead bird was no longer lying out there on the step.

CHAPTER 14

Diane

Saturday drags on forever. Every hour feels like a week, every minute a day. I keep checking my phone for news updates: 'Police officer missing'; 'Body found in burned-out car'; 'Edinburgh murder investigation launched'. But there's nothing. Just the usual political nonsense, celebrities I've never heard of doing things I couldn't care less about, and a load of stuff about football that I gloss straight over.

I flick through the local news sites, scroll through Twitter. Nothing about Marcus, or a body, or a burned-out BMW. Nothing about me.

The clock crawls forwards, and the silence from the news outlets begins to feel like a weight being slowly lifted from my shoulders.

Could we have got away with it?

The thought makes me feel sick. Even if we did get away with it, a man is dead. A horrible man, I'll give you, but that's not the point. And all I'm worried about is if I'll escape punishment for it. When did I become the kind of person who thinks like that?

Since Thursday, I remind myself. Since I helped dispose of his body.

Music is playing downstairs, the thrum of a bass line vibrating up through the floorboards. I can hear the swish and rumble of a paint roller on Chloe's ceiling and the occasional grunt of effort when she's presumably stretching to reach a difficult spot.

At one point, she sings along to a song, her voice clear and childlike. I wonder if it's an act, this whole young, innocent, vulnerable routine. I wonder what else about her isn't real.

Did she kill Marcus?

I hope not. She seemed genuinely shocked. Genuinely upset.

Is that why I helped her, though? Or did I think that, even if she did kill him, the bastard probably had it coming?

I've known men like him. I've been *trapped* by a man like him. Suffered at his hands, and his feet, and his—

I check my phone again. Scroll through the news sites.

Nothing.

I flick over to my messages, checking to see if there's anything back from Ronan yet. He didn't reply to me last night. That's not totally unheard of, but there'd usually be something the following morning.

There's no response from him yet. The message is still sitting there, delivered but unread.

I try to call, but it goes straight to voicemail. He's never been great at answering, especially when he's working, so I'm still not overly surprised. I shoot him a text after the beep.

Call me when you can. Need to talk.

I don't elaborate. I don't want to sound too desperate, too clingy. That's not what we are to each other these days.

Exactly what we are, I don't quite know. But it's not that.

I barely know him these days. Not the way I used to. He's usually available whenever I text and quick to come over, but aside from the sex, what do we actually share? We don't talk about our hopes or dreams or fears. We don't discuss politics or religion or anything. We don't even sit and watch Netflix.

He's just a body in my bed, occasionally in my kitchen making tea, rarely in my life beyond the physical.

And yet, right now I'd give anything to see him walking through that door, to feel his arms around me. The shadow of a boyfriend is better than no boyfriend at all.

I check the phone again. Both messages sit unread.

It's not like him, and something about it makes a tension form in the lining of my stomach.

Downstairs, the radio changes to some chirpy pop song, and the roller starts moving across Chloe's ceiling faster, harder.

Swish. Swish. Shwum.

I turn on the TV and crank up the volume, flicking through the channels until I find something suitably mind-numbing. I don't care what it is, I just need something to drown out the paranoid voices whispering in the dark corners of my brain.

I find an American baking competition. It's a twelve-episode marathon, and I've only missed the first two.

Perfect.

I'm eight episodes deep when my eyes start to feel heavy. I've spent the day drifting from sofa to kitchen to bathroom and back again, not accomplishing anything, barely even able to concentrate on the TV. Just existing in a fog of anxiety and fear. And biscuits. Quite a lot of biscuits. That whole 'never eating again' thing didn't really stick.

I'm just starting to drift off when my phone pings, snapping me back to the here and now. I grab for it, hoping it's Ronan, but it's just the Duolingo bird passively aggressively letting me know that I haven't done a language lesson in over a month.

I introduce the stupid bird to some language even it probably hasn't heard before.

The messages to Ronan still haven't been read.

And the *swish, swish, shwum* of the paint roller beneath my feet eventually lulls me back to sleep.

The sound of a door closing jolts me awake. Was it my door? Is someone in here?

I sit up, disorientated and with a puddle of dried-up drool sticking the side of my face to a cushion. I'm still on the couch, a throw blanket tangled around my legs that I don't remember pulling over me.

Through the window, the pale light of dawn creeps over the rooftops. The battery on my phone is nearly dead, but it has enough juice to tell me it's 6:24 a.m.

'Hello?' I croak into the silence. Nobody answers. Nobody's here.

I'm starting to think I imagined it when there's another sound from outside. Footsteps.

I get up and peer through the gap in the curtains. Chloe is walking away from the building, dressed in sports clothes – leggings and a crop top that shows off her flat stomach – with a small shoulder bag. It's Sunday morning. Where the hell is she going at this time?

Logically, I know it must be the gym, but the idea of dragging myself in for a workout at this time on a Sunday is so alien as to seem completely absurd.

Still, I feel my shoulders slumping with relief as she rounds the corner and disappears out of sight. She hasn't bothered me since Friday, but she's always been there, ever-present, moving around, or singing, or painting.

For a moment, I'm jealous of her energy.

I check my messages while I put the phone on to charge. Still nothing from Ronan. Weird.

Maybe he's with someone else. I've never asked if he sees other women. I've never really wanted to know. But there's something about the silence that's prickling at my suspicions. Something feels… off.

I try calling again, but it goes straight to voicemail. Again.

'Ronan, it's me. It's, eh, it's Diane,' I say, though I'm not sure why I feel the need to clarify. 'Call me back when you get this, OK? It's… it's important.'

I hear the neediness in my own voice, and I hate it, so I quickly hang up. With the phone tethered to the wall by the charging cable, I open Instagram and go to his profile. His last post was Thursday, a picture of a new deck he'd built for some client. Nothing since then.

Maybe I'm overthinking this. He's probably just busy. Or his phone's dead. Or he's sleeping off a hangover.

I flick over to the news apps, and I yawn and scratch as I scroll through the headlines. Still nothing about a body, or a car, or a missing police officer.

Still no mention of me, or of Chloe.

Maybe we really are in the clear.

I should be happy about that, I suppose. Relieved. But mostly I just feel hollow, like I've left something vital behind in that clearing in the woods. Some essential part of me that can't be retrieved.

I drag myself into the shower and stand under the scalding spray until my skin is pink and my fingertips are wrinkled. The bathroom still smells faintly of chemicals from last night's frenzy, but I've scrubbed the tub clean, removing any obvious trace of what I'd done.

Once I'm dressed in leggings and a baggy jumper, I decide I need to get out of the flat. I've been cooped up since Friday night, spiralling down into my own dark thoughts. A walk might help clear my head. Maybe I'll treat myself to a light breakfast at that little café on the corner. Or, even better, a heavy one. Full Scottish. Square sausage, tattie scones, the works.

Death row inmates get a last meal, right? Maybe this will be mine. Before the police come knocking. Before the arse falls out of my life entirely.

I stand and stare at my reflection in the mirrored door of the wardrobe. Nothing has changed about me physically in the last week, and yet it's not the same person looking back at me. Not remotely.

My reflection and I turn our heads left and right, each sizing the other up. Neither of us likes what we see.

I'm about to slap on some make-up when my phone starts buzzing by the bed. My heart leaps when I see the screen. It's a FaceTime call.

Ronan!

I snatch up the mobile and all that excitement collapses like a burst balloon. It's not Ronan. It's my mum's face filling the screen, her pink, round cheeks flushed with excitement.

I take a deep breath and answer. 'Hi, Mum.'

'Diane!'

She practically shouts my name, though her face is only inches from her iPad screen. She's never quite got the hang of video calling and feels the need to project so her voice is heard all the way on the other side of the city.

'There you are!' she says. 'I've been trying to get a hold of you for ages.'

'You have?' I frown. I've had no missed calls.

'The buttons weren't working,' she says, which is her catch-all explanation for any technical issues she encounters on anything, from the iPad to the microwave. 'Anyway, you're going to… God, you look like lukewarm shite,' she informs me, but she doesn't bother waiting for a response. 'You're going to laugh at this. You know them old toys of yours? The ones that were up in the loft. Weird little squirrels and rabbits and the like?'

'The Sylvanian Families,' I say.

'Aye, them. Right freaky wee things. Hedgehogs and whatnot. Otters.' Even with her face that close to the camera, I can see her give a shudder. She never did like them. 'You know we put them up for sale on the Facebook?'

I sigh. 'It's just Facebook. And, aye, you said you were going to. But I'm getting the money,' I remind her.

'Yes, yes,' she says in a way that suggests we'll cross that bridge when we come to it. 'Anyway, someone came round to buy them. She waited here while your dad went and got the boxes out of the upstairs cupboard. With the boiler. You know the one.'

It's an irrelevant detail. Most of what my mum says is irrelevant detail. I just nod, saying nothing, hoping the story is going to reach some sort of conclusion soon.

'Anyway, we waited down here for him, and then she saw our photo. From Tenerife. You, me and your dad. Remember? Twenty-seventeen. You got the sunburn. Remember?'

'Yes, Mum,' I say, struggling to sound interested. 'I remember.'

'Course you do! You were all wee blisters. Anyway, she sees that and she's like, "Oh my God! I know her! That's Diane!" Turns out she knows you. What are the chances?'

My mum laughs. Her eyes sparkle with delight.

And yet, my stomach does a slow, nauseating roll.

'Who is it?'

'See for yourself!' Mum turns the iPad around.

The movement is a blur at first, a smear across the screen.

And then it settles on a familiar face. Sitting on my couch. Between my parents. In my childhood home.

'Hi, Diane!' Chloe waves enthusiastically, her face splitting into a wide grin. She has a mug of tea in her hand and raises it like she's toasting me. 'Surprise!'

CHAPTER 15

Diane

I am raging. No, more than that, I am rage itself. The concept of fury made flesh.

How dare she? How fucking *dare she* go to my parents' house?

I stand by the kitchen window, hands pressed on the worktop on either side of the sink, fingers splayed, eyes locked on the pavement outside.

What was she doing there?

How did she find them?

What did she say?

Oh, God. What did she say?

It's not long before I'm given the chance to ask her myself when I spot her through the glass. She comes strutting around the corner carrying a big dusty cardboard box with 'Diane's wee squirrels' scribbled on the side in faded black marker pen.

She's got an earphone in. A smile on her face. A bounce in her step.

What the hell is wrong with her?

I race outside, determined to catch her before she disappears downstairs into her flat. I pull the door behind me, but not hard enough to fully close it. It bounces back off the frame an inch or two, but I don't have time to go back.

'What the hell do you think you're doing?' I demand, throwing open the door to the tenement, just as she reaches the top of the steps that lead down to her front door.

She freezes, wide-eyed, like one of the Milk Rabbit children caught in the headlights of the Sylvanian Families Cruising Car. 'What's the matter?' she asks, surprise in her voice. 'What's wrong?'

'You know fine well what's wrong,' I shout, charging down the steps. 'My parents? What the fuck, Chloe? How did you even find them? What kind of weird, creepy shit is that?'

I'm practically vibrating with rage. The words are tumbling out of me, tripping over themselves in the rush to get out, to get at her. I don't even care if the upstairs neighbours or the people in the next-door flats hear me. Let the whole damn street know.

Chloe takes a step back, all innocence and confusion.

'What? No, I… Sarah showed me these Sylvanian Families on Facebook Marketplace last night. She knew I used to collect them, and the price was good.' She holds out her phone, opening up Facebook to show me. 'Look.'

I don't look. I'm not interested in seeing her screen. 'And what, they just happened to be mine?' I ask. 'Bullshit!'

She shakes her head. There's a desperation in her eyes. She wants me to believe her. She needs me to.

'I swear, Diane, I had no idea they were yours until I saw the photo in the living room. I freaked out a bit myself.' She looks down at the box, then back up at me. 'It is a bit weird, yeah, but it was just a crazy coincidence. I mean, Edinburgh's not *that* big, is it?'

I want to tell her to go to hell, to get away from me, to stay away from my family. But something about her expression makes the words catch in my throat. Could it really just be a coincidence? Is that possible?

'I mean, what did you think happened?' she asks, tilting her head in confusion. Her blue eyes bore into me, and I notice the bruise on her cheek is starting to fade. 'Did you think I was stalking you or something?'

She lets out a little laugh, and I'm suddenly six inches tall, beetroot with shame. I'm a thirty-seven-year-old woman, standing on the street in too-tight leggings and a shapeless baggy jumper, shouting at a girl half my age that she's... what? Obsessed with me?

Why the hell would she be? What would she possibly see in me?

'So it was just a coincidence?' I say flatly.

'A total fluke,' she chirps, nodding enthusiastically. 'I was as surprised as you were. That's why I told them, and we decided to phone you. We thought you'd find it funny, like we did.'

My tongue flits across my cracked lips, like I'm building up to say something, but my head is empty, my throat dry.

'Your parents are so nice,' Chloe prattles. 'Your mum made me tea, and your dad showed me all these old baby photos. There was one where you were about three, running naked through a paddling pool,' she says, grinning. 'You were so cute. Oh, and...'

With some effort, she shifts the box beneath one arm, fishes in her shoulder bag and then hands me a fifty-pound note. 'Mum said just to give it straight to you.'

Mum. That's what she says. Not 'your mum'. Just mum.

'I'll take good care of them,' she assures me. 'Oh, by the way, you find Cowboy Meowboy yet?'

I stare in surprise, trying to adjust to this sudden change of topic. Eventually, I just shake my head.

'I'm sure he'll turn up,' she says, offering me a supportive smile. Then she heads down the stone steps towards her front door.

She's almost at the bottom when I finally find the words to call down to her.

'Chloe.'

She stops and looks up. Her smile is dazzling, and for a moment I almost forget what I was going to ask.

But only for a moment.

'The other night. Thursday. After…' I don't bother to fill in the blanks. 'What were you and Ronan talking about out here?'

She frowns, as if trying to remember. 'On Thursday? After *you know what?*' She pulls a face and stares blankly up at the sky just past my head. 'God, can't remember. Just thanking him for the lift, I think.'

I stare down at her. I can't tell if she's lying. Not about any of it.

'Right,' I say. 'Thanks.'

I watch as she disappears into her flat and closes the door behind her. Seconds drag on as I linger there before I head back into the tenement block towards my own front door.

I'm halfway across the close when I spot it.

A small brown shape on the doorstep. A mouse. A dead one.

Its head has been torn off, leaving a ragged stump of a neck, just like the bird.

I stepped right over it in my rush to come outside.

Like before, the flesh and fur have been ripped at and torn. The limp, lifeless body is just rags of flesh and fur.

I look back to the door of the tenement, half-expecting to see Chloe standing there smiling at me.

But there's nobody in here but me.

CHAPTER 16

Diane

I need to find Ronan.

It's been nearly three days since I heard from him, and his silence feels like a metal band tightening around my chest. Another one to add to the growing collection.

I've called. I've texted. I've stared at his social media accounts like some lovesick teenager, willing a new post to appear.

Nothing.

I don't know his exact address these days, just that he's no longer in the same pokey wee flat he used to share with a couple of mates. I'm pretty sure he's now in one of those little cul-de-sacs off Restalrig Road in Leith. He mentioned it once when he was talking about a job he'd done for a neighbour. He showed me photos of his front garden, too, and the decking he built.

I could find it. I know I could.

But should I? Is it weird? I was practically accusing Chloe of being a stalker a few minutes ago, and now here I am thinking about sneaking round to Ronan's house and peeking in the windows.

But I need to know if he's OK. Even as I'm pulling on my jacket, I'm convincing myself that's all it is. Concern for a friend. Nothing more.

The bus journey over there takes nearly forty minutes. I spend it staring out of the rain-streaked window at the passing city streets, my mind whirring with the thoughts of what might await me when I get there.

Maybe he's ill. Maybe his phone's broken. Maybe he's avoiding me because he's somehow figured out what we were up to on Thursday. What if he knows? About the car. About the body. What if he knows?

What if Chloe's said something to him?

What if she's done something?

I push that thought away. It's absurd. He's about twice her size. Several times stronger. The worst she could do is tell him the truth. And if she did, I suspect the police would come racing round to arrest us in no time.

The cul-de-sac is tidy, a row of semi-detached houses with neat front gardens and well-kept hedges. It's more boring and conventional than I'd expect from Ronan.

I spot the van immediately, parked in a driveway three houses up on the left. My heart does a little flip, and I whisper a quiet, 'Thank God,' in relief.

He's here. He's home. He's safe.

The house is a two-storey terraced, with a stylish front door and the same decking Ronan showed me the photo of a few months back. The curtains in most of the windows are open, aside from one of the windows upstairs.

He's sick. That must be it. That must be all.

I hang back, hidden from the house by the shadow of the van, and take out my phone. It takes a few seconds for the call to connect.

Voicemail. Again.

Shit.

I should turn around, go home, just wait for him to call me back. He'll get in touch when he's feeling better. I know he will.

But I've come all this way. And his house is right there.

And I've never felt quite so alone.

Well, maybe once.

Gravel crunches under my feet as I approach the front door. The house is nicer than I expected, with hanging baskets full of artificial flowers on either side of the door. Through the large bay window, I can see a living room with a flat-screen TV on the wall. It's on. There's a cartoon playing. *SpongeBob*.

I stop at the front door, right on the step, and try calling him again. It goes straight to voicemail, just like before.

I glance back along the path, as if I might still be thinking about leaving, but I'm lying to myself. I can't leave. Not now.

The door is a sophisticated shade of grey, with a brass knocker shaped like a lion's head. I lift it and let it fall against the plate with a sharp *thwack*.

Then I wait, shifting my weight from foot to foot, rehearsing my lines, already regretting this decision.

I hear footsteps getting closer. They're fast, like someone is hurrying to get to the door.

It swings open and I start to blurt out my hastily prepared explanation before I realise it's not Ronan standing there. It's a woman, probably around my age, with dark circles under her eyes and a frown that deepens when she sees me.

She's holding a baby, no more than a few months old, propped against her shoulder. Behind her, a little boy of about four peers around her legs, his hands streaked with paint, his eyes wide and suspicious.

'Aye?' the woman asks, her tone immediately defensive. 'Can I help you?'

'I, uh…' I'm completely off balance. Adrift. I peek past her, and she shifts to block me.

'What do you want?' she demands.

I smile, like this is all some sort of misunderstanding. 'Is, eh, is Ronan in?'

Her eyes narrow, and she shifts the baby to her other shoulder. 'Who's asking?'

'I'm… a friend of his,' I manage to stammer out. 'From work. Sort of. I mean, we don't work together, but I've… hired him. For jobs. Construction. Renovations. Building… things.'

I'm babbling, and I know it. The woman's expression doesn't change, but the contempt in her eyes hardens.

'Oh, a *friend*, are you?' she says, drawing out the word like it's something offensive and dirty. 'Right. I bet you are. And you're here looking for him because…?'

'He, um, he wasn't answering his phone, and I was worried.' My voice sounds far away, like I'm hearing it from down a long, narrow pipe. 'I just wanted to check if he was OK.'

She lets out a bark of laughter, sharp and humourless. 'Oh, he's just fine, I'm sure. Probably just off with another one of his wee side pieces.' Her eyes rake over me, her judgement scraping at my skin. 'You another one of his wee fuckbuddies, then?'

I recoil as if she hit me. 'What? I… no, I…'

I can't finish the sentence. Whatever I was going to say, we both know it would be a lie.

'Have to say, I thought he'd be strutting about with some pretty young thing,' she says, sneering as she looks me up and down. 'Not *this*.'

The little boy tugs at his mother's jeans, looking up at her with confusion on his paint-smeared face. 'When's Daddy coming home?'

And there it is. The final piece of the puzzle slides into place with a sickening *click*.

I sometimes wondered if he was seeing other women. He is. And I'm one of them.

'I'm sorry,' I whisper, already backing away. 'I didn't know. I didn't… I had no idea he was…'

'Married?' she says, her voice bitter. 'Aye, that'd be right. He never mentions it, does he? Not to any of you.'

Any of you.

How many others are there?

'I'm so sorry,' I say again, already turning to leave. 'I wouldn't have… if I'd known…'

I don't look back. I can't. I just hurry away down the street, my face burning with shame, my eyes stinging with the tears I'm trying desperately to hold back.

'And if you see the dirty waste of space,' the woman calls after me, 'tell him not to bother his arse coming home!'

I walk for hours, headed back towards the city centre, back towards the flat, but not following any set route. Walking more for the sake of it than to reach any particular destination.

It's raining. I can see it pooling on the uneven pavements and slicking the faces of the people rushing by, but I don't feel it. Not really. Not even when a bus speeds through a puddle just a few feet from me, throwing up a spray of oily water that finds its way in through my jacket.

OK, maybe I feel it a little then.

I pass shops shuttering up for the evening. Restaurants where families, friends and lovers share candlelit meals and Quarter Pounders with Cheese. Voices roar from pubs as I pass. People with cigarettes pinched between fingers gather in tight knots by the doors, huddled together beneath their canopies of smoke.

None of them matter.

I'm passing a bank at the Waverley Station end of Princes Street when I catch the reflection in the angle of a window. A woman. Skinny. Blonde. A dozen steps behind me and keeping pace.

Tracking me. Following me.

I'm in no mood for her shit. I stop. Spin. I can feel my face contorting, my anger rising like hot, fiery bile.

'What are you doing here?' I cry. 'Leave me alone!'

It's not her. It's not Chloe. The girl glances warily at me as she hurries past, as if I'm some crazy woman ranting on the street.

Yeah. *As if.*

I check my phone, but the screen stays dark when I tap it. I only gave it a short blast of charge earlier, and it's clearly given up the ghost.

Probably just as well. What would I have done? Texted Ronan to tell him I never wanted to see him again? Begged him to come round?

I shove my hands in my pockets and lower my head as the rain gets heavier. I'm almost back at the flat now. Almost home.

I'm thinking of the shower I'm going to have when I eventually waddle up the steps and unlock the front door of the tenement. I can feel the squelching in my shoes, the wetness of my socks squidging up between my toes, rubbing the skin red raw.

I'm cold. I'm wet. I'm drained, both physically and emotionally.

I peel off most of my clothes at the door, dart into the bathroom, crank on the shower.

I'm shivering the whole time – big, whole body shakes that turn my breathing into a series of shaky, shallow sips and big, gulping gasps.

The shower helps. My skin is so numb that I don't feel how hot the water is to start with, and I'm already out and wrapped in a towel before it starts to sting.

I leave the bathroom in a swirl of steam and head through to my bedroom, already shivering again. Climbing under the covers, I bury my face in the pillow and do what I should have done a long time ago.

I scream. I direct all my anger, all my sadness, all my shame into a long, drawn-out shout that is swallowed by the folds of the pillow and absorbed into its polyester stuffing.

I scream, and I cry, and I crush the pillow around my head like I can suffocate myself with it.

I scream. For a full five minutes, I just scream.

And when the voice comes from the end of the bed, I scream even louder.

'You alright?'

I twist, whip around, all bare breasts and raw panic, a hand held up like I can fend off whatever horror has materialised here in my bedroom.

Chloe.

Of course it's Chloe.

She isn't smiling for once. Instead, she's looking at me with concern in the sparkling centres of those bright blue eyes.

'What the hell are…? What are you doing here?' I gasp, wrenching my damp towel out from beneath me, desperately trying to hide my nakedness. 'Why are you here? Why are you in my room?'

She raises a thumb and points it back over her shoulder. 'You left your front door open.'

'No, I didn't!' I cry.

Did I? I can't remember.

'You did. It was open, and I heard…'

She looks at the pillow I've been screaming into. God, how long was she standing there? How much did she see?

'A noise,' she says in a rare display of diplomacy. 'I, um, wanted to check you were OK.'

'I'm fine!' I snap, despite what must seem like quite a lot of evidence to the contrary. 'But you can't just come in here! Get out, alright? Get out!'

'Sorry, right. Yes.'

She nods and moves to go but then stops. There's something furtive and mouse-like about her movements. Her usual bounce and confidence are both missing.

'Have you, uh, have you looked at your phone?'

Something about the way she asks the question stops me yelling at her to leave.

'My phone? No. It's off,' I tell her. 'Why?'

She looks down at her hands. At first, I think she's just fiddling with her fingers, but then I see that she's holding her mobile, tapping at the screen, pulling something up.

'It's just…'

She holds the phone out, screen facing me.

I hear her taking a breath. 'This came up. On the news. I, uh, I thought you'd want to see.'

There's a headline, but I don't read it. Not yet.

Instead, my eyes are drawn to a photo.

A car in a clearing, surrounded by police tape, burned to a blackened metal skeleton.

All my thoughts about us having got away with it reveal themselves as the silly fantasies they always were.

They've found it.

They've found Marcus's body.

And soon my life as I know it will be over.

CHAPTER 17

Diane

'What's the matter, Diane? Forget who you are?'

The world swims back into focus. I see my hand, tightly gripping the pen, the nib of which is frozen on the paper in front of me.

I can hear Lucy's voice prattling away. She's sitting behind the reception desk, making some inane, jovial small talk about the fact I've been standing here at the sign-in sheet for a full minute without writing anything.

I quickly scribble my name and the time – ten minutes late – then set the pen down like the metal is red hot.

'Sorry. Miles away,' I say, straightening up.

She looks up at me from behind the desk. I see her eyes flick over me, a quick up and down that settles into a look of puzzlement. She doesn't say anything, though, thank God.

I must look a state. I haven't showered. Barely slept. After Chloe left, I spent the night alternating between crying, pacing the room and emptying my cupboards of all the junk food that had accumulated in them recently.

The fact I emptied it all into my mouth means my stomach feels like it's been ripped out, kicked around on a sawdust floor, then forcibly reinserted, upside down.

It was the six Creme Eggs that broke the camel's back. That or those three tubes of Pringles.

I wasn't going to come to work. It wasn't even a thought until about half an hour ago, since I assumed that my front door would be smashed in by armed police long before now.

But no. Nothing. The news articles about the discovery remained vague. They mentioned the burned-out car, but not the body. There was still nothing about a missing police officer, and no mention of a manhunt.

The not knowing is almost worse.

Half a dozen times during the night, I thought about texting Ronan, either to call him a scumbag or to ask how he was.

But my other messages are still sitting there unread.

And I can still feel the eyes of that little boy staring at me from behind his mummy's legs.

Kids. He has *kids*. I'd never have hooked up with him again, had I known.

There wasn't time for a shower. I sprayed on deodorant, pulled on the same work outfit I'd chucked on a chair on Friday afternoon, and tried to wrangle my hair into something presentable. The results, judging by the number of times Lucy has glanced up at it, are mixed at best.

'Are you even meant to be in today?' she asks.

'Bollocks!'

The word snaps out of me with enough force and volume to make Lucy jump. I hear her knees hitting off the underside of her desk.

It's Monday. I've been given the day off in lieu of a couple of Saturdays ago when I had to come in to cover for a staff shortage. I'm not supposed to be here today.

All that rushing, all that effort, and I could still be in bed.

The alarm on Lucy's face jerks back into her usual welcoming smile. 'It's good, though! There's an induction to do. Colin was going to have to do it and, well, you know…'

She looks at the doors on either side of us, leans in closer and whispers, 'He can be a bit…' She pulls a face that I can't quite describe, but which I immediately understand the meaning of. Everyone does. Everyone who's spent more than a few minutes in Colin's company.

Nothing he says or does is *quite* enough to call out as inappropriate workplace behaviour, but most of it skims pretty close. It's why Emma, in HR, is always so strict on him about his egg sandwiches. If she can't get him for being a sleazeball, she'll someday get him for that, like Al Capone being jailed over tax evasion.

I hoist my bag onto my shoulder and sigh. 'Right, fine. Training room?'

'Training room,' Lucy confirms.

Her eyes dart across me again. I can almost feel her gaze like the warmth of a spotlight, sweeping over every inch of me, scrutinising every pore.

When she smiles again, there's something pitying there.

'But uh, you should absolutely go ahead and get yourself some coffee first!'

'What are you trying to dredge up in there, then? A corpse or something?'

I blink, suddenly alert, suddenly alarmed. Carol stands before me, blowing onto her tea, gesturing with her eyes to the mug of coffee I've been standing here stirring for the past however long.

'You're not going to find any treasure in there, you know?' she says.

I laugh – somehow, I laugh – pull the spoon out, then rinse it under the tap and stick it in with the others in the mug by the draining board.

'You won't mind me telling you that you look like shite,' Carol says, as direct as ever. 'What's the matter? Hot flashes keeping you up? They nearly ruined me, them bloody things.'

'I'm thirty-seven,' I remind her, but she just puts a hand on my arm and assures me that it gets better. A bit. Though, not quickly, and not all the way.

I can't be doing with her today, so I make my excuses, take my coffee and my bag and head for the training room. I can hear Colin rambling away in there as I approach the door and check my watch. He should be onto the first of the induction videos at this point but, of course, he likes the sound of his own voice too much.

If nothing else, at least I can do one good deed today and rescue whatever poor kids are stuck in there with him. I'm not saying I'm great at my job, even on my best days, but I'm not Colin, and that must count for something.

He turns to look at me, eyes widening in surprise when I open the door. I start telling him that it's fine, that I'm here, that he can go, but the words shrivel up and die in my throat.

There's only one trainee in the room.

Blonde hair. Blue eyes. The slightest suggestion of bruising on her cheek.

She's wearing a cream shirt, like mine. She's already got a name badge, *like mine*. She's here, in my work, and she's looking at me, smiling at me, *dressed like me*.

'Diane? You alright?' Colin asks. He slides down off the desk he was sitting side-saddle on. I flinch at the touch of his hand on my arm. At the note of concern in his voice. 'You look like you've seen a bloody ghost.'

Coffee sploshes onto Emma's desk when I throw the door open without knocking.

She gasps, setting her mug down and hurriedly scrambling to clear papers from the path of the rapidly spreading brown puddle.

'What the fuck is she doing here?' I bark.

Emma looks up from her hasty clean-up job. 'Diane?'

'Chloe!' I stab a finger back at the door, past all the curious faces watching from behind their computer screens. 'What is she doing here?'

'Training!' Emma, usually unflappable, practically shrieks the word. 'She's training. With Colin. Why? What is all this? What's the matter?'

'Everything alright?' Carol asks, sidling into the room.

She shoots a meaningful look at the agents trying to lug in from their desks, then closes the door on them before turning to me.

'You alright, love?'

'No. I'm not alright. It's her. Chloe. What's she doing here?'

Emma and Carol swap puzzled looks.

'I told you. She's training with Colin,' Emma explains, her voice settling back into its usual calming rhythm. 'I didn't think you were here today.'

'I'm not. I mean, I am, obviously,' I say. 'But *why is she here*?'

'She's starting work,' Carol says, like it's the most obvious thing in the world.

And it is. Of course it is. Why else would she be going through the induction process in the training room wearing a company name badge?

'She's infiltrated my job,' I mutter, turning away and massaging my temples, trying to fend off the headache that reached its peak when I locked eyes with Chloe across that room. 'I can't get away from her, not even here.'

'What are you talking about?' Emma asks.

Carol shakes her head at her and whispers, 'It's all hormones,' so quietly I'm clearly not supposed to hear it.

'No, Carol, it's not *fucking hormones*!' I shout.

Her eyes widen a fraction, then narrow like she's about to go for my throat. Thankfully, she doesn't.

I point at the door again, more emphatically this time, trying to make them understand, trying to make them see.

'She won't leave me alone. She was in my house. She's… She's following me, I'm sure of it.'

'Doesn't she live in the same block of flats?' Emma asks.

'Yes! And she's there. She's always just there!' I cry, as if this somehow proves my point. When it's clear from their faces that it doesn't, I continue. 'There was a bird. And a mouse. On my doorstep. She… she *meowed*.'

They're both looking at me like I've lost my mind. Like they should be getting me help.

'Friday! What about Friday?' I yelp. 'Just bumping into her like that? At random? And then she stays with us all night!'

'I mean…' Another look passes between the two women before Emma continues. 'She didn't want to come, did she? I sort of dragged her along.'

I stumble over the next few words. I hadn't actually realised that, but it doesn't matter. It doesn't change anything.

'Yeah, well, did you drag her along here, too?'

'Pretty much,' Carol says.

That takes the wind from my sails a bit.

'What?'

'I told her on Friday we were short. Took her number. Called her last night and asked if she fancied a job.'

A hurricane of anger carried me in here, but the winds continue to drop, and I feel the first prickles of embarrassment.

'She was a bit worried it would be weird for you, but I, uh, I said it'd be fine and that Emma would call you today to explain,' Carol continues. 'You're not even meant to be in today.'

'No, I know that. I just… Why? Why her?'

'She seems like a nice girl,' Carol says. 'And she's had it rough, bless her. You hear about her ex?'

My insides freeze into blocks of ice. 'Her ex?' I ask, my voice hoarse. 'What about him?'

'Knocking her around, he was. The bastard.' Carol waves a hand. 'Oh, but you know about that, don't you? I heard all about what you did to him.'

I swallow. Stare. 'What I did?'

'The water. Over his head?' She cackles at that. 'Beautiful stuff. Well done.'

'Right. Right. I mean, yes, OK. I did do that,' I concede, relieved that it's only that she's referring to.

They're not getting it, though. They don't understand.

'She was at my mum and dad's house! Yesterday! She went to my mum and dad's.'

That gets their attention. 'What?' Carol asks.

Emma frowns. 'What for?'

'To… to buy some old stuff they were selling,' I say, and when I see them both relaxing, I double down. 'That's not the point! She was in their house. They made her tea!'

Even to my ears, it sounds pathetic. Deranged, even. *They made her tea* is not the killer twist it felt like when it was in my head.

'Well, so would I have. She's a nice girl,' Carol reiterates. 'And she's had it rough, like I say. I'd take the poor soul under my wing and bring her home myself, if I didn't think my Frank'd try and fire it up her as soon as my back was turned.'

'You hear about her sister, too?' Emma asks, lowering her voice like she's not sure if she should be sharing this. 'Awful. Horrible. I shouldn't say.'

She says, anyway.

'The poor cow's in a coma.' She silently mouths that last word, like this somehow protects her from any breach of privacy claim. 'Has been for years. It's just the two of them, too. Parents died in the same crash. They were all going to pick Chloe up from her dance class.'

'Christ alive,' Carol says, but I barely hear her over the ringing in my ears.

'It was her birthday, too,' Emma says, still whispering. 'Can you believe that? I mean, happy sweet sixteenth, or what?'

Carol mutters something else, but I cut in, talking over her, practically elbowing her aside as I approach Emma's desk.

'Wait. Hang on,' I say, and the shake in my voice is worse than ever.

I can't believe I don't know this. I can't believe I never asked.

I can't believe I didn't recognise her.

'What's Chloe's second name?'

CHAPTER 18

Diane

Emma is phoning again. She's tried to get me twice already this morning. Carol, too, though just the once. They want to know where I am, why I'm not in work. I rang in sick on Tuesday and Wednesday, after heading straight home on Monday, but I haven't called in today to say I won't be in.

Her name is right there on my mobile's screen. 'Emma', it says, then, in brackets '(HR)'. I had to write it like that so I'd remember who she was. Because I forget things sometimes. Mostly, it just happens. Other times, I have to try really, really hard.

Chloe left just after eight. I watched her go through the slits of the living room blinds. She was wearing a grey skirt suit, like the one I used to wear. The one I'd been wearing the day we burned up Marcus's body.

It looked identical from what I could see of it.

Is it mine? Is it the same one? Did she save it from the fire? Are there bloodstains all down the front, and sweat on the armpits?

No. No, it wouldn't fit her. She's too small. Or I'm too big, or… I don't know. I can't keep it straight in my head. I'm struggling to remember what's what.

Maybe I should take my tablets. You're not supposed to just come off them. The doctor always told me that.

I think I was still taking them until Monday. I can't remember, but there were fewer of them in the box every day, so I must've been. Right?

They weren't working, though. Not the way they were meant to. I was still getting things all muddled up.

That's why I didn't recognise her.

That's why I didn't figure it out.

Ronan is gone. I've come to accept that now. He's vanished. Poof. Sometimes, I wonder if he was ever even here.

The phone stops ringing. Emma gives up. For now, at least.

I let out the breath I've been holding. Fifty-seven seconds. A new record.

Breathing is important. That's what the doctor told me at the time. Breathing is how you slow the panic, how you narrow it down, make it smaller, smaller, smaller. Breathing is how you bring the world under control.

But breathing is hard sometimes. In. Out. I feel like I'm not getting enough air. Like there isn't enough oxygen in the room. In the world.

So I hold it. I keep it in, keep it to myself.

And by doing that, and staying quiet, maybe Emma and anyone else who calls me won't know that I'm here.

Quiet.

Quiet little mouse.

The news is on. Two channels. I bought a second TV specially. Had it delivered. They're set to BBC and Sky News right now, but I flick through them sometimes, checking the others. CNN. Al Jazeera. GB News, even.

There's nothing more about Marcus, or his car, or his carpet, or his house. But I can feel their net drawing in, closing around me. It'll trap me, in the end, like a fish flopping on the deck of a boat, mouth gasping, eyes bulging. Too much air then. Far too much.

Why didn't I recognise her?

Why didn't I figure it out?

Chloe Quinn. Their daughter. Her sister.

For a moment, I can see them. What's left of them. Through the glass. Through the smoke. Through the twisted tangle of metal. I can watch the life drain out of them.

And then I'm back here again, back now. Back in the room.

I need to stop scratching my arms. I can see the blood, even through my sleeves. But the itch only goes away when I scratch them. Even then, not for long. Just for a little while.

There is a van outside. Plain white. It's small – one of those vans that's more like a car that's been cut in half and had a storage compartment welded onto the back. Not a big van. Not like Ronan's.

Where is Ronan, I wonder? Did he leave me? Did I do something to scare him off?

There's a man in the van, too. He was downstairs with Chloe before she left. I tried to listen to what they were talking about, put my ear to the floor and shut my eyes, but I couldn't hear much. Just a mumble. Just a whisper.

Were they talking about me?

Was she telling him everything we did?

Do the police drive vans like that?

I bet they could, if they wanted to. I bet they can do anything.

I'm not sure how long I watch him, but after a while he gets out of the van and looks straight up at my window. Straight up at me. I jump back into the shadows, closing my eyes, holding my breath again.

One. Two. Three.

I count all the way to twenty-two before the buzzer sounds. It's a short, sharp *bzzzt* that makes me think the man from the van is annoyed at me.

She must've told him.

He must know.

I check the news channels. Scan the headlines on my phone. Nothing.

He buzzes again, holding the button for a bit longer this time, and I suddenly know, in my bones, that he's never going to leave. He'll stand out there forever, buzzing the buzzer. A busy bee that will never fly off.

I float through to the hall, lift the handset, and say, 'You're welcome.'

I don't know why I say that, why I say *those words*, but I press the button that opens the door to the block and hear the *ka-thunk* as he comes inside.

He knocks on my door a few seconds later. I'm already watching him, though, through the peephole I had installed on Monday. His face is oddly stretched, like I'm looking at a reflection in a spoon. Like I am him, with his brown skin and dark eyes, and his beard that's a different colour to his eyebrows. Black beard. Grey brows.

I know he must dye one. Right now, though, I can't think which it would be.

He's wearing a blue boiler suit with 'Scottish Gas' written across the lapel. He has a name badge, like mine. Not the same name, though. Not my name.

'Hello?' I say, and he steps back in surprise. He looks the door up and down, like that's what spoke to him, not me.

'Uh, hi. Miss Shelley?' he asks. Which would be a funny name for a door, when you think about it. 'I'm here to read the meter.'

He's not the police. Unless he's pretending. They do that sometimes. But the police wouldn't dye their hair, I don't think, so I open the door and let him in.

'In you come. Quick,' I say, and he looks a little surprised by this. He shoots a look back at the main door, and I think he's about to make a run for it, but then he steps inside.

'Do you know you've got a dead bird out there?' he asks. 'On the step? Right mess, it is.'

'Cat,' I say, and he looks at me strangely.

'I'd have thought so, aye,' he agrees.

He takes a few steps into the hall, then looks around at the walls, his head creaking slowly in a big semicircle, up one wall, across the ceiling, down the other.

There's a question behind his smile, but he doesn't say it out loud.

'Just through here, aye?' he says, pointing towards the living room.

He enters without waiting to be told, headed for the door that leads to the kitchen. That's where the meter is, in a little cupboard on the back wall. I watch it sometimes. There's something hypnotic about the slow, steady blinking of its little red light.

The meter man has stopped again. He looks around. At the walls. The floor. The pictures hanging from all their hidden hooks.

He shuffles his feet, like he's testing the carpet. Like he's worried he might sink into it and get trapped.

A lamp catches his attention. The overhead light, too.

He doesn't seem to notice the two TVs. Or, if he does, he's not interested in them.

'Well, this is a new one on me,' he says, turning to look at me. He's smiling. Almost laughing, even though there's nothing funny. 'Who was first? Or did you both get together and plan it out?'

I don't know what he's talking about. I don't understand. When he doesn't explain, I'm forced to ask him.

'What do you mean?'

He does laugh then. It's just a little one. I can see the question behind that, too. The confusion in his eyes.

'Well, I mean, it's a bit weird, isn't it?'

I look around, trying to see my flat through his eyes, trying to figure out exactly what it is he's talking about. But his eyes aren't my eyes. And I can't see a thing.

'What's weird?' I ask.

He doesn't laugh this time, but he keeps his smile there. Like a mask. Like a shield to hide behind.

He scratches his head, and I remember that my arms are itchy. So itchy. Is it the tablets, or is something under there, inside me, worming away beneath the skin?

'Well, I mean, this place. And downstairs,' he says.

He looks around again, like he's double-checking. When he looks at me again, his smile has faded, just a little.

'The paint. The carpet. The pictures, even,' he says.

I stare at him, scratching my arms, trying to figure out what he's telling me. Trying to work out what he means.

His smile is gone. There's only the question now.

'They're both exactly the same.'

CHAPTER 19

Chloe

Seven Years Earlier

I'm fifteen years old, standing outside the leisure centre on a mid-September day, wishing I'd brought my jacket.

Class has been finished for twenty minutes now. The other girls have gone, wandering off in giggling ones and twos, or whisked away in family cars and prebooked taxis.

A couple of them hung out with me for a while, chatting about today's choreography, the music choices, and how hideous Miss Harper's new jumper is. She said her husband knitted it for her, which threw up all sorts of questions, mostly about whether or not he was blind.

I didn't even know men could knit. My dad definitely can't.

Anyway, there's nobody waiting with me now. Everyone's gone. Everyone but me.

I check my phone again. I've messaged Mum and Isabelle twice already. There are no replies from them, though. No missed calls. Nothing.

It's weird. Mum's usually so punctual it borders on obsessive. If we're meant to be somewhere at ten, we'll arrive at nine forty-five. Dad jokes that she has a watch inside her instead of a heart, like the Tin Man in *The Wizard of Oz*. He's nearly as bad, though. They're almost never late. When they are, they always call to let me know.

But not today.

My bare legs have broken out in goosebumps. The chill is seeping through my shorts and T-shirt and the leotard below. The rain that was threatening on the way here has finally arrived, starting as a fine mist that beads in my hair and clings to my eyelashes.

I check my phone. Nothing.

I turn it off and back on again, in case there's a backlog somewhere. A blockage in the network. I don't know if that's even a thing, but it's worth a go.

No slew of messages comes through. No voicemails, no missed call notifications. Not a word. Not a cheep.

I rattle off messages to Mum and Isabelle again, then send one to Dad, too, even though he'll be driving.

If they don't reply to these, then I'm going to have to think about actually *phoning* them. Ugh. Hopefully, it won't come to that.

Miss Harper comes out, shouting a goodbye over her shoulder to someone in the leisure centre. She's got her jacket on, hiding her awful jumper, her car keys already in hand. She slows when she sees me.

'Everything alright, Chloe?' she asks. She looks around us, like she's hunting for something. 'Your parents not here to pick you up?'

'They're coming,' I tell her. 'They're just running a bit late.'

'Ah. Right. Do you want me to wait with you?'

She checks her watch, and I get the impression she desperately wants me to decline the offer. I am more than happy to do so. She's nice and everything, but standing talking to her one-on-one? No, thanks.

'No, it's fine,' I say, forcing a smile. 'They'll be here any minute.'

She hesitates, looking uncertain. 'You're sure?'

'Totally,' I assure her. 'They were picking Isabelle up from work, so she probably just got held up.'

Miss Harper frowns but draws a blank. 'Isabelle?'

'My big sister. Much bigger. Older, I mean. She's thirty. Like, literally double my age.'

'Wow. That's quite an age gap.'

'I know. I keep reminding her.'

Miss Harper laughs at that.

'I bet you do. And what does she say to that?'

I open my mouth to reply, but then think better of quoting one of Isabelle's foul-mouthed outbursts.

'She's not a fan,' I say, and Miss Harper just nods and smiles.

She checks her watch again. 'Well, if you're certain you're OK waiting…'

'I am, miss. I'm fine, honest. On you go.' I shoo her away with a smile that's starting to ache at the edges.

She heads to her car, glancing back once before climbing in. I wave as she drives off, keeping the smile plastered on my face until she's out of sight.

Then, despite how much I prefer to text, I try calling. Mum first. No answer. Dad next. Straight to voicemail. Then Isabelle. Nothing.

I look over to the spot where Miss Harper's car was, part of me wishing she was still here. That I'd asked her to stay.

But she's gone. The car park is practically empty.

The rain is getting heavier now, and I'm the only one left outside the building. I huddle closer to the wall, trying to find shelter under the narrow overhang.

A taxi pulls up and, for a moment, I think it might be for me – that they've sent one because the car's broken down or something. But a woman gets out, hurrying towards the building with her umbrella tilted against the rain. She barely glances at me as she disappears inside.

I check my phone. Forty minutes now. This isn't like them at all.

I try calling again, cycling through all three numbers. Nothing. The knot in my stomach tightens.

I can't stay here much longer. I've got no money for a taxi, and the leisure centre will be closing soon. It's Friday night and they shut early.

Home is just over two miles away. It's not that far. I've walked it before, just never in the rain, never in dance clothes, never alone with the sky starting to darken at the edges.

But I've got a house key. It'll be dry and warm there. Familiar, too. I can figure out what's going on and wait for them to come home.

Taking a deep breath, I step out from under the overhang and into the chill of the worsening rain. It soaks through my top almost immediately. My thin dance shoes squelch with each step, water seeping in through the fabric.

While I walk, I try Mum again, then Dad, then Isabelle. Nothing. Nothing. Nothing.

The route takes me down the main road first, where streetlights cast their orange glow and cars rush past, throwing up sprays of water from puddles. Some drivers slow down when they see me – a soaking wet teenager in shorts and T-shirt – but nobody stops.

I cross beneath the railway bridge, where the noise of the rain amplifies, drumming against the metal and concrete above me. The sound is almost comforting, creating a barrier between me and all the thoughts spinning around in my head.

Where are they?

Why won't they answer me?

After twenty minutes of walking, I try calling again. I've tried each number at least a dozen times now, but still nothing.

Something's wrong. I know it is. But I keep moving because I can't think of anything else to do except get home. Maybe they'll be there. Maybe they've just forgotten me.

It's not a very nice thought, but it's more comforting than some of the others that have been whirling around inside my head.

The rain is coming down in sheets now. My hair is plastered to my face, my clothes clinging to my skin. I'm shivering, teeth chattering so hard I'm sure they might crack.

A car slows beside me. It's silver, old, with rust speckling the wheel arches.

'You alright there, sweetheart?' the driver calls, leaning across to speak through the passenger window. He's older – forty maybe – with thinning hair and glasses that reflect the streetlight. 'You need a lift somewhere?'

There's a smell coming from the car. Old cigarette smoke, I think.

For a moment, I'm tempted. So tempted. I'm cold and wet and miserable, and home is still about half a mile away.

It'd just be a few minutes in a car. No time at all.

He stretches over and opens the passenger door a little. The smell gets worse. I see rubbish in the footwell – crisp packets, sandwich wrappers, empty beer cans.

'Uh. No, thanks,' I say, forcing a polite smile. 'I'm fine.'

He doesn't drive away, though. The car crawls alongside me as I walk.

'Come on, you're soaked through,' he insists. 'I'm just trying to help. I'm not a weirdo or anything. Where are you headed?'

'I'm meeting my dad just up there,' I lie, pointing vaguely ahead. 'Thanks anyway.'

'I don't see anyone waiting,' he says, and there's an edge to his voice now that wasn't there before. Something cold and hard. He tries to disguise it with a smile. His teeth are stumps of yellow and brown. 'Come on, get in. Don't be stupid.'

I walk faster. The car speeds up, matching me.

'I said no, thank you,' I repeat, firmer this time.

'Well, fuck you then, you stuck-up little bitch,' he snarls, all pretence of kindness gone. 'Walking around dressed like that and then acting all innocent? What do you think you're playing at?'

I don't answer. I just keep walking, staring straight ahead, my heart hammering in my chest.

'Hey! I'm talking to you!' he shouts. 'Think you're too good for me, is that it?'

I glance around. The street is empty. No other cars, no pedestrians, no open shops. Just me and him.

'Dirty wee cock tease,' he spits. 'You think you're special? You're not.'

Even if I wanted to say something now, I couldn't. My throat is too tight. There's no air in my lungs. The rain disguises the tears that run down my cheeks.

He keeps talking, keeps shouting at me, calling me names. I can still hear him. Still smell him.

Every instinct, every part of my brain is screaming at me to run, to get away from this man, with his horrible teeth and dirty car.

I see an alleyway up ahead – a shortcut between streets not too far from my house. It's too narrow for cars. If he wants to chase me, he'll have to get out. And, on foot, I bet I can outrun him.

Without warning, I break into a sprint, darting down the narrow passage between buildings. I hear him swearing, hear the revving of an engine, then the squeal of brakes.

I don't look back. I just run, my wet shoes slapping against the concrete, my breath coming in sharp, painful gasps.

When I stumble out the other side, I keep running, down another street, across a road, through a small park. I only stop when my lungs are burning and my legs feel like they might buckle beneath me.

A police car passes. I wave frantically after it, forcing myself to run again, trying to catch up and flag it down. I'm close to home, but if nobody's there, I'm worried the man might come after me. Might come inside.

The police can help me. I just need them to see me, to stop.

'Hey! Please! Don't go!' I shout after them, but I don't have enough breath left in me to project the words loud enough for them to hear.

I lose sight of the car as it rounds the corner onto my street. When I reach the bend a moment later, though, I can see it crawling along just a short distance ahead of me, indicator flashing as it slows.

Next to my house.

It disappears as it turns, pulling onto our driveway. My pulse quickens, but my pace slows. My feet plod me onwards, but hesitantly. Uncertainly.

Although each step is slow and shuffling, I eventually reach the entrance to my garden.

The police car is in the driveway. A uniformed officer stands by the front door, talking into his radio.

Something inside me wants to run, to get away from here. But my feet are on a mission, guiding me home. They move slowly, like I'm wading through treacle. The officer looks up as I approach, his expression shifting into something careful and neutral.

I don't speak. Even if I knew what words to say, I've forgotten how to make my voice work.

'Are you Chloe Quinn?' he asks finally.

I nod. It's all I can do.

'I need you to come with me, sweetheart,' he says.

His voice is gentle. Kind. It terrifies me more than the man in the car ever could.

'I'm afraid there's been an accident.'

CHAPTER 20

Chloe

I am eighteen years old, sitting by a hospital bed, counting the clicks from the ventilator.

I've already gone through the usual conversations. I've told her about the house sale, and the job hunt, and all the funny little things that have happened this week. I don't mention my failed exams, or the debt collectors, or those guys outside the pub.

Instead, I ask her how she's doing, then nod and smile as the machines beep, and click, and wheeze out a response.

'Well, good to hear you're keeping busy,' I say, and then I laugh. It's become a weird little tradition between us, whether she knows it or not.

Some people say she can hear me. I've never seen anything to suggest that's true, though. I've played her favourite music, read her favourite books, whispered scandalous rumours about people she knows.

She's never so much as twitched.

Her hair is getting long again. The nurses let me cut it last time, and they were polite enough not to comment on how much of a mess I made of it. I did mention it, though, a big, over the top 'Oh God, what have I done?' that came out like a squeal of horror.

Isabelle always fussed over her hair. Part of me hoped that the thought of me butchering it would be enough to wake her up. I'd have happily taken the slagging. I'd even have accepted a slap.

Anything, if it meant her being back here with me.

There's a trickle of drool on her chin. I get up and wipe it with my sleeve before any of the nurses can come in and see. I'm sure they've seen a lot worse, but still. She wouldn't like them seeing her like that.

I hesitate, leaning over her, looking down. She's Sleeping Beauty, not dead, but not all the way alive, either.

I plant a kiss on her forehead. Her skin is cool and slightly clammy. She smells clean, but *hospital clean*, not like a normal person. Like she's been scrubbed and disinfected. Like she's a dirty floor, or a stain on a wall.

I can't remember what she used to smell like. I can't remember how she used to sound. If she opened her mouth and spoke to me now, would I even recognise her voice?

I sniff and wipe away a tear, then settle back into the chair beside her. There's nothing more to say, so we enjoy a comfortable silence. Or as close to silence as we can get with a backing track of life support machines doing their thing beside us.

She's lost weight. She didn't need to. Her skin seems to cling to the contours of her face, like it has been draped carelessly across her skull. There's a tube up her nose and a pipe down her throat, and a web of cables and wires tethering her to the bed. To life, if that's even what you can call it.

Some days, I can sit looking at her for hours. Other times, being in the room makes me want to scream, and I can't get out of here quickly enough.

Tonight is different. Tonight, I want to get away, but not because I can't bear being here. It's because for the first time in a long time I've got something I need to do. Somewhere important I need to be.

I lean in closer to my sister and place a hand on top of hers. There's no response to my touch, of course, but I entwine our fingers together.

'Listen, sis, I need to go, OK? I'm supposed to be meeting someone. Someone I think can help me. He reckons he might be able to help me figure some stuff out about that day. About what happened.'

I give her hand a squeeze. I hope she can feel it. I know she can't.

'I'll tell you all about it tomorrow, OK?' I say, then I get to my feet and grab my jacket from the back of the chair. 'But I've got a good feeling about this one, Isabelle. This could be the one. This could be the lead we've been waiting for.'

I give her another kiss on the head and look down at her face. She seems to be at peace.

That makes one of us.

'But even if it isn't, I'll never give up,' I tell her. 'I won't stop until I find out who did this. To you. To Mum and Dad.'

I straighten up. The machines beep, and click, and wheeze.

'And then, whenever that is, however long it takes, I promise, I'll make them pay.'

CHAPTER 21

Chloe

I am twenty-two years old, standing on a street corner, fighting back a full-blown panic attack.

Every day of the last seven years has been leading me to here. To now.

To her.

I pace back and forth on the pavement, checking my phone, making myself obvious. It's mid-October, far too cold to be dressed like this, but I need her to notice me. The crop top. The shorts cut high enough to display the curves of my arse cheeks. The bare legs that draw looks from the dirty old men who slow as they pass in their cars.

The cold doesn't matter. Nor do the lecherous looks. Nothing matters except making this work.

I've spent months planning this. Finding the flat. Befriending and manipulating Sarah. Arranging to stay here. Making it look natural. Making it look like nothing but random chance.

'Today's the day, Isabelle,' I whisper to myself.

I run my hand over my eye – the make-up is thick and precise, a carefully crafted bruise that I'll carefully fade over the coming days, just like a real one would. I practised for hours to get it right, watched countless YouTube tutorials. The shading, the edges, the colour gradation. It needs to look convincing.

I need her to feel sorry for me. Assuming she's even capable of such a thing.

I wonder if she even thinks about it. About what she did. About the lives she destroyed.

I don't need to look to know she's standing there at her window. I can sense her watching me. I've studied her habits enough to know she's usually home by this time on a Wednesday. I've been walking past this building for weeks, noting her comings and goings, waiting for the perfect time.

My curiosity gets the better of me. I half turn, pretending to look along the street, and catch a glimpse of her from the corner of my eye. There's movement through the kitchen window. She's there. Watching me.

I pretend not to notice, continuing my performance, strutting around, drawing her out.

Her shadow moves away from the window. I wait, my heart hammering. This is it. Finally, this is it.

The main door to the tenement opens, and there she is, after all this time. After all this searching. Diane Shelley. In the flesh.

My chest tightens at the sight of her. She looks different from the photos on her social media – heavier, more worn down by life. But it's definitely her. She can't deny it.

Soon, she won't be able to deny anything.

'Um, excuse me,' she says. Her voice is hard. Confrontational.

I turn to her, wide-eyed, feigning surprise, letting her see the bruise on my face. I notice her eyes drift to it, then quickly away, then back again.

'Yeah? Hello! Hi,' I reply. It's not what I practised, but it all just slips out.

I'm nervous. Far more nervous than I expected to be.

What if this is a mistake? What if I've got this wrong? Or what if she sees straight through me, realises who I am, and figures out what I'm doing here?

But then, I see the moment her expression shifts from suspicion to something softer. Pity, maybe. I congratulate myself on a good job with the make-up.

'I, um, I don't think… that is… this isn't really the sort of area where people, you know… wait for… business opportunities.'

I feel a surge of relief washing over me. She's completely fallen for it, hook, line and sinker. This is going to be easier than I thought.

'Sorry?' I ask, tilting my head and putting on my best confused expression.

'You know. *Clients*,' she whispers, giving me what she clearly thinks is a meaningful look.

Her face is pale and pudgy, like it's been fashioned out of old dough. Her eyes are sunken. Her hair is lank and greasy.

Is this it? Is this really the monster I've been hunting all this time?

I expected some terrifying force of nature, but she's pathetic.

I stare at her, trying to hide my disgust, then go back to playing my part. 'Oh my God. You think I'm a…?' I glance down at my outfit, making a show of my dawning comprehension.

The look of embarrassment that spreads across her face is delicious. I can almost see her shrinking into herself, mortified. Her obvious discomfort bolsters me.

'I'm just waiting for my delivery,' I explain, holding up my phone to show the tracking app I have open. 'Removal van. It was supposed to be here twenty minutes ago.'

'Delivery?' she repeats dumbly.

'Yeah. For my stuff.'

She turns and shoots a look at the basement flat, her face a picture of dawning realisation and horror.

I'm going to make sure I see that look again when I finally reveal who I am and why I'm here. When she finally realises that her past has caught up with her.

But not yet. Not until I have everything I need. Not until there's no chance of her worming her way out of it.

'Your… stuff?' she asks, just as the sound of a diesel engine rounds the corner. The removal van I hired pulls up, right on cue. Not too early, not too late. Precisely when I arranged for it to arrive.

'Sorry we're late, love,' the driver says, playing his part perfectly. 'Traffic was a bastard on the bridges.'

'No worries,' I tell him, flashing a smile, and I introduce Diane as my new neighbour.

'You here to help with the heavy lifting, aye?' he asks, and she just stares at him, blankly, like she's a dumb animal.

She has no idea.

Everything is going according to plan. Step one, complete. I've breached the perimeter. I'm in.

I'm going to ruin her life.

I'm going to dismantle it, bit by bit.

I'm going to take away everything she holds dear. Just like she did to me. And then…

Well, we'll cross that bridge when we come to it.

'I'm Chloe,' I tell her. I thrust out my hand, plastering on my brightest, bubbliest smile. 'I'm your new downstairs neighbour.'

CHAPTER 22

Chloe

I hoped the wine might loosen her tongue. God knows, she necked enough of it.

Technically, she has been talking. She's talked a lot, in fact, about nothing of any interest or importance. Her cat. This horrible basement flat. The removal men.

She watched them, eyes darting after them as they lugged the boxes and furniture down the front steps and into the rooms. They weren't exactly perfect specimens of manliness, but there was a hunger in the way she watched them. A longing in the dark hollows of her eyes.

Pathetic.

The flat is grim, though I've stayed in worse places. Much worse. The furniture, gathered from second-hand shops and recycling centres, has seen better days. That's an understatement, actually.

But I don't have a lot of money to spend. What little inheritance I got is long gone, and I can't access Isabelle's while she's still alive.

Alive. That's what they call it, at least. But all those tubes and pipes and wires make me wonder how much of her is still left in there. How much of my sister still exists?

We were never that close in a sisterly way. She was more like a second mum, fussing over me, bossing me around. We weren't friends. Not really.

But I miss her, I think, most of all.

Diane is asking me about the black eye. I spin her a sob story about an abusive ex. I know it'll strike a chord. All my digging in her past has thrown up at least one violent boyfriend. That's what the fake bruise is for. If she has any empathy, any real emotion, she'll connect with it. With me. One abuse survivor to another.

'He doesn't know where you are, right?' she asks when I tell her all about the terrible things he's done to me.

I shake my head but try to look scared. To look small. 'I don't think so. But he's…'

'Connected,' she says.

I nod. 'And persistent.'

I want her to be worried for me. And, if all goes well tonight, she will be.

Marcus isn't going to be happy when he finds out where I am. He's going to be livid, in fact. At least, I hope so. I'm counting on that fact to help sell the story.

When she's almost ready to leave, she takes a breath, then offers to let me stay with her, upstairs, until I get the place in a better state.

The offer catches me off guard. What is she doing? What is she playing at? Has she figured out who I am? Is this a display of dominance, or is she trying to mess with my head?

I tell myself it's none of those. It's just my strategy paying off. She's genuinely concerned. I've hooked her in.

I'm almost tempted to take her up on the offer. Being that close, being in her flat, maybe even in her bedroom… The things I could find. The secrets I could uncover.

But no. Not yet.

Stick to the plan.

I decline politely, insisting I'll be fine down here on my own. She looks relieved but makes it clear that the offer remains open.

She suggests we swap numbers and gives me her phone. I hesitate. My emails, my texts – there are so many secrets in my mobile that would give the game away.

But she's staring at me now, hand out, and unless I want her to get suspicious, I've got no choice but to give her my phone.

I look at her phone in my hand and wonder what secrets of hers it holds. Is there evidence in here that would end all this? If I ran with it now and gave it to the police, could it all be over?

Could justice finally be done?

She finishes typing her number. I add mine to her contacts, and, just before we swap back, a text comes through on my phone.

Marcus.

Shit.

Did she see it? Did she read what he said?

'Everything OK?' she asks.

'Yeah, fine,' I say, and I shove the phone into my pocket. 'Just spam.'

We chat a little longer. Niceties, really, nothing more, as she edges closer and closer to the door.

'Just give me a shout if you need anything,' she says, like she's just some friendly neighbour. Like she's just a normal person. 'Even if it's just to borrow a cup of sugar, or whatever.'

The words shoot out of me like gunfire. 'Or to see your pussy.'

I don't know why I said that. To make her uncomfortable, I think. To embarrass her. To make her feel small, and shamed.

Or to tease her with something, maybe. To lead her on with a promise of something. To sink another hook into her flesh.

She nearly chokes, and I watch her cheeks sting red with embarrassment. She does feel things, then. She's not completely dead inside. That will make things easier.

And more fun.

'Cowboy Meowboy,' I remind her, and she splutters with relief.

'Right! Yes! The cat!'

She hurriedly opens the door then and steps out onto the tiny square of patio, waving at her face, as if trying to cool it down. The sound of traffic rumbles by on the street above, painting the little courtyard with slow-moving shadows.

'Uh, so... See you around, then,' she says, and suddenly, I don't want her to leave. I've spent all this time tracking her down, and I'm terrified she's going to disappear, run away. Vanish, all over again.

I lash out and grab her wrist. Holding it tight, my fingers locking together. A handcuff, holding her in place.

She looks frightened by my sudden turn of speed and by the strength of my grip around her arm.

I despise this woman. She ruined my life.

And revenge has been a long time coming.

'I've got a feeling we're going to be great friends, Diane,' I tell her.

Then, as my smile begins to shake, and pinpricks of pain in my eyes bring tears rushing to fill them, I release my grip, close the door, and slide the lock closed with a *clunk*.

I stand there in silence, listening to the heavy plodding of her feet on the steps, the opening and closing of her door, the creaking of her floorboards directly above my head.

I am here now.

I am inside.

Finally, I can begin.

I see the headlights sweeping across the front of the building and hear the rumbling of the car's engine go silent.

I have the lights off and sit in the shadows behind the door, waiting.

My phone is still in my hand. He's tried texting, calling, there's even an email from him, garbled and ranting, demanding to know what the hell I think I'm doing.

I know how he must be feeling. Used. Like I took advantage of him and used his connections for my own ends. He thought I was writing an article. He had no idea what my actual plans were.

Not until I spelled them out in that text message half an hour ago. Not until I told him what I was going to do and where he could find me.

I hear the sound of his feet on the stone steps. He's muttering, his anger frothing up, bubbling over. Me being here, all this, it could cost him his career. There was a time, I'm sure, when I would've felt bad about that. But that was before. None of that matters now.

He knocks. It's firm and insistent, but not too loud, like he doesn't want to draw the attention of the neighbours. One in particular.

I sit there, saying nothing, listening to him as the volume of his knocking and his voice grows steadily louder, as his questions become requests, become demands, become threats.

He really doesn't want me to go through with this.

He really doesn't get a say.

His police connections were what first drew me to him. The string of one-night stands that led to the collapse of his marriage flagged him as a potential target.

But it was his temper that sealed the deal.

The door shakes in the frame as he kicks it or drives his shoulder against it. The letterbox snaps open, and his voice is suddenly no longer trapped outside. It's right here with me in the room, a whispered hiss that alternates between begging and threatening.

'This is madness. You can't do this!' he spits into the darkened flat. 'You're going to get me in deep shit!'

He doesn't realise that I'm right here, so close to him that I could reach up and grab the fingers that hold the letterbox open, then snap them one by one.

The thought of it fills me with an overpowering urge to laugh, and I bury my face in against my knees so as not to give myself away.

He goes back to hammering on the door and shouting again. I hear movement upstairs. The creaking of floorboards. The thudding of footsteps.

A voice, I think. Just one. Just hers. She must be calling the police.

She's up. She's aware.

A wave of euphoria hits me, and I have to bite down on my hand to stop myself whooping with delight.

It's working. All my planning is paying off.

It's a few minutes later, right in the middle of another burst of angry ranting, that I hear Marcus howl. It's a raw, animal sound that catches me off guard, and I let out a little cry as I jump with fright.

Luckily, he's too preoccupied to have heard me. He shouts something, and from upstairs I hear Diane calling down to him, warning him to clear off, letting him know that the police are on their way.

I take a chance and creep to the kitchen window, staying low, keeping to the shadows. Peeking out, I can see him standing there, hair plastered to his face, water running from his elbows and his wrists and the tips of his fingers.

She dumped water on him. Of course she did. The psycho. He's lucky it wasn't boiling.

He shouts back to her, and that's when I brace myself. This is the risky bit. Will he tell her? Will he reveal who I am and why I'm here? Will he ruin everything?

He does warn her, but it's nothing specific. It just sounds like more threats, and when she stresses again that the police are on their way, he stares at my front door, then retreats up the steps.

A moment later, his car goes speeding off.

I almost feel bad about it all. He never asked for any of this. And I might still need him.

I'll go round tomorrow and explain. I'll apologise. I'll do whatever is needed to get him back on side.

He's a simple creature, really, like the rest of them. It won't take much.

But first…

I think back to that day seven years ago. To the man in the car. To the policeman on the doorstep. To the moment that everything was torn away from me.

The tears come, just in time.

'Chloe?' She knocks. 'It's Diane. From upstairs.'

Her voice couldn't sound more different to Marcus's. It's soft. Considerate. Kind, even.

If you didn't know better, you would swear she was almost human.

CHAPTER 23

Chloe

The stench hits me out of nowhere. It's thick. Pungent. Metallic. I can taste it, as well as smell it. Like old pennies on my tongue, in my nostrils, sticking in my throat.

And then…

And then…

Oh, God.

Oh God oh God oh God!

Marcus is on the floor. He's on the floor and there's so much blood. So much, too much. It's everywhere. On the carpet, on his clothes, on his face. His eyes are open, staring blankly at the ceiling, at the sky and the Heavens beyond it. His shirt has been torn, split apart, like the flesh below it. He's covered in stab wounds. Deep ones. Too many to see, too many to count.

I stand frozen in the doorway. The carpet between us shifts and stretches, impossibly moving him further away and right up close at the same time. It's like I'm miles away, somewhere else, but staring straight down into his open eyes and twisted mouth.

I'm not here, in this room. I'm there in his body, looking up through his eyes. Seeing nothing. Seeing me.

This isn't real. It can't be real.

Even as I'm thinking that, though, some other voice in my head is arguing back.

It is real. This is happening.

Marcus is dead. Marcus has been *murdered*.

But what if he isn't? What if he's still in there? What if there's still time?

My legs give way, and I'm on my knees beside him, my hands hovering over his body, not sure where to touch, what to do.

'Marcus?' I whisper, as if this is all some sick prank, and he might suddenly sit up and laugh.

But he doesn't move. He doesn't breathe. Of course he doesn't.

I press my fingers to his neck, searching for a pulse I know I won't find. His skin is cold. Not freezing to the touch, but cooler than it should be.

'No, no, no,' I mutter. My fingers press harder, searching desperately for the signs of life I know I'm not going to find.

CPR. I need to do CPR.

How the hell do you do CPR?

'Come on, you've seen this. You know this!' I babble. It's not much of a pep talk, but it's all I can manage.

I place my hands on his chest, one on top of the other, and press down. The pressure causes something wet and warm to seep out from a wound in his neck, coating my fingers in the thick red tar of his blood.

His blood is on my hands. Literally.

I get a sense then, just fleetingly, of everything unravelling. All my carefully constructed walls. All my plans. All my hard work. I can feel it all teetering – on the brink of collapse.

Marcus is dead.

Very, very dead.

And this wasn't part of the plan.

I scramble backwards, dragging myself across the bloodied carpet until my back thuds against a wall. I stare at the body until

I can't look any longer, and then turn my attention to something else, anything else.

My hands. The dark red stains on my fingers, under my nails. They swim out of focus, until I'm looking at him again. At the ruined carcass on the carpet.

Is this how my parents looked that night?

I was never allowed to see them. The police wouldn't let me.

Is this what they were like? Broken and bloodied, their life draining away while I waited impatiently for them outside the leisure centre? Dying in a tangle of wreckage while I silently cursed them both?

I've thought about it so often. Imagined the scene from every angle. The twisted metal. The shattered glass. The blood. Always the blood.

I've been haunted by the thought of it. I always hated the police for that, for not letting me see them. For denying me my chance to say goodbye.

But I get it now.

This is what death looks like. This is what it smells like. It's raw. Visceral. Each ragged wound only serving as a reminder of what fragile creatures we are.

The room spins and grows smaller, bringing the body nearer again, up close.

I'm going to be sick.

I stagger to my feet, making it to the downstairs toilet just as bile burns its way up the back of my throat.

I don't let it out, though. I swallow it back down at the last possible moment.

This isn't the time to freak out.

Let me think. Let me be smart about this.

Calling the police is one option. I can just tell them I came in here and found the body.

That's what a normal person would do.

But if I call them, they'll investigate. They'll want to know who I am, why I was here, how I got in. They'll dig into my background, my connections, my motivations.

They'll find out about my sister. About the accident. About my obsession with Diane Shelley.

And then what? They'll tell me to leave it all in their hands. To trust the system that's already failed us for seven years.

That's assuming they don't throw me in jail for Marcus's murder. And, right now, that feels like a risky assumption to make.

No. None of that can happen. Not until justice has been served. Not until she's paid for what she did.

But I need help. I can't do this alone.

I take out my phone and open the contact list. I had friends once, I'm sure of it. I remember them. They fussed over me after the funeral. They promised to be there for me, no matter what.

That was seven years ago. I haven't spoken to any of them since. There's been no time for friends. No time for anything except the hunt. Would they still come running? Would they even remember who I am?

Not for the first time since that night, I feel utterly, completely alone. There's nobody I can turn to. Nobody I can count on to help me with this.

Nobody, except…

I think back to the flat, to the woman living above me.

To the woman whose life I fully intend to destroy.

But not today. Not yet.

She offered to help me. Did she mean that?

There's only one way to find out.

I open up the messages app.
I select Diane's number.
And then, after a shaky breath, I start typing.

PLS COME QUICK

CHAPTER 24

Chloe

The fire crackles, the flames already consuming all the soft materials inside the car. The upholstery. The carpet. The body.

I step back as the heat starts to sting my skin, watching the flames dance higher, stretching toward the night sky. The smell of burning petrol and melting plastic fills my nostrils. Sharp. Acrid.

There's another smell, too. Like barbecue.

I try not to think about that.

Diane stands beside me, her face illuminated by the orange glow. The light flickers over her, and the moving shadows turn her momentarily demonic. She's staring at the burning BMW, intensely focused. There's something unsettling about how calm she is about all this.

'How long until it all burns up?' I ask, my voice barely audible above the roaring of the flames.

'It won't *all* burn up.' She says it so matter-of-factly that a shiver runs through me, despite the heat from the blaze. 'But I think it should destroy any evidence that might lead them to us.'

There's no emotion in her voice. No tremor of fear or regret. It's like she's standing at a bus stop, discussing the weather.

I still don't quite know why I texted her to come to Marcus's house. Of all the people to ask for help.

I'd expected her to have a complete meltdown and to point-blank refuse to help me. I even thought she might try to turn me in. And maybe she would've, had she not thrown up everywhere and connected herself to the scene.

She changed after that. The hysteria never fully materialised, and instead she took charge and outlined our options for getting rid of the body. There was a coldness to it all that I really should have been better prepared for.

After all, I've known for a while that I'm dealing with a monster.

'We should start walking,' Diane says, turning away from the fire. 'Someone might see the smoke soon.'

I nod and follow her down the narrow path that leads away from the clearing. She strides along, not rushing, exactly, but confident. In control.

This is not the Diane Shelley I've been studying. That one was fragile and easily manipulated. A clueless mess of a human being, bumbling through life with no consideration for her actions.

I always thought what happened to my parents was an accident. A drunken smash on a secluded road. Something I was going to make her pay for, yes, but not something deliberate.

But what if I haven't been giving her enough credit?

I look back at the flaming wreckage of the car, at the body blackening and blistering in the back.

What if Diane Shelley is a ruthless, cold-blooded killer?

'I'm going to call Ronan,' she says when we reach the main road. She pulls out her phone. The shadows it casts on her face make her look monstrous again, like a grotesque old puppet in a Punch & Judy show. Like she's wearing a horror mask.

Or maybe her face has been the real mask all along.

'He can pick us up,' she continues.

'Your boyfriend?' I ask.

'He's not really my boyfriend,' she says, though there's a bit of hesitation there, like she isn't quite sure what they are. 'It's… complicated. But he'll come if I ask him.'

As she dials, I notice her hands are steady. Mine have been shaking for hours.

We step back into the shadows while she waits for the call to connect. I catch her looking at me with an expression I can't quite put my finger on. Is it concern? Suspicion?

Or recognition, maybe? One predator acknowledging another?

I turn away, pretending I haven't noticed.

And, for the first time since all this started, I can't help but wonder which one of us should be more afraid.

The idiot almost messed this whole thing up.

When Ronan arrived to collect us, he almost let on that he recognised me. It was only the sharp warning look I shot him that made him snap shut his dangling jaw and turn his attention to Diane.

He didn't ask any questions on the drive back to the flat. We barely spoke at all, in fact, just sat staring out of the window at the darkened city streets passing on the other side of the glass.

Diane, in particular, was quiet. I think she was just processing the day's events, but I got the feeling that she was angry with me, too. Not that I could really blame her, given what I'd dragged her into, of course. It was fair for her to be upset.

And yet, some part of me didn't want her to be. I told myself it was because, for the plan to work, she has to like me. She has to trust me.

But was that all it was?

Now, Ronan is coming dangerously close to ruining everything again, and it's taking all my willpower not to lash out.

We're out on the street, under the lamppost, right next to his van, and his voice has a pleading edge to it that makes my skin crawl.

'Please, babe. I can't keep doing it,' he whispers. 'I can't keep coming round and shagging her. Have you seen the state of her? I can hardly keep my dinner down some nights.'

I fight the urge to shout at him, and keep my voice low and soothing.

'I know. I know,' I tell him. 'You've done amazing. We're nearly there.'

'I just want us to be together,' he says. 'Just me and you, like we talked about.'

'We will,' I assure him. 'It's almost over. It won't be long.'

He looks down at his feet, and I realise he's fighting back tears. *Ugh.*

'She kicked me out. Of the house. Mairi. She kicked me out. She let me see the kids.'

'Aw, babe,' I say, and I hope it sounds more sincere to his ears than it does to mine. 'But that's good. If we're going to be together, then it would have to happen at some point.'

He sniffs, rubs his eyes, then looks up and meets my gaze.

'Now, chin up. Eyes on the prize,' I say, putting my hand on his arm. 'Keep it together and everything will be fine.'

He starts to reply, then something just past my head catches his eye. Diane. She must be watching. I can see him struggling to remain composed.

'So, eh, nice to meet you, anyway!' he says. It sounds obviously fake, like he's a bad actor playing a role.

I hope he's more convincing when he's in bed with her.

Without waiting for an answer, he jumps in his van and speeds off.

I turn and head down the stairs, pretending not to notice the face watching from the window above.

And imagining what the look on it will be when her whole damn world falls apart.

CHAPTER 25

Diane

I'm feeling much better now. I think the tablets are out of my system. My arms have stopped itching, and things are less jumbled now than they were yesterday.

Or was it the day before?

Whatever, it doesn't matter. Things are on the mend. It's actually a pretty good day.

Right up until the point when *he* arrives.

'Diane Shelley?'

He's standing at the door of my flat. Someone else must have buzzed him in. Or maybe he has a key. He looks official, so it's a possibility.

'Um, yes,' I tell him, after running through a handful of excuses and lies and deciding that none of them sounded convincing enough. 'Who's asking?'

He's in his thirties. Neat and tidy, well put together. His stubble is shaved with careful precision, so it draws a straight line from just above his mouth to just below his ear on both sides.

There's a weariness to him, though, like he hasn't been sleeping much. Do I look like that, I wonder? Do I have that same air of exhaustion about me?

He holds up a slim leather wallet. There's a photograph of him tucked away behind a layer of see-through plastic, along with all his identifying details.

'I'm Detective Sergeant Martin Brompton,' he says, and his name jumps out at me from his ID card like it's been upgraded to a bolder font. 'Do you mind if I ask you a few questions?'

I let him inside, guide him through to the living room, and then offer him tea. I don't expect him to say yes, but he asks if coffee is an option, and then looks delighted when I tell him that it is.

Maybe it'll wake him up a bit.

I make it in one of the fancy cups from the back of the cupboard. I wish I hadn't, because the way it rattles in the saucer tells him how badly my hands are trembling.

Does he know?

Is this it?

Are these my final moments of freedom?

He takes it gratefully, but when he sips, a little look of concern troubles his otherwise smooth forehead.

He moisturises, I bet.

'It's powdered milk,' I explain. I feel my smile growing too wide, but I can't stop it. 'Don't worry, I haven't poisoned you or anything!'

It's probably not the best thing to say, given the circumstances, but the words just came out all on their own. I try to laugh it away, but the sound is too loud, too harsh, too braying, and he sets the cup down on the coffee table without drinking any more.

I sit – perch, really – on the arm of the couch, watching him, waiting for him to tell me why he's here.

I already know why he's here. They've found some clue we overlooked. They've tied us to the body and the burned-out car.

But he's come here alone. He took the coffee. If they were arresting me for murder, would he have done either of those things?

'Diane. Can I call you Diane?'

I nod. He smiles at that. It's a nice smile. Nicer than Ronan's, even. Something about him tells me he's gay, though. He takes way more care of his appearance than any straight men I know.

'Diane, I'm sorry to bother you like this, and I appreciate you giving me a few minutes of your time.'

'Of course,' I say.

That sounds promising. A few minutes of my time is better than fifteen years to life.

'What can I do for you?'

He scratches at the back of his head and stifles a yawn, which he apologises for.

'Long day?' I ask, even though it's not even noon yet.

'Aye, most of them,' he says, and he smiles again. Good teeth. Gay or not, a girl could really fall for a guy like him.

'I'm following up on a call you made around a week ago, Diane. Last Wednesday night. You called nine nine nine to report a disturbance.'

They're all statements, but I can sense the shape of the question lurking below them.

'That's right,' I confirm. 'Some drunk guy kicking off. It was a lot of fuss about nothing. Shouldn't have bothered calling. He moved on a few minutes later, it wasn't really an issue. I regretted phoning in and wasting everyone's time. Not like you don't have enough to be getting on with!'

I'm babbling. I can't seem to stop the words tumbling out of me. DS Brompton just sits there, nodding along, saying nothing. Just observing.

'So, yeah, it was nothing. I told the other policemen that already.'

'You did. Thank you for that,' he says.

His tone is kind. Friendly. I bet he's a nice person. I bet he remembers everyone's birthday, and always gets them a card.

Maybe he makes them by hand. I can imagine him doing that. I can picture him being good at arts and crafts. Good with his fingers.

I realise that he's talking and that I haven't been paying attention. I pinch my chin between thumb and forefinger and nod, trying to act like I've been following along and am deep in thought.

He goes silent and looks at me like he expects me to say something. I have absolutely no idea what he might be waiting for, though, and I don't want to accidentally confess to murder or anything, so I tell him the truth.

'I'm so sorry,' I say, 'I wasn't listening. I was thinking of something else. What did you say?'

There's confusion in his eyes, but it doesn't hang around for long. Instead, he laughs. 'Aye, I bore myself, sometimes,' he says, then he glances at the notebook I now see he clutches in his left hand. 'Your call, that night, you said your neighbour's ex was the one making all the fuss. You seemed concerned for her welfare.'

Did I say that? I run a hand through my hair, buying myself a few moments to think. It feels thick and oily. I haven't washed it in days. It's stuck together in places with clumps of pastel green and light grey.

'I don't remember,' I tell him.

'You don't remember what you called about?' he asks.

I give my head a shake. 'No, I mean, I remember, yes. I remember calling. I'm just not sure exactly what I said.'

'I am,' the detective sergeant tells me. 'I've got a transcription of it.'

He holds the pad a little further away from him, then brings it a smidge closer, trying to find the right focal length. Once he's settled on it, he begins to read.

'"He's here, he's right downstairs, he's hammering on the door. Her ex. It's her ex. He's already roughed her up, and he's trying to kick the door in. You need to get here. You need to get here now."' He lowers the pad and looks up at me. 'That ring any bells? There's more, but…'

'I remember,' I tell him.

'That was you, then?' he asks. 'Who said all that? That was you?'

He's still smiling, but it's fainter now. He doesn't look nearly as kind. I wonder if I was wrong about him being friendly?

Maybe DS Martin Brompton isn't such a nice man, after all.

'It was,' I confirm. 'But I was wrong.'

'You were wrong?' He points to the pad. 'That sounds pretty certain.'

'I know, but—'

'I could get the audio recording for us. See how you sound on that.'

'I'd only met her that day. I had no idea who her boyfriend was.' Something about the statement feels like an admission of guilt. 'Or *is*, or whatever. She'd just mentioned that night that she'd run away from him, so when I heard the knocking, I put two and two together and got five.'

I know I'm saying the words, but part of me is just sitting back, listening in, impressed by how smoothly the lies are coming out of my mouth. DS Brompton is nodding slowly, like he needs a few seconds to process this information.

I instinctively want to keep chattering and fill the gap in the conversation, but I sit on my hands, bite my tongue, and wait.

He can't prove I'm lying. He doesn't know anything. This is a courtesy follow-up call, nothing more.

'Do you know a Marcus Fraser, Diane?' he asks.

And the world winds down into slow motion.

I can feel the smile fixed on my face, but every part of it is wrong. Wrong size, wrong shape. Wrong everything.

I frown, still grinning, then shake my head. It takes forever. It takes an age.

'Nope,' I say with a forced enthusiasm.

I cross my arms, but is that the wrong thing to do? Does crossing your arms make you look like a liar? Or is that looking up and to the left?

'Should I have heard of him?' I ask because it feels like the sort of thing people say.

The steam swirls from his coffee on the table. The way he's looking at me makes me want to hold my breath and start counting. To pretend I'm not here, like I do when Emma and Carol call me.

'He's been in the news. Well, not directly. Not as such,' the detective sergeant says. He's watching me closely now, waiting for me to slip up. 'You hear about that car that was found? Burned out. East Lothian. Few miles this side of Tranent.'

I shake my head, too scared to speak, in case the crack in my voice gives the game away.

DS Brompton pulls a face like he's surprised to hear this. 'It's been everywhere,' he says. 'Locals. Nationals. BBC. ITV. They all covered it.'

'I don't watch the news,' I tell him.

'No?'

'It fosters feelings of helplessness and can lead to a worsening of mental illnesses like depression and anxiety.'

He looks surprised by that answer, too. It's true, though. The doctor told me that once. Word for word.

'Right. I see,' he says, after a moment's pause. 'Well, Marcus Fraser was a police officer. We have reason to believe he was... involved in an incident.'

'Murdered, you mean?' I ask. Even as the words are coming out, I can feel my throat tightening, trying to trap them. Feel my stomach upending itself, and my blood beginning to curdle in my veins.

Stupid.

Stupid, stupid, stupid.

He shifts in the seat, like a snake getting ready to strike.

'Why would you say that, Diane?' he asks.

I try to keep calm. To stay casual. I shrug. 'I just… I don't know. It just sounded like it was something bad, that's all, so I thought…' The explanation runs out of runway then, and all I can do is bookend it with another shrug.

'So, you just guessed he'd been murdered?'

I stare back at him, heart thumping in my throat, lips dry. When I go to speak, my mouth makes a weird clicking sound.

'*Was* a police officer.'

DS Brompton raises a carefully sculpted eyebrow. 'Sorry?'

'You said he *was* a police officer, past tense, which made me think he was dead. And you said his car had been burned out. So, I just…' I lick my lips, trying to moisten them, but my tongue has turned to sandpaper. 'Was he?' I ask. 'Murdered?'

He scratches at his chin, considering the question. Considering me.

Finally, his shoulders slacken, and he seems to relax.

'I'm afraid I'm not at liberty to say. But his car was spotted on CCTV cameras on Wednesday evening, not far from here. Just around the corner at the top of the street, in fact. Black BMW.' He's studying me again, watching every movement of every muscle. 'You see it?'

I tell him I didn't. Not that I remember, anyway.

'It was around the time of your call, which is what flagged it up,' he says. 'Seems like a big coincidence.'

'It does,' I agree, but I don't say any more than that.

'You didn't see it, though? The car?'

I shake my head, more firmly this time. 'No.'

He reaches into the inside pocket of his jacket, doesn't find what he's looking for, so checks the pocket on the opposite side.

This time, he finds it. This time, he pulls it out.

'What about him?'

He holds up a photo, and suddenly I'm staring into the same eyes I looked into less than a week ago. This time, though, they're glossy, and bright, and alive, not the empty dark hollows of a dead man's.

'Was this the man who was causing the disturbance?'

Marcus stares back at me, *smiles* back at me. He looks like he's laughing, or maybe just about to.

For a moment, I'm back there in his living room, kneeling beside him, staring down into the open wound in his throat as I pull the shroud of bubble wrap around him.

Pop. Pop. Pop.

'Diane?'

'Hmm?' I give myself a shake. 'Sorry, no. No, I don't think so. It was dark, but I'm sure the guy downstairs had lighter hair. Longer. Bald on top. And a moustache, maybe.'

I stop talking when I realise I'm describing the American wrestler, Hulk Hogan. The story already sounds flimsy enough without adding the former WWF World Heavyweight Champion into the mix.

'It wasn't him?' the detective asks.

'No. Definitely not.'

'Definitely not? Because you just said you didn't *think* so, but it was dark.'

'It wasn't him,' I say, tearing my eyes away from the photograph. 'It was nothing like him.'

He keeps the picture held up and facing me for a few more seconds, then nods and returns it to his pocket.

'Right. Fair enough. It was a bit of a long shot, but worth a try.'

He gets to his feet, flipping closed his notebook.

Is that it?

Am I safe? Is he done?

'Thanks for your time, Diane.' He doesn't so much as glance down at the barely touched cup and saucer on the table. 'And thanks for the coffee.'

He hands me a business card. The paper feels warm, like he's been sitting on it.

'If anything comes to mind, or… Whatever. Just give me a call.'

'I will,' I tell him.

I won't.

He smiles, thin-lipped, then nods. 'I'll see myself out,' he says, though he only makes it as far as the living room door before he stops and turns back. 'Oh, just one more thing,' he says, like he's Columbo.

'Yes?'

'His car was picked up on CCTV on Thursday evening, headed for the bypass.'

There's something about the way he says it. Something about the way he looks at me.

'Oh?'

He nods, slowly, still watching me. 'It's hard to tell, the picture's not that clear, but it looks like there are two people sitting in the front seats.'

I swallow. It burns all the way down.

'Women, we think.' He's staring at me, staring *into me*. Then, without warning, he shrugs and breaks into a smile. 'Like I say, though, the quality on these isn't great. So, who knows?'

I feel like he expects me to joke along, or laugh, but nothing comes out.

'Anyway, your neighbour. Downstairs.' He points to the floor like I don't know what direction that is. 'You think she'll be in for me to pop down and have a chat?'

'Why?' I ask. 'What for? I've told you everything.'

'I'm sure you have, Diane,' the detective says, and he's looking at me again in that same way, like he can see straight through me. He winks, as if he knows a secret. 'But it never hurts to check.'

CHAPTER 26

Chloe

The rain started about a minute after I left work – a sudden, vicious deluge that's turned the uneven pavements and cobbled streets into a series of tiny ponds and lakes.

I huddle under the pathetic excuse for an umbrella I bought from the pound shop on the way back to the flat. It's cheap shite that keeps folding in on itself every time there's so much as a breath of wind.

Just another thing that isn't going according to plan.

It's been three days since Diane locked herself away in her flat. Three days of silence. No response to my calls or texts. No answer when I press the buzzer. She doesn't even leave for work. I've been told she called in sick on Tuesday, after rushing out of the training room the day before, and now her phone just goes to voicemail.

It's so inconsiderate of her. How am I supposed to ruin her life if she won't even talk to me?

I turn onto our street, already mapping out my next move. Maybe I could tell her I'm in trouble again. Would she buy that? I can't use Marcus, for obvious reasons.

Or… what if I came clean and told her the truth? Some variation of it, anyway, leaving out a few details. Would that work? Could I break through her defences that way?

Maybe. But she'd have to actually talk to me first.

I look up at her window as I approach the flat, in case she's standing there, and I can wave for her to come outside.

She isn't. Her curtains and blinds are all closed. The place looks like it's in darkness. If it wasn't for the squeaking of her floorboards through the day and night, I'd be starting to think she'd run away.

But dead things are still turning up on her doorstep, which assures me that she hasn't gone anywhere.

I'm about to start down my steps when I spot a figure standing at my front door. A man. Smart suit and shoes. Nice hair. Well turned out.

He has his back to me as he presses the doorbell, holding his finger on the button.

My heart lurches. Instinct screams at me to turn around, to walk away, to run.

He hasn't noticed me yet. I could still do it. I could still get away.

The rain hammers on my flimsy umbrella, matching the rapid rat-tat-tat of my pulse. It's a drumbeat. An announcement.

He turns, looks up, and spots me.

He's a cop. I can tell. These days, I can recognise them a mile off.

'Chloe Quinn?'

Shit.

Shit.

I hesitate, but only for a fraction of a second. 'Yes?'

He produces a leather wallet from his inside pocket and flips it open, revealing his warrant card. I descend the steps and make a show of studying it. Rainwater beads on the clear plastic that covers the ID.

'Detective Sergeant Martin Brompton,' he says. 'Sorry to bother you, but I was hoping I might be able to have a word.'

'Is something wrong?' I ask. There's concern in my voice. Not too much, not too little.

'I just need to ask you a few questions, if that's alright?'

He didn't answer the question. My chest tightens, but I plaster on my best smile and fish my keys from my pocket.

'Of course,' I say, opening the door into the dark and silent hallway beyond. 'Please, come on in out of the rain.'

'I appreciate you taking the time to speak with me,' DS Brompton says.

He's sitting on the couch, scooched forward so he's more or less balancing on the front of the cushion.

When he first entered the living room he hesitated, his eyes darting to every nook and every corner, then roaming slowly across the walls like he was taking in every inch of the place.

There was something about his expression that seemed strange. Off. Like he was seeing something there that I wasn't, spotting some detail that I'd missed. I found myself following along, my gaze tracking the route that his eyes had taken just a moment before.

Whatever he was seeing, though, I was blind to it.

I don't know why, but it made the skin prickle on the back of my neck.

'No problem at all,' I tell him. 'Always happy to help the police.' There's a twitch at the corner of my mouth, like my smile is malfunctioning. 'Not that I talk to them very often.'

He offers a thin smile of his own in return. 'I don't blame you. We can be hard work. You should see some of the people I work with,' he says, then he pulls out a notebook, flips to a page that's marked with scribbles and wet spots, and sets it down on the coffee table.

'You'll want to get dried off and changed, I'm sure, so I'll get straight to the point, Chloe. I'm investigating an incident involving a police officer,' he says. 'A detective constable named Marcus Fraser.'

A detective constable? The bastard told me he was a sergeant.

'I don't know anyone by that name,' I say, offering a shrug in support of that statement.

'Right. OK.' He nods, but I get the feeling it's not the answer he was looking for. 'He's about six foot, late thirties, dark hair, drives a black BMW.'

'No, sorry,' I say after an acceptably thoughtful pause. 'That's not really ringing a bell. Marcus…?'

'Fraser,' he says, matter-of-factly. 'With an S.'

I shake my head. 'No. Sorry.'

He makes a low 'Huh' sound at the back of his throat, and his whole face pulls downwards into a frown. 'That's strange.'

My heart stutters. My insides squirm. From where he's sitting, though, you'd never be able to tell.

'How is that strange?'

The detective leans forward slightly. 'Just that we have reports of a woman matching your description entering and leaving his house in Howden Hall Road several times over the past few weeks.'

'Howden Hall Road?' I say, holding his eye. 'Where's that?'

He doesn't reply. I hold his gaze, calculating away inside my head. How many reports? How credible? Was I seen from a distance through a hedge, or caught in the high-definition gaze of a doorbell camera? That could be the difference between sightings of a random blonde woman and a positive ID of me.

And there are a lot of random blonde women in Edinburgh.

He's about to say something when a muffled thud comes from somewhere nearby. It sounds to me like it came from the direction of my bedroom, and, judging by the way he turns to look, he thinks the same.

'Is there someone else here, Chloe?' he asks.

'No,' I say. My eyes dart to the ceiling. 'It must've been my neighbour. The floors are pretty thin…'

'Diane,' he says, and it takes all my effort to hide my surprise.

'That's right. Have you spoken to her?'

'I have.'

My pulse speeds up again. Though I try to stop myself, I swallow hard, like I can force down the heartbeat that's suddenly thumping in my throat.

What did she tell him? What does he know?

'Oh?' I say, trying my best to sound disinterested. 'She's been keeping to herself lately. I haven't seen her in a few days.'

I regret it immediately when I see how this piques his interest.

'Why's that?'

'She's, uh, I'm not sure,' I tell him. 'She's not been well, I think. She's off work. Sick. Flu or something.'

'She seemed alright,' the detective tells me.

I put everything I've got into a big, bright beamer of a smile. 'That's good to hear. Hopefully she'll be back to work tomorrow.'

'You work together?'

The question sounds innocent enough, but I'm sure I sense a trap in there somewhere, just waiting for me to activate it.

'Yes. No. I mean, not really. Same company, but different departments.'

There's another sound from somewhere nearby. A thud, like before. I'd swear it's not from upstairs.

But how is that possible? There's nobody here but us.

Is there?

DS Brompton is looking past me, at the door, when I turn back to him. His gaze lingers there for a second, then returns to me.

'Where were you on Thursday, Chloe?' he asks, changing the direction of the conversation so suddenly that I stumble over my response.

'Thursday?'

'Aye. Thursday. Can you give me an account of your where-abouts that day?'

I rub at my forehead. The sweat rolls into tiny balls of dirt beneath my fingertips.

'What time?'

'Just take me through the day, if you can,' the detective says. He reaches for his notebook and takes a pen from an inside pocket. 'Be as detailed as you can.'

'Thursday,' I say again, stalling for time. He's staring at me, seeing straight through me, making it hard for me to concentrate. 'Thursday. So…'

'She was with me.'

I jump to my feet in surprise as Ronan comes strolling into the living room, wearing nothing but his boxers and a lopsided smile. I struggle to hide my shock. What the hell is he doing here? How did he get in?

'We spent most of the day in bed, didn't we, babe?' he says.

Before I can form any sort of reply, he crosses to my side, plants a kiss on my neck, and drapes an arm around my shoulder. 'Sorry, were there noise complaints? We were making quite a racket,' he says to the detective. 'Thin walls and all that.'

DS Brompton regards him in a slow, curious sort of silence, then glances between us, his expression guarded. 'You were together all day Thursday?'

'All day and all night,' Ronan confirms.

He slaps me on the arse. It's hard. Shocking. I cry out, then try to turn it into a laugh, like I'm used to this, like it's *what we do*. 'Didn't even leave for food, did we, babe?'

'Uh, no. No.' I slip an arm around his waist, leaning into the lie. 'We didn't even leave for food.'

'And you are?' the detective asks, pen poised over his notebook.

'Ronan McIntyre. I'm Chloe's boyfriend.' There's something possessive in his smile when he turns it on me. It makes me want to slap him, or go for his throat, or gouge his eyes out.

But all I can do is go along with it. All I can do is smile back.

'Can anyone confirm your story?' DS Brompton asks.

Ronan snorts. 'Not unless they were pervy bastards peeking in through the windows.'

His hand is on my waist, fingers trailing up and down my hip. I keep smiling. It doesn't feel like he's saving me so much as claiming me.

'I see.' DS Brompton makes a note, then closes his book. There's a reluctance to it, like he doesn't want to but doesn't have a choice.

His eyes scan the room again, taking in the artwork on the walls, the furniture arrangement, the colour of the carpet. 'Interesting flat you have,' he remarks.

'Thanks,' is all I can think to say.

He nods, pulls out a business card, and places it on the coffee table.

'Well, thank you for your time, Chloe. Ronan.' He stands, straightening his jacket. 'I may need to speak with you again, so please don't leave town without letting me know.'

'Of course,' I say, detaching myself from Ronan so I can show the detective out.

He glances up at the rain, then hurries off up the stairs.

I close the door behind him and wait until I hear him go splashing off down the street.

Only then do I turn to face Ronan. He's leaning against a wall, arms folded, looking far too pleased with himself.

'OK, Ronan,' I say, drawing in a breath. 'Let's start by you telling me what the hell you're doing here.'

CHAPTER 27

Chloe

Ronan laughs at me. He shouldn't do that. I don't like it when people laugh at me.

I grin and bear it, though. I need to find out what he's doing here, how he got in. How much he knows.

'I don't know what the big deal is, babe,' he says, still wearing nothing but his silky red boxers.

He opens the fridge, planning to help himself to the contents, and then stands there looking surprised by how empty it is. There's nothing in there. Nothing at all. He settles for a glass of water. Even the way he glugs it, then discards the glass in the sink, feels like an act of dominance.

'We always said we were going to move in together.'

'Eventually,' I say.

Never, I think.

He grins and scratches his balls through his underwear. 'No time like the present, eh?'

'No, not yet. You can't be here. You'll ruin everything,' I tell him. I shake my head. It's emphatic, but he doesn't seem to care.

Clearly, he's not the sort of man to take 'no' for an answer.

He moves in closer, lowering his voice into what he presumably believes to be a seductive purr. It makes my skin crawl.

'Listen. Babe. I know it's not ideal, but I've got nowhere else to go. The missus has turfed me out, hasn't she? She knows about me and Diane. About what you've been making me do with her.'

He tries to put his hands on my waist, but I draw back from his touch. It doesn't deter him, though, and he keeps coming closer until he has me cornered against the front door.

'She knows about us, babe.'

Us. He says the word like it means something. Like it's a thing. I want to push him back, scream at him, make him see that there is no *us*, that there's never been an *us*, and there never will be.

But I'm not done with him yet. I still might need him.

He's been instrumental in my plan to destroy Diane. He was the love of her life once upon a time. He still is, I think. It didn't take much for him to charm himself back into her bed. It didn't take much for me to convince him to do it, either.

For months, Ronan has been a reliable source of information about the woman who killed my parents. He's also her main weakness.

Much as I'd love to be done with him, I'm not. Not yet.

But that doesn't mean he's staying here.

I remember that Diane is still upstairs, and put a finger to my lips before leading Ronan through to the living room. He takes my hand when we reach the door, and tries to pull me in the direction of the bedroom, but then follows when I tear myself free of his grip.

It's only when the TV is on that I dare speak again.

'What do you mean *she knows about us*?'

Ronan shifts his weight from one bare foot to the other. For the first time since he came striding into the room in just his underwear, he looks a little self-conscious.

'I mean, Mairi knows about us. About me and you.'

'What *about* me and you?' The question is a hiss through my gritted teeth. 'What *exactly* does she know, Ronan?'

'No. I mean, nothing. Not really. Not any details,' he says, backtracking. 'Just, you know, that I've been seeing someone else.'

'So, Diane, then?'

He rubs at the back of his neck and shivers, suddenly aware of how cold it is in the flat.

'I mean, yeah. Mostly. Not just her, though. We, eh, we had an argument, and it just sort of slipped out about, well, us.'

There's that word again. I wish it was a tangible thing that I could grab hold of and ram back down his throat.

'I didn't mention your name or anything. Nothing like that. I just said there was more than one other person I'd been shagging.'

My skin crawls. Though I try not to, I think of his wife. The mother of his children. I imagine how she must've felt in that moment.

And then I flip a switch in my head, and I don't think about her any longer.

'But we haven't *been* "shagging". Have we, Ronan?'

He smirks, his eyebrows waggling suggestively, like I was offering up some sort of invitation.

'I mean, not all the way. Not yet,' he says, sidling in closer again. 'But no time like the present.'

'Don't touch me!' I warn him, drawing back.

He looks shocked. No, more than that. He looks outraged.

'What the fuck is wrong with you?' he asks. He looks me up and down, and I suddenly feel even less dressed than he is. 'What's with the attitude?'

'I just… This messes with the plan. You being here.'

'The plan?' He scoffs at that. 'Did your plan involve the police coming to your door and asking you what you've been up to?

Pretty much accusing you of God knows what? Was that part of your plan?'

He moves closer again. It's not seductive this time, though. It's an animal on the prowl. A predator closing in on its prey.

'What would have happened if I hadn't been here?' he asks. 'What were you going to tell him? Because it sounded to me like you were struggling there.'

He jabs a finger against his chest. It's so fast and sudden that I jump with fright.

'I stepped in and saved you there. You'd be in the shit if it wasn't for me. And everything I've done? With that mental munter up there? For you?'

His face twists into a scowl. The finger that was pointed at himself now stabs at me.

'You need to be more grateful. You should be on your knees thanking me for everything I've done for you. You should be kissing my feet!'

His bare chest rises and falls. The sour tang of his sweat taints the air around him.

'You want me to go up there and tell Diane everything? Tell her how you talked me into dredging up the past and becoming her fuckbuddy? You want me to go up there and spill the beans?'

'No,' I tell him.

He steps in closer and presses a finger to his ear, cocking his head towards me. 'What was that? Didn't hear you.'

'No,' I say, louder this time. I want it to sound defiant. I want it to put him back in his place.

It doesn't.

'No. Thought not,' he says.

He holds a hand out. I stare at it, knowing exactly what it is. Knowing precisely what it means.

It's not an invitation. It's not even a request. It's an order.

'Right, then,' he says. 'Come on.'

It's seven years ago, and a man in his car is shouting at me for being a tease.

It's seven days ago, and a man in his house is pushing me down and calling me a psychopath.

It's now, and a man in his underwear stands waiting for my answer.

I need him. To end all this, I need him.

So, I take his hand, and I let him lead the way.

CHAPTER 28

Diane

I stand outside the door, on the front step, clenched fist raised like I'm ready to knock. I don't, though. Not yet. I need to prepare myself first.

It's only been a couple of weeks since I last saw them, but a lot has changed in that time. I've come off my medication. I've got a new neighbour, lied to my work, and set fire to a policeman's corpse.

It's been a busy old fortnight, all in all.

Parents aren't meant to judge us. That's what they say, isn't it? Of everyone in the world, your mum and dad are the ones meant to love you for just who you are. Despite all your flaws and your faults, they're always meant to be there.

And mine are there. Always. Even when I don't want them to be. Breathing down my neck, watching over me, telling me I'm not doing things properly, that I'm doing things *wrong*.

I'm sure they don't mean it like that. I'm sure they're just doing their best to protect me and keep me safe.

I'm almost certain that's all it is.

The door opens suddenly, and my dad is there, squinting back at me like he doesn't know who I am or why I'm here. Even before he speaks, there's a gruffness to him. That's his default, though. In both looks and general demeanour, he reminds me of Brian Cox.

The actor, I mean, not the science one.

'Diane?' he says, looking me up and down. 'What are you doing?' He points to the doorbell. It's one of those camera ones that he must've recently had installed. 'I thought this thing had glitched, or frozen, or something. You just been standing out there?'

'Um, not really,' I say. I shoot the doorbell a dirty look, like it's all its fault.

Then my dad beckons me in, and I've got no choice but to step over the threshold and into the house.

It smells. Not bad or anything. The opposite, really. It's my dad's aftershave and my mum's baking. It's home-cooked dinners and finger paints and birthday parties. It's Sunday roasts, Sunday papers, Mother's Days and Father's Days, and breakfasts in bed.

It's exam results. It's arguments. It's cocktail nights, and barbecues, and cookies for Santa on Christmas Eve.

It's home. Or it was, anyway. Once.

'Everything alright?' Dad asks as I follow him through the narrow hallway lined with cluttered floor-to-ceiling bookcases. 'Not like you to just drop round.'

He stops so suddenly I almost walk straight into him.

'You're not pregnant, are you?'

'What? No!' I splutter the words out like I'm embarrassed by the idea. Or maybe just by the horror in his voice when he asked the question. 'I'm not pregnant.'

He glances at my stomach like he's not convinced, then meets my eye again.

'Are you ill? You look ill,' he says. 'Are you dying?'

'Course I'm not dying!'

Again, he seems dubious, but he shrugs and goes shuffling through to the living room.

My mum looks up from where she's doing a jigsaw at her little fold-out crafting table. She's nearly blind these days, especially when it comes to seeing things up close, and the glasses she's wearing make her eyes appear twice their actual size.

'Oh! Was it you right enough?' she asks, fiddling with a puzzle piece, turning it over and over in her hand like she's sensing where it should go. 'We saw you on your father's phone, but thought maybe it was a whatchamacallit?'

'A glitch,' Dad says.

'Aye. A glitch.'

It would have to be quite an impressive technical error to conjure up a fully 3D version of their own daughter on the doorstep, but I choose not to point that out. It'd only confuse them. Technology isn't their strong point.

I clock the front of the jigsaw box. It's an image of the Last Supper. That makes sense. Once finished, she'll no doubt frame it and hang it next to the one of Christ on the cross on the staircase wall.

'What's the matter?' Mum asks, giving me the same once-over that Dad did out in the hall. 'Are you not well or something?'

'I'm fine!' I insist.

'Are you pregnant?'

Unlike Dad, who seemed positively distraught by the idea, she sounds almost hopeful. I feel bad for disappointing her.

'No. I just thought I'd pop round and see you,' I say. 'Can't a girl swing by and see her mum and dad?'

'Thirty-seven-year-old woman,' Dad corrects.

Mum gets up from the table and places down the puzzle piece without looking. I don't know if it's in the right place. Having spent an infuriating three weeks trying to do the Christ on the cross jigsaw with her a few years back, I highly doubt it.

'Och, wheesht yourself, you,' she says to him. 'She's always our girl. I'll go get the kettle on. I've just made scones.'

'I shouldn't,' I say, but she ignores me.

She hurries past, headed for the kitchen. She's a feeder, my mum. Always has been. It's why me and my dad are the shapes we are, whereas she's got the build of a pencil that lives on caffeine and nerves.

Dad doesn't say anything until we hear the water sloshing into the kettle in the room next door.

'So. You alright?' he asks. There's more meaning behind it this time. It's a genuine question, not a simple greeting.

'I'm fine,' I tell him.

He nods. It's slow and methodical, just like him. 'You taking the tablets?'

I tell him that I am. I'm not sure if he believes me, but he doesn't call me a liar.

'That's good. You know how important they are.'

'I know,' I tell him, then I look away, searching for a change of subject. 'Is that a new rug?'

His gaze sticks on me for a few seconds before following the tilt of my head. 'That one? No. We've had that years.'

'Oh, yeah,' I say, pretending to remember. Acting like I can recall seeing it before.

You'd think I would remember it. It's a horrible bloody thing, all browns and burgundies, with raggedy tassels at two of the ends.

It reminds me a bit of the flying carpet from *Aladdin*, only I'd imagine this one would suffer a malfunction and nosedive straight into the side of a mountain halfway through 'A Whole New World'.

'Listen, Dad,' I say, and I can see him tense, fearing I'm about to make the big announcement he's been bracing himself for since he saw me frozen out there on the step.

He doesn't relax any when I tell him I'm just going to go upstairs and take a look at my bedroom. If anything, the concern lines just etch themselves deeper on his face as I hurry out of the room, smiling at him the whole way.

There's only one bathroom in the house, right at the top of the stairs. My room is the next one along. You can still see the vague remnants of childhood stickers – rainbows, and ponies, and all things pink.

I can't even remember if they were my choices or my parents'.

Then again, there's a lot I don't remember.

The room hasn't changed much since the last time I was in here. It was a couple of years back, when I'd come down with the flu and come crawling home to be fussed over and taken care of.

Before that, it had been almost five years. I came back here after the accident. I couldn't stand being alone with their lifeless, bloodied faces.

Mum keeps the bed made, just on the off chance. Just in case. Dad says she misses me being around the house. He doesn't tell me if he does, but that in itself probably says all I need to know.

Everything about the place looks the same. The bedside table – the first bit of flat-packed furniture I assembled myself – with the handle on upside down. The wardrobe door with the crack across the bottom corner of the mirror.

The carpet, the curtains, the lightshade, the bed. Even the crucifix Mum fixed to the wall above the bed after I finally relented. It's all the same.

And yet, it isn't.

Something has changed. Maybe not in the fittings and furnishing themselves, but in the space between them. The air is different.

But that's not all. If I squint, if I use a bit of imagination, there's an imprint of a figure on the duvet on one side of the bed. Shorter than me. Smaller than me. Like someone has been lying on it. Some curious little Goldilocks, poking around, making herself at home.

I find the hair on one of the pillows. It's slap bang in the centre, like it's been left there on purpose for me to find. Long. Blonde.

Curious little Goldilocks, trying me on for size.

I should be angry. I want to be angry, but all I am is tired. I climb onto the bed, taking care not to disturb the outline, and I lie down next to it. Facing it. Imagining someone there.

My eyes are heavy. I lay my hand lightly across the outline's middle, being careful not to mess it up. Not to wake her.

And not even the slow, steady creaking of footsteps on the staircase can prevent me from falling asleep.

CHAPTER 29

Diane

This is not a flashback.

It's not a dream, either. It's some half-remembered memory of a memory, buried by the pills, and the shame, and the therapy.

It was hazy enough the first time around, when it happened. That was the booze. The stress. The panic of it all, making it all seem vague and faraway, like it was happening to someone else. Like someone else was responsible.

I'm not sure if I remember any of it, or if I'm only remembering some version of it I imagined much later. I don't know what bits are real and what parts only ever happened in my head.

But I know two people died and one might as well have. That bit's real. That bit's a fact.

It all happens so fast. I'm driving – from where, going where, I don't remember. It's not important. I'm driving. My hair's wet, and thick with salt. There's sand in my shoes.

A beach? Have I been at the beach?

It doesn't matter.

It all happens so fast. There's a bend in the road. There's music playing. Or... no. Voices talking on the radio. They're saying numbers, I think. Counting, maybe. I can't tell.

It's raining. The wipers *tha-thunk* back and forth across the glass. Not a day at the beach, then. You don't go to the beach when it's raining.

So where have I been?

It doesn't matter.

It all happens so fast. There's a car on the road, up ahead. Crawling along, tail lights like smears of red across the windscreen.

Tha-thunk.

Tha-thunk.

Tha-thunk.

They're too slow. Whoever's driving is taking the piss. Do I say those words out loud? Do I hear them? Do I just think them inside my head?

I blast the horn. It makes me jump. It's so loud, so sudden, so out of nowhere that I grip on tight, my nails digging into the steering wheel so hard that my knees hurt.

Does that make sense? Is that possible?

It doesn't matter.

It all happens so fast. I see the driver looking up at me as I swing past him. Our eyes meet through the side windows. He looks angry, but scared, too. I give him the finger and laugh at him, all the way down there, hunched behind the wheel of his teeny, tiny car.

More lights spread across the rain-dappled glass in front of me. The wipers seem to sense this and speed up, trying to bat away the spreading white glow that grows and grows as it rushes towards me.

Tha-thunk-tha-thunk-tha-thunk-tha-thunk.

The lights are too close, though. Too close, too fast. Nowhere to go. Nowhere to hide.

The man on the radio keeps saying names and listing off numbers.

'One.'

'Four.'

'Two.'

'Three.'

And the lights are too bright, too blinding. And the man in the car beside me is so angry, so scared. So very, very small.

There's a sound of metal on metal. A squealing of tyres. A sharp, sideways shudder as I swing in, narrowly avoiding a head-on with the oncoming vehicle.

Tha-thunktha-thunktha-thunktha-thunk.

'Two.'

'One.'

'Five.'

'One.'

I scream. I grip the wheel and hiss at the pain. Bottles *clink* together in the footwell at my feet.

'Shit, shit, don't look back! Don't look, don't look!'

Do I say that out loud? Do I hear it? Or is it only in my head? It doesn't matter.

It all happens so fast.

From behind me comes the sound of thunder.

'What are you doing? What are you doing? *What are you doing?*'

'Diane? What are you doing?'

I gasp awake, eyes wide, hands clawing at the air like I've just been dragged back to life after drowning. I'd imagine it feels much the same, too.

I'm not there driving, or at the roadside, or tangled in the wreckage of that car.

I'm here, on my bed, with my dad looking down on me. There's concern in his eyes, but it's a hostile, impatient kind, like he's worried but would really rather not be. Like whatever's wrong, I've no doubt brought it on myself and most likely just to inconvenience him.

'Is there something the matter, Diane?' he asks. 'You're being…'

He gestures vaguely to me, lying there on top of the bedcovers, as if the state of me neatly concludes his sentence for him.

'Are you ill again?'

'No,' I tell him.

'Because me and your mum can't run after you like last time. We've stuff to do.'

'I'm not ill,' I assure him.

He steps back as I clamber off the bed. I don't know why I'm so careful not to disturb the imprint on the duvet. Preserving evidence, maybe. Let's go with that.

I'm taller than him these days, so he has to look up to meet my eye. I can tell this displeases him greatly. Something else he no doubt considers my fault.

'Have you been drinking?'

'No.'

He nods to signal that this is good, but he's not done with me yet.

'Are you on drugs? Is that what this is?'

'I'm just tired,' I say.

'That's not an answer.'

I sigh. He looks surprised by it. Shocked, even. 'I'm not on drugs. I'm just tired.'

He looks past me to the bed. 'You're tired.'

'That's right.'

'So, you travelled forty-five minutes across town from your own flat to have a two-minute kip, did you?'

'Tea's ready!'

Mum's voice is a reedy cry from the bottom of the stairs. I hear her humming to herself as she bustles on through to the living room, cups rattling in their saucers.

I make a move to step past my dad, but he stands his ground.

'Let me look at you,' he says, putting his hands on my shoulders. 'Head up.'

I want to shrink, to wriggle away, but thirty-odd years of training kick in, and I tilt my chin upwards until I'm staring straight ahead. He cups my face in his hands, and I can feel his fingers prodding around under my jaw, crawling across my throat while he stares deep into my eyes.

'Open.'

My mouth opens on command. My tongue unfurls like a flag of surrender.

'Hm,' he says, and I can't tell if he's pleased or disappointed. 'Nothing swollen. There doesn't seem to be anything obviously physically wrong.'

'I told you, I'm fine,' I say, rubbing at my neck. I can still feel his fingers tap-tap-tapping at my throat.

He studies me for a long time. Downstairs, Mum calls for us again.

'If you say so,' he finally concedes, and I think that's the end of it.

It isn't.

'But after scones, I think it's best that you had a word with the doctor.'

'No, there's no need, Dad. I'm—'

He holds a finger up. Like an obedient dog, I go silent.

'The doctor, Diane,' he says. 'I really think that's best.'

· · ·

He is no longer my father. Not in here. Not in this room.

In this room, he is less than that. And more. Much, much more.

His certificates line the wall behind his desk. Degrees, diplomas, regulatory boards. Black and white proof that he knows best. That I should listen and do as he says.

The desk was expensive. I don't know how much, but I remember Mum's reaction to the credit card bill, and that was before the additional cost of having to remove the window to get the thing inside.

That was thirty years ago and, to be fair, the desk doesn't really show its age. It's still the same polished oak, with the same green leather trim on the top. The drawers are all on his side, but I'd imagine the little brass handles look much like they did when the desk was first delivered.

On this side, there's just a featureless length of solid wood that hides everything below the desk. When he sits behind it on his big leather chair, he's just a chest, head and shoulders. Barely even human any more.

My seat is smaller, made of synthetic fabrics and scratchy plastics. The arms dig into my sides, squashing me, making it harder for me to breathe.

His chair rocks and tilts and twists from side to side. Mine is fixed in place, facing forwards, eyes front. *Ten-hut!*

'Have you been sleeping OK?'

It's an innocuous enough question. It's the sort of thing parents everywhere probably ask their children. But he's peering at me over the rim of his glasses, a fountain pen held above a leatherbound journal, the point pressed against the page.

'Fine,' I tell him.

The office is compact, and with the door closed behind me, there's a strange texture to the sound. It makes our words feel like dirty secrets whispered in the half-dark.

'You said you were tired. You look tired,' he tells me.

'Thanks a lot.'

His chair creaks. He scribbles a word or two, still watching me over the frames of his specs.

'I can't help you, Diane…'

He leaves it hanging. Waits for me to close the loop.

'If I won't help myself. I know.'

He nods, but his face doesn't change. It's not a nod of agreement. An instruction for me to continue.

How can I tell him any of it, though? How can I explain the face of a dead man keeps me awake at night? The smell of his burning body. The sizzle and pop of his blistering flesh.

Although, that might have been the bubble wrap.

But he's waiting for me to tell him something. And, from past experience, I know I won't leave this room until I do.

'I've been having these… dreams,' I tell him.

I expect him to write something, but he doesn't. He just watches me from above the rim of his glasses and below the forests of his eyebrows.

'They're about…' I blow out my cheeks and tap my thumbs together. 'Death, I suppose.'

He still doesn't write anything. 'Uh-huh,' is all he says.

'Not mine. I don't mean mine,' I continue. 'There's a guy. In the dreams. He's dead, and I have to… get rid of him.'

'Dispose of the body?' he asks.

I avert my eyes and nod.

'And how do you do that?'

I almost blurt it out. The car. The carpet. The bubble wrap, and the flames. But that's too much detail. That could give the game away.

'We dump him in the water. Off a pier,' I say. 'Wrapped up with rocks around his feet.'

He does write then. It's a short scribble with a question mark at the end. I try to see what it is he's written, but I needn't bother, because he asks it out loud a moment later.

'We?'

Damn.

Damn.

'The royal we, I mean. Me. I. I dump him in the water.'

'And who is he?'

'I don't know,' I say. He holds my gaze. I'd shift in my seat, but the arms are too tight, so all I can do is jiggle my feet around. 'I don't. I've got no idea.'

'It's not…' He tilts his head to the left. He's not indicating someone in the room, but someone in the past. We both know who. 'Is it?'

'No. No, it's not him. It's not them. It's nothing to do with all that,' I insist.

But it is, of course. It's all connected. I realise that now.

Chloe Quinn. The little sister. The orphaned girl. I can't believe it took me so long to figure it out.

'Then who is he?'

'I don't know,' I tell him. 'Honestly, I've got no idea. He's just a guy. Just some guy.'

'Just some guy you kill repeatedly in your dreams?'

'I don't kill him!' I say, taken aback. 'He's dead when I get there!'

'Well, who else is killing him, Diane?' he asks. 'This is your dream. He dies in your head, no one else's. If you're not responsible, then who is?'

I don't have an answer for that. He's right, I suppose. Every time Marcus dies again, I'm the one who's killing him.

'Is there anything else bothering you? Work? Relationships? Are you having intercourse?'

I can feel my cheeks stinging red at the question and don't quite know where to look. Across the desk, he tuts and sighs.

'We're adults here, Diane. This is important. Remember, you're not chatting with your father here, you're talking to your doctor.'

He's not my doctor, of course. Not in any official sense. I'm fairly sure that wouldn't be allowed, even if he wasn't retired. I know he had to rope in an old colleague to prescribe my medication. I'm not even convinced that's legal.

'I'm not seeing anyone. Well, not really. It's complicated,' I tell him. I should probably keep the next bit to myself, but part of me wants to shock him. To make him even more disappointed in me than he usually is. 'Remember Ronan?'

He stiffens. His pen leaves an involuntary mark on the page.

'You're seeing Ronan again?' he asks. 'I'm not sure that's wise, Diane.'

Nor am I, to be honest, but I'm not going to give him the satisfaction of saying as much. 'It's nothing too serious,' is all I tell him, then I quickly move to change the subject. 'Chloe. The woman that came round for the Sylvanian Families.'

He's still thinking about the Ronan situation and struggles to keep up. 'The what?'

'The toys. She came round that Sunday to buy them. Lives downstairs from me.'

'Yes. What about her?'

'She went upstairs, didn't she? When she was here?'

He looks blankly back at me, as if he has no idea what I'm talking about.

'To use the toilet or something,' I prompt, which dislodges something in his head.

'Oh. Yes. I think she did. Why?'

I think of the imprint on the covers and the hair on the pillow. Drinking tea with my parents, taking my toys, lying on my bed.

Infiltrating my home, my work, my friend group. Last time I saw her, she was even dressing like me.

In my dreams with Marcus, she's always already there. She's always on the floor with the knife and the blood on her hands.

'No reason,' I say.

He sets his pen down, takes off his glasses, and interlocks his fingers across the curve of his belly.

'Does she know?'

The question catches me off guard. I have no idea what he's getting at.

And yet, there's something about the way he says it that makes my heart beat faster.

'Does she know what?'

He tuts again. Sighs again. 'Come on, Diane. I know who she is. I knew the family, remember? We all did. Seven years isn't that long. She's changed, but not that much.'

I feel like he's kicked me in the stomach, and all the air has been knocked out of me. He rubs at his forehead. Dead skin rolls into little black balls beneath his fingers.

'Does she know? About what happened?' he asks. He hesitates, just for a moment, like he needs to take a run-up at the next question. 'Does she know what you did?'

'No,' I say. It's too quick. Too certain. He doesn't buy it.

'Are you sure?'

I can't stop my head shaking. 'No,' I admit.

The office is hot. Punishingly so.

'I think… I think I should talk to her,' I say, slowly and carefully, feeling my way through this conversational minefield. 'I think I should tell her.'

'Jesus *fucking* Christ, Diane!'

The words are a sharp hiss. A swipe from a claw. A swing with a blade.

He looks up like he's offering an apology to the big man upstairs, then diverts his attention back to me.

'Do you want to kill your mother?' he demands, pointing to the door behind me, as if she's standing there waiting for me to punch a fist through her chest and rip out her heart. 'Do you want to send her to an early grave? Is that what you want?'

'No. No, of course I don't, but—'

'Because that's what'll happen. You know this, Diane. We've spoken about this! If she finds out – if she finds out what you did, and what you really are – there'll be no coming back from it for her. You will break that woman in two.'

I don't answer him. I daren't. Not when he's like this.

He half turns in his chair, not looking at me. His gaze sweeps across his framed certificates, like he might find some solace or inspiration pinned there beneath the glass.

Something to alleviate the shame he feels at having me for a daughter.

'You were blind drunk and made a stupid decision. You messed up. We both know that. There's no getting away from what happened,' he says. His voice is level now, not quite all the way professional, but headed in that direction. 'But what's done is done. It's awful what happened to that family. It's a tragedy that I'm sure you will carry with you until your dying day.'

He points at me, then presses the fingertip against the top of his desk. Suddenly, I have a flash of sitting there on his knee, leaning on that exact spot while I drew pictures on old bits of scrap paper. Ponies. Rainbows. Bright smears of pink.

Those seemed to make him happiest.

'But God gave you and you alone this burden to carry, Diane. It's yours. Not mine, and certainly not your poor mother's.'

He gives that a moment to sink in. To really let me dwell on it.

'So, whatever you have to do, whatever steps you have to take to get this ridiculous notion about confessing out of your head, then I suggest you do it, and do it quickly.'

He leans in closer. His finger screws into the desktop, like he's stubbing out a cigarette.

'Take care of this, Diane. Quickly.' It's an order. A commandment. The doctor's decree. 'Because it won't just be your own life you're destroying, if you don't.'

CHAPTER 30

Chloe

His snoring is a guttural, choking racket that makes me think of wild animals. Of pigs rooting through mud and filth.

He lies starfished on the bed, expanding to fill the space I left when I snuck away to clean myself up.

The sight of him, all that bare flesh and hair, forces me to swallow something hot and sour that rises in my throat. I feel it burning all the way back down.

I pull a blanket over him. It's not for his sake – I couldn't care less how cold he gets – but for mine. I don't want to see him like this. I don't want the reminder of what just happened.

I gather up my clothes and get dressed in the bathroom, where there's less risk of waking him. The way he's snoring suggests he'll be out for a while yet, but I don't want to take any chances.

I heard Diane leaving around ninety minutes ago. It's the first time she's been out of the flat in days, and the first chance I've had since then to go poking around. It's time I started setting my trap. It's time for Diane Shelley to pay.

It's only when I catch sight of myself in the bathroom mirror that I feel a treacherous little pang of doubt.

What is my trap, exactly? After all the planning to get this flat and infiltrate her life, things get a bit vague. I know I want to punish her for what she did. I want to annihilate her for it. But the details of exactly how I'm going to do that weren't yet fixed even before everything with Marcus.

I was going to play it by ear. String out her suffering for as long as possible, before getting her locked up.

Or taking matters into my own hands.

Now, there's a detective involved. Now, we're connected.

Can I use that? I pull a hoodie over my head and wrestle my arms into the sleeves. Can I pin the whole Marcus thing on her?

Risky. There's no way she wouldn't grass me up, too. But if I spin the story, if I make it look like she killed him and then forced me to help her get rid of the body…?

I might do a few months. A year or so, possibly. But Diane? She'd be sent down for life. It would be deserved, too. It would be just.

She is a killer, after all.

Getting a copy of her keys was easy. She gave Ronan a set so he could let himself in, and I got him to make duplicates for me.

He knows I'm out to get Diane. He doesn't know why, and I'm not sure he even cares. It's possible he loved her when they were together, but I had to talk him into their current arrangement. He finds her difficult to be around, but he was desperate to please me and win my affection.

I thought I had him under control. I thought he was on a tight leash. But the rattle of his snoring through the wall tells me how naïve I've been.

It's raining lightly when I step outside, a cold drizzle that baptises me, washing me clean of sin. I raise my face to it, eyes closed, mouth open, drinking it in. Then I hurry up the stone steps and slide my stolen key into the front door of the tenement building.

. . .

A pale ghost of my reflection stares back at me, half-there in the door's dirty glass. My hair is a mess. There are smudges of black under my eyes, dried tracks of tears.

I push on inside. The air in the close is thick and pungent, like someone has left bags of rubbish out on one of the floors above, and the smell is seeping down through the stairwell.

I hold my breath as I jab the key at the lock on Diane's door, hands shaking.

And then, the key goes in. The door opens, revealing the space beyond.

The breath I've been holding escapes me as a soft, whispered, 'What the hell?'

This isn't just her hallway. It's mine, too. The door is in a different position, but the narrow corridor stretching out in front of me is identical to the one in my flat. Same pastel green walls. Same grey vinyl flooring. Same lightshade hanging from the ceiling.

The smell of paint still lingers. I get the feeling that, if I reached out and touched the walls, I'd find them tacky.

I don't, though. I'm suddenly gripped by the feeling – no, by the knowledge – that touching anything would be a very bad idea.

The door closes behind me as soon as I step inside. I consider turning around and leaving, but my curiosity isn't having it. It leads me down the hallway, stopping at every room to peek inside.

I come to the bedroom first, and the sight of it freezes me to the spot.

That's my duvet cover. Those are my pillow cases. Not just similar, but the same. Identical.

The rest of the décor matches, too. Same light grey walls. Same bedside lamp. Same everything.

The hallway feels like it's getting narrower as I continue down it, as if the building itself is closing in around me, tightening its grip.

I check the bathroom. Same blue walls. Same shower curtain. Same pyramid of the same toilet paper standing in the corner.

The cold tap in the washbasin drips, just like mine does. Something about that fact cuts through the growing thunder of my heartbeat. Something feels off.

I step inside and tighten the handle on the tap. Unlike mine, this one stops dripping immediately.

My skin prickles at this attention to detail, and I retreat back to the narrow confines of the hall.

I should get the hell out of here. I should leave. This is…

This is…

I don't know what this is. It isn't something I was prepared for. How could I have been?

I need to regroup, rethink. But my curiosity still has other ideas. Rather than head for the exit, I inch on through to the living room. I'm braced for it this time, but the shock of it still hits me like a cold hand on my warm back.

The walls, the flooring, the throws on the couches. They're all the same as mine. It's more than that, though. It's worse.

In my flat, there's a picture on the wall across from the door. It's a stupid illustration of a Highland cow I picked up at a shop on Princes Street, just to make the flat a bit more homely.

It's here, too. Same picture. Same frame. Same spot on the wall.

My eyes creep to the other pictures. Cheap prints picked up around Edinburgh. They're all the same as mine. I remember buying all of them.

A few of them are slightly blurry and less defined, like she's taken photographs of my artwork and printed them out on sheets of plain paper.

I feel as if I'm looking at a work in progress of someone taking over my life. Becoming me.

It's all too much, it's too messed up. I am suddenly filled with the sense that I should not be here. I need to leave. I need to get out of here, get back to my flat, figure out what the hell all this means.

And I'm about to. I really am.

But that's when I see it.

That's when I see the knife.

It sits on the draining board in the small kitchen that's tucked away through the door off the living room. The kitchen cabinets are the same as mine, too, but then I think they always were.

Weren't they? Surely, she wouldn't have gone that far?

I creep closer to the sink. The blinds are closed on the window behind it, but I can see a little gap between two of them, one side slightly raised where she's been peeking out.

The knife is a standard kitchen knife. Six inches long, maybe, with a straight back and a curved blade.

There's blood. It beads on the polished steel. Clings to the curve. Dots the metal of the draining board below it.

What is this?

What has she done?

And just what the hell is she actually capable of?

I thought I knew her. I thought I had a handle on all this. But I suddenly get the sense that I am floundering, far out of my depth, miles and miles from shore.

I shouldn't have come here.

I should have stayed away.

It's when I turn to leave, though, that I notice the fridge. There's a smear of blood by the handle. Not a fingerprint, exactly, more like a scuff mark. The dark red stands out against the yellowing plastic.

I shouldn't be here.

I should go.

I repeat that in my head like a mantra as I shuffle over to the fridge. I don't have gloves, so I cover my hand with the sleeve of my hoodie and grip the fridge's handle.

I pull the door open.

The light blinks on.

And the full horror of what's in there is revealed.

Birds. Mice. Some ravaged and torn apart, others perfectly intact, their glassy eyes gazing up through the condensation-coated plastic of their little Ziploc coffins.

My heart, which has been beating in my throat, now stops. Goes silent. There's only the ringing sound in my ears. It's an alarm, a warning.

Go. Run. Leave. Now.

The eyes of the dead things seem to stare up at me, plead with me, urge me to get away, to save myself, to not end up like them.

I close the fridge and run to the sink, my stomach gripped by a sudden urge to purge itself.

I swallow it back, force it down. I can't be sick. I daren't. She'll know I've been here.

Until right now, I didn't care about that. Part of me wanted her to know that someone had been in, so she'd be uneasy. I wanted her anxious and freaked out. That's why I let myself in last week, when she was in bed. I wanted her to feel vulnerable and exposed, even in her own home.

Now, though, I don't want to leave a trace. I had pegged her as responsible for the accident that killed my parents and left Isabelle in her current state.

But I'd always assumed it *was* just an accident. That she made a terrible mistake that ruined my life, and then she covered it up so she'd never have to face the consequences.

What if she's more than that, though? What if meek, mild-mannered Diane Shelley is a full-blown psychopath?

I hurry through the open-plan kitchen and living room. Part of me is noting that the cushions on the couch are the same as mine, too, but the rest of me no longer cares. Matching soft furnishings now feels like the least of my problems.

I'm halfway down the hall when I hear the bang of the building's front door closing. I skid to a stop, holding my breath, listening to the shuffle of unenthusiastic footsteps in the tenement's close.

My heart starts beating again then. It's deafeningly loud in the silence. So loud that I almost don't hear the other sound, even though I'm listening for it. Even though I'm braced.

Metal on metal.

A key sliding into the lock.

She's here.

Diane is home.

CHAPTER 31

Diane

Dad's lecture is still ringing in my ears when I make it back to the flat. Well, that and the hymn that Mum made us all sing.

She never used to be all that religious. Neither of them were. They always identified themselves as Christians, but only in the loosest possible sense. It's only in recent years, as old age started to creep up on them, that they've begun hedging their bets. They're no longer just Christians, they're *churchgoers*.

Mum seems much more into it than Dad is, but he goes along with it to keep her happy.

I have a lot of issues with my dad, but I've never once doubted how much he loves my mum. I just wish I'd felt even a fraction of it from him myself.

I replay our conversation as I dump my keys in the bowl, shrug off my jacket, and hurry to the bathroom. I've been bursting for a pee since about thirty seconds after leaving my parents' house, but I couldn't face going back in, so I held it all the way home.

Now that I'm close to the toilet and the end is in sight, my bladder is screaming in protest, forcing me to hobble, cross-legged, along the hallway.

Take care of it.
Deal with it.

That's what he said. But what did he mean? What does he want me to do?

Ignore her? Confront her?

Does she even actually know anything, or am I just projecting?

I dash into the bathroom, already hauling at my jeans and underwear. The relief, when I sit, is palpable. I relax my shoulders and let out a long, leisurely sigh. It's genuinely the happiest I think I've been in over a week.

Though I don't really believe in any of that stuff, I find myself singing Mum's hymn below my breath. It's mostly to stop myself thinking about what Dad said and what he might have meant by it.

Take care of it.

Deal with it, Diane.

'He's got the whole world in His hands,' I whisper, reaching for the toilet paper. 'He's got the whole wide world in His hands.'

I wipe. Stand. Reach for the flush handle.

'He's got the whole world…'

My voice tails away into silence. Total, absolute silence.

That's not right.

Something is different. Something is wrong.

I close my eyes, trying to pinpoint what's changed. There's something missing. Something that should be there in the texture of the background.

I don't move. Don't breathe. I just stand there listening for a sound that is only notable by its absence.

And then it hits me.

The tap.

The tap isn't dripping.

There are still water splashes in the basin, but the handle has been turned, shutting off the drip.

Someone has been here.

Someone has been in my flat.

And something in my gut tells me that they still are.

CHAPTER 32

Chloe

'Hello?'

I press my hands over my mouth, clamp them hard, stifling any sound that might otherwise escape.

Her voice is muffled by the walls and the wardrobe door, but I can hear her as if she's right here with me, hiding deep down in the dark.

Her footsteps creak in the hallway. I've heard the exact sound of those steps before, but from below. Now, they're right outside this room.

'Helloooo?'

There's a sing-song tone to her voice. She's not shouting. It's barely more than a whisper, but it's clear that she's searching for someone. She knows someone's here.

She knows *I'm* here.

'Here, kitty-kitty.'

Her voice is clearer now. Louder. It comes from the doorway of the bedroom. I screw my eyes shut, bite my lip below my hand, stay as still and as quiet as I possibly can.

'He's got you and me, brother, in His hands…'

There's something about her singing that makes my skin crawl. The floorboards creak beneath her weight. My hands shake. I choke back the urge to sob.

How did I get here? How did it come to this? How did it all get so out of control?

Diane Shelley isn't the monster I thought she was. I know that now. She's more than that. She's worse.

I should've grabbed the knife. I should've picked up something, *anything* to protect myself with. Instead, I ran away, and I hid, like I did seven years ago when that policeman came to tell me what had happened.

Like I did when I first saw Isabelle lying there on that bed, with all those tubes and cables.

Like I wanted to do when I sat in the front row of that church. When I watched those coffins being lowered into holes in the ground. When I shook those hands and matched those sad smiles and knew that *this was it* and my life, as I'd known it, was over.

I have that same feeling now. The same tightness in my chest, like it's swelling up, filling out, getting ready to explode. The same sense of a black hole opening up beneath me, swallowing me down, down, down into an impossible darkness.

She left me alone then.

Why won't she leave me alone now?

'He's got you and me, sister, in His hands…'

She's right there, right outside the wardrobe. I can hear her breathing, see her shadow as it blocks the narrow strip of light between the doors. The wardrobe moves as she shifts her weight from foot to foot.

And I brace myself for the end.

CHAPTER 33

Diane

I don't really know what I'm doing. There's a panic rising in my chest with every step further into the flat I take. I've taken to shouting out, to singing below my breath – anything to keep my nerves under control and stop me running right back out the front door.

It's that bit that I can't explain. I *should* be running. Or, at the very least, I should be creeping through the place in silence, peeking around doorframes and listening for movement, not calling out. Not singing.

And yet, I'm back mumbling Mum's stupid hymn as I stand in my bedroom, looking the place over. There's no imprint on my bed this time, although it would be hard to tell given how the covers lie tangled on top of it, the pillows pummelled by angry, sleepless fists.

The curtains are open like I left them. Through the grimy window I can see the square of overgrown grass out the back and the lopsided shed that nobody seems to have a key for. A six-inch tall *Funko Pop!* figure – Jeff Winger from *Community* – sits on the windowsill, the lifeless black circles of his eyes watching on, like he's trying to make sense of me.

You and me both, Winger.

I rock my weight from foot to foot, building up the courage to continue on through the flat. Calling out another 'Hello?', I shuffle out of the bedroom, glancing back at the front door in case it's standing open, signalling that whoever was in here has now done a runner.

No such luck.

The living room is empty. Nothing seems to have been disturbed. The knife is still on the draining board, where I left it. I don't like how it feels in my hand, but I pick it up, anyway.

I feel better for having it. And worse.

'He's got the little tiny baby in His hands…'

I check the fridge. It's big enough for someone to hide in. Of course, nobody is. Everything's fine in there. Everything's normal.

There's nobody in the living room, tucked behind the couch. There's nobody behind the curtains. Nobody folded up beneath the coffee table.

My pulse slows. I feel my grip on the knife start to relax. There aren't many hiding places in the flat. If someone was here, then it looks like they've already left.

Unless…

There is one place that I didn't check.

The place where I stuffed Marcus's clothes. The only hiding place there is in an apartment this size.

The wardrobe.

The hymn dries in my throat and dies on my lips. My fingers flex, then tighten around the moulded plastic handle of the knife.

Slowly, keeping as quiet as I can, I tiptoe out into the hall, gaze fixed on the next door along.

The floorboards creak beneath me, but there's otherwise no sound at all as I return to my bedroom. My heart is steady. My hands don't shake.

Take care of it, Diane.

Deal with it, Diane.

My fingers find the little metal doorknob. My reflection watches me from the mirror, silent and stoic in her judgement.

I draw back the blade and pull the door open, ready to thrust, and stab, and slash at anyone hiding in there.

There's nobody. Just clothes, and dust, and shadows.

I close the door again. My reflection almost looks disappointed.

Over on my windowsill, Jeff Winger lies on his side, toppled over.

I run to the window, look out onto the postage stamp of grass. There's nobody there. Just the grass, and the shed, and three high fences blocking it all in.

And the steps, I realise, leading down to the back of the flat below.

Chloe.

CHAPTER 34

Chloe

I can see her standing out there, through the patterned glass. She's bigger than me at the best of times, but now, distorted by the pattern of frosted bumps, she seems enormous. A leviathan. A Japanese kaiju.

Godzilla on my doorstep.

I try to slow my breathing, bring it back under control. My clothes are dishevelled from the mad dash to escape. My hair, already messy, now feels like it's standing on end.

The doorbell rings again, reminding me, like I needed it, that she's out there. *Ding-dong.*

I came in through the back door and immediately felt better being on home turf. If she'd caught me upstairs, I dread to think what she could've done. Down here, though, she doesn't have the same power. Down here, I can call the shots.

I retreat to the kitchen, slide a knife from the block and tuck it behind my back. Diane knocks on the door this time, a slow, steady *thud-thud-thud*. Keeping the knife concealed, I head along the hallway, arranging my expression into something friendly and relaxed.

'Diane!' I cry when I open the door, maybe overegging it a bit. 'How are you feeling? Work said you haven't been well. I would've come up to see you, but I didn't know if you'd be sleeping, or…'

Her silence interrupts me. It's so heavy, so calculated, that it cuts between my words, slicing off the end of my sentence.

She's not smiling. That, in itself, is unusual. Smiling is generally her default. Apologetic smiling, embarrassed smiling, awkward smiling, desperate to please smiling. Aside from when we were wrapping up Marcus's body and burning it, I don't think I've ever seen her without a smile of some sort on her face.

She's not wearing one now, though. Not by a long shot.

She's looking at me. Not staring, because that implies a fixed, steady gaze. Instead, her eyes dart around in a series of tiny twitches, like she's searching my face, scanning it, copying it like she did the pictures on my wall.

That briefly gets me wondering when she was in here. *How* she was in here. But those are worries for another time.

I lean on the doorframe with my free hand. The other keeps hold of the knife behind my back.

'You alright, Diane?' I ask. It's easy for me to sound concerned – I am *very* concerned right now, but for different reasons. 'You still not feeling great?'

'I know who you are,' she tells me.

Her voice sounds different. Flatter. The abruptness of it catches me off guard.

'What? Who?' I ask.

She finishes her scan of my face and looks down. I realise her fingers are twisting together, shifting and squirming like they're fully independent of her. Like they're alive.

'I was really sorry,' she says. It's barely a whisper. Hardly a squeak.

And yet, it echoes around inside my head like she screamed the words in my face.

'What?' I ask, suddenly more aware than ever of the weapon hidden behind my back. 'What did you say?'

'Your mum and dad. Isabelle,' she continues, still not looking at me. Still not daring to. 'I was so sorry.'

There are pins and needles in my legs, like the blood has stopped reaching them. My grip tightens on the doorframe. On the knife.

'I was so sorry to hear about what happened.'

I try to answer her, but I can't speak. I can barely breathe. It's all I can do to nod and mutter a guttural, 'Huh,' that doesn't mean much of anything.

'Isabelle and I were in school together,' she says. 'We weren't friends, exactly, but we shared a lot of classes. I'd seen her just a few months before the accident. At our reunion. She seemed like she was doing well. Always knew she would.'

I can't feel my body now. It's like I'm detached from it, floating a few steps behind, watching the monster on the step and the knife in my hand.

The sound of Isabelle's name in her mouth is an affront. An outrage. It makes me want to scream, to lunge at her, to plunge the knife into her chest and neck, over and over and over again. To bathe in the bitch's blood.

But there are cars passing on the road and people walking on the pavement, and though killing her here would be a fair and fitting revenge, the courts wouldn't see it that way.

And who'd be left to look after my sister then?

'I thought I might go and see her.'

The words snap me back into my body with such force that I eject a spluttered cry of shock.

'What?'

'Isabelle,' she says, meeting my eye. 'I thought I'd go and see her in hospital.'

'No. What? Why?'

'There's a few things I'd like to say to her.'

'Like what?'

She finally smiles. It's not like her others, though. There's no apology in this one, or desire to please. It isn't the smile of someone desperate to be liked.

Quite the opposite.

'That's between me and her,' she says.

I'm about to push her on it when a loud, guttural snore reverberates along the hallway from the half-open door of the bedroom.

Shit.

I try to pretend not to have heard it, but she looks at me curiously, head tilted to one side, like she's waiting for an answer to a question she hasn't asked.

'Uh, new boyfriend,' I tell her.

Her eyebrows rise a fraction of an inch. Even after everything we did with Marcus, I can feel her judging me. Or maybe it's because of all that.

'Fast mover,' she says.

The buzzsaw of Ronan's snoring snortles off into silence, and my heart rate picks up at the thought of him stumbling out of the bedroom in just his underwear, stinking of sweat and of sex.

'Yeah, well, you know…' I say, though it's not really an answer to anything. I nudge the door with a foot, bringing it closer, blocking as much of the hallway as I can.

Diane looks at the shoulder of my arm, the one folded in behind my back. The one holding the knife.

A lifetime seems to pass before she meets my eye again. The smile has gone now. It was so fleeting I start to wonder if it was ever even there.

'I'm sorry again for your loss, Chloe,' she says, taking a step back. The rain, which the angle of the flat had been sheltering her from, now hammers down at her. She doesn't seem to notice. 'You know where I am, if you need me.'

I don't say a word. I daren't. I just stand there in silence, watching as she plods back up the stone steps and listening as she unlocks the front door of the building and carries on inside.

It's only then, as I'm about to close the door, that I spot the dead bird on my doorstep. It's been cut neatly into two mirrored halves, right down the middle.

CHAPTER 35

Diane

I have been here before. In this hospital. On this ward. Standing outside the door to this room.

When? I can't say. I don't remember. But I've been here. I know I have.

Isabelle and I were never friends. Not even close. We weren't so much in school together as in school at the same time. There were no funny encounters between us, no shared tales of bad teachers, or teenage crushes, or wacky school trip adventures.

She wasn't a bully or a victim. She wasn't one of the popular pupils or languishing with me among the nobodies. She was just there, sitting in mid-tier. Ironically, that made her one of the most forgettable kids of all.

I'd seen her at the reunion a few months before the accident. It was the first time I'd thought of her in years. It would not be the last.

We didn't speak that night. We didn't speak again. I don't recall how I felt when I discovered she'd been in the car that day. The medication and therapy have dulled the memory. Did I feel worse? Could I have?

Was that what triggered the full breakdown and the months of rehabilitation that followed?

I'd always thought, until today, that I'd pulled over. I would've sworn I stopped and looked in at them, that I saw their faces, the blood and the life draining out of them. The saggy marshmallows of the airbags. The glass, like precious gems, across their laps.

Until today, I'd have sworn I'd tried to help them.

But whether it's the effect of the tablets wearing off, or just the fact my mind is so full with thoughts of that day, I'm not so sure now. I thought I had it fixed, that I had logged it all in the ledger of my brain, but some of those memories now don't feel like memories at all.

I think I drove on. I think I left them. I think my panic screamed at me like it was an external voice, warning me that we had to get going, had to get away. Urging me not to look back at the damage that had been done.

That version is true. I can feel it deep down in my gut somewhere. I wish it wasn't. I wish the version I used to believe was the right one. I feel like I wanted to stay with them. To look them in the eye, and hold their hands, and say how sorry I was.

But that voice in my head wouldn't let me.

I've been here before, I'm sure of it. Outside this room. Maybe I came to apologise then. Maybe I came to ask Isabelle for her forgiveness.

I wish I could remember. I wish I hadn't taken all those pills for all those years. I wish things were different.

I'd know if I ever stepped inside or if this is as far as I made it.

She's sleeping when I enter. Of course she is.

The door clicks shut behind me. It sounds far too loud, like the slam of a prison cell. My breath catches at the noise, and I stand there, frozen, like it might jolt her awake.

It doesn't. Of course it doesn't.

Isabelle lies in the bed, covered by a pale green hospital blanket that's tucked neatly around her. Her hair is longer than I remember – though I'm not sure if I even really remember it at all. It's brushed flat across the pillow, combed into submission by nurses who treat her like she might wake up at any second.

She's thinner than I expected. Almost frail. Although, that makes sense given her feeding tube.

Her face is pale and still, slack with sleep or sedation or whatever mix of chemicals they pump into her to keep her alive. One arm rests on top of the blanket, curled gently at the wrist, like it's been posed that way by someone who's trying to make her look peaceful. The other is beneath the covers, its outline barely visible beside the shapeless lump of her body.

The machines around her hum and bleep and throb. A tiny digital heartbeat flickers in green on the monitor beside her head. She's alive. Still. Somehow.

I feel something tighten at the back of my throat. Not a sob, exactly. More like a knot of guilt that's working its way up, trying to choke me.

Her lips are parted. Dry. There's a sheen to them that looks like gloss but is more likely lip salve or ointment. Her eyelashes are dark against her skin. Her chest rises and falls, shallow and rhythmic, like the breathing of someone playing dead.

For a second, I wonder if she *is* faking it. If this is all just some elaborate revenge. If her eyes will snap open in a second, and she'll sit upright, crowing, 'I remember everything,' and damning me for my lies.

She doesn't. Of course she doesn't.

I inch closer. My footsteps are almost silent on the waxed floor, but every breath I take feels loud enough to rattle the windows. I stand beside her, look down at her face, trying to find some trace of the girl I went to school with.

There's nothing there. Nothing I recognise. Nothing I understand. Just this... damaged woman, frozen in time, like her soul got encased in amber seven years ago and has been trapped there ever since.

Seven years ago. The day I hit her.

There's a padded chair beside the bed, jammed into the corner of the small private room. I lurch towards it, head spinning as the memories of that day once again come bubbling to the surface.

I can smell the alcohol on my own breath. My eyes are heavy. The whole world is fuzzy around the edges.

How drunk was I? Are these memories accurate?

Why the hell did I get behind the wheel of that car?

The wipers. The rain. The voice on the radio.

'Three. One. Two. One.'

Isabelle's father's face, beside me, through the glass. Looking up. Angry. Scared. Something about it is wrong. Something doesn't make sense. But there's no time to dwell on that. No time for anything.

Headlights.

Thunder.

Got to go, got to go!

Get a grip, Diane. You can't do anything! You can't save everyone!

Got to go, got to go, got to go!

'I'm sorry,' I blurt, then I bite down on my lip, silencing myself, like I'm worried she might hear me. If she hears me, she'll know what I did. She'll know what sort of person I really am.

And I don't want anyone to know that. Not even me.

I put a hand on hers. I expect it to be cold to the touch, but it isn't. She's warm. Warmer than I am.

'I'm sorry about what happened to you and your family, Isabelle,' I say, covering my tracks.

I give the hand a squeeze. She doesn't react.

Of course she doesn't.

Then I adjust the angle of the chair to give myself a better view of the door.

And I wait.

CHAPTER 36

Chloe

She's sitting there, in the corner, when I enter the room. Lurking like a spider at the edge of its web, ready to pounce on its tangled prey.

Is that what this is? A trap? It has to be. She must've known I wouldn't let her come here alone. She certainly doesn't look surprised to see me.

'Took your time,' she says.

I don't answer her right away. Instead, I check Isabelle's monitor, watch for the rising and falling of her chest, look her over to make sure she hasn't been hurt in some way.

'What do you think I am?' Diane asks when she realises what I'm doing.

'I don't know,' I tell her, taking the hard plastic chair from behind the door and placing it across the bed from her. Isabelle lies between us, eyes closed, ventilator clicking with every breath it feeds her. 'You tell me.'

She looks away, across to a blank patch of wall where a window might reasonably be expected to be. Seconds pass as she stares at it, like she can see through the imagined pane of glass to a brighter world beyond.

'Listen. Chloe.'

She's still looking at the wall, and I get the feeling that she's building up to something. If she is, she's in no rush to get there.

'Yes?'

'It's been a messed-up couple of weeks,' she says, finally giving me her full attention. 'You moving in. Everything that happened afterwards. It's been a mess. And…'

Her gaze darts away again, but only long enough for her to sigh.

'I don't handle messes well,' she says.

I don't say anything, just leave space for her to talk. I want her to own up to what she did. That's all I need now. No more games. No more trying to unravel her life. She's too dangerous for that.

I just want her to admit what she did, out loud, so I can hear her saying it.

'I've got a confession to make,' she tells me.

'Oh?'

We both lean in a little closer, narrowing the gap between us. We're eye to eye across my sister's motionless form, and, for a moment, the beeping and clicking of her life support is the only soundtrack to the room.

Diane chews her bottom lip, eyes widening, like she's about to burst into tears. She swallows. She opens her mouth.

I lean in closer. When she speaks, it's barely a whisper.

'I don't have a cat.'

The remark catches me by surprise. I blink and stare at her in confusion. 'What?'

'Cowboy Meowboy. I-I said I had a cat. But I don't,' she explains, and I watch the pink tinge of embarrassment creeping up her cheeks like a rising tide. 'I just… I said I did that first day because I wanted to go, but I didn't want to seem rude, so I made up an excuse. I made up a cat. I'm sorry, I shouldn't have lied to you.'

She's being so sincere about it that I laugh. I can't help it. It's all too absurd for me not to. She starts to smile, too, and chuckle a little, but I can tell she doesn't quite know what's so funny.

'I know you don't have a cat, Diane,' I tell her. 'I saw your fridge.'

She winces, but there's a smile mixed in with it, like she's owning up to some mortifying mishap. A wardrobe malfunction, maybe, or an ill-timed fart.

Like she's *Wacky old Diane, always up to her antics* instead of a killer who keeps dismembered animal corpses in chilled plastic bags.

'I don't really know what that was about,' she admits, and something about the way she says it makes me believe her. 'I take things too far sometimes. It's always been one of my problems. I lied about having a cat, and then I sort of felt like I had to keep up the deception. I didn't want you to know I'd lied to you, and since I didn't have a cat, I thought I could just sort of… leave evidence. I just… I just wanted you to believe me.'

She looks away again, back to the window that isn't there. She's insane. There's no doubting that now.

'I wanted you to like me,' she whispers.

Like her? After what she did? After everything she took from me? She's even more deranged than I thought. And, after everything I saw today, that's really saying something.

'That's why I stayed when I came to Marcus's house. Not because I'd been sick. I didn't really care about that. I stayed because I thought you needed me.'

I did need her. I don't admit that, though, I just let her talk.

'But then I realised something wasn't right. Bumping into you on that night out. You going to my parents' house. Sitting with them. Lying on my bed.'

That last one surprises me. I had no idea she knew about that. She wasn't meant to. I don't even know why I did it.

'I tried to tell myself you were just being clingy, after everything. Maybe you were grateful for my help and didn't quite know how to show it. Maybe that was all it was.'

She drags her eyes away from the imaginary window and meets mine.

'But then I found out who you were. That's when I knew what all this was really about,' she tells me, and there's a weariness about her, like every word is a struggle. 'How did you work it out?'

I shrug, like it was no big deal. Like I didn't dedicate five years of the last seven to finding out who was responsible.

I consider not telling her. I should leave her wondering, let her dwell on it, let her stew.

But I can't help myself. I want her to know how clever I've been. Part of me, for whatever reason, wants her to be impressed.

'You came here six months after the accident,' I tell her, and I note the fleeting look of surprise that darts across her face. 'I didn't know who you were, but you came back, and I followed you.'

'I don't remember,' she tells me.

'Yeah, well, it happened. I dug around, found out that you were in school with Isabelle and thought that's all it was. I sort of forgot about you for a while.'

The chair is becoming uncomfortable. She watches me as I shift around in it.

'Then I saw you at the graveside. My mum and dad's, I mean. You were with someone. A guy. Older.'

'My dad,' she mumbles, though it sounds like a guess. I get the impression she doesn't remember this occasion, either. Or she's pretending not to, at least.

'I hung back and watched you. You seemed really upset. Like, *way more* upset than you should've been,' I tell her. Her face stays blank. Emotionless. 'I thought it was weird, so I did some more digging.'

I stand up. My bum's about to fall asleep, and I need to jiggle the blood back into my legs. She tenses, as if she's expecting me to fly at her, hands grabbing for her throat or gouging at her eyes.

I wouldn't do that, of course. Not here. Not in front of Isabelle.

'You stopped posting on Facebook the day of the accident,' I tell her. 'That was what started me thinking. Nothing on Facebook, nothing on Instagram, nothing on Twitter. You'd been pretty active before then. I learned a lot about you from the stuff you used to share.'

I give that a minute to sink in before I go for the jugular.

'That's how I knew I could use Ronan to get close to you.'

That one hurts her. She flinches, and I swear for a second she bares her teeth at me.

'He doesn't love you,' I tell her, twisting the knife. 'He doesn't even like being around you.'

She swallows and grips the arms of the chair. She almost cries, I think. Almost, but not quite.

I could keep going. I could keep hurting her, breaking her down. But there's a pang of something in my chest. Something heavy that pins me down and stops me going for the kill.

Guilt?

Surely not.

Not for her. Not after what she did.

'I see,' she says. That's it. Nothing more than that. No hysterics, no drama, no wailing or gnashing of teeth. Just those two words.

'Why did you paint your flat like mine?' I ask her, lowering myself back onto the hard plastic chair.

'Why did you break in?' Diane fires back.

'I didn't break in. I had a key.'

She flares her nostrils. 'OK. Why did you enter without my permission?'

'Would you have let me in?'

Diane shrugs. 'Maybe.'

It's my turn to look away this time, shaking my head, making it clear that I don't believe her.

'I just really liked what you'd done with the place,' she tells me, and it's so preposterous a statement that I laugh. She doesn't join in.

'So, you were in my flat, too,' I point out. 'After I decorated. When?'

'Monday. The night I ran out of the call centre. But I wasn't snooping,' she tells me. 'I was just checking up to make sure you were OK.'

'While I was out at work?' I guess.

'While you were sleeping,' she tells me, and the cold, matter-of-factness of it sets my skin crawling.

'That is seriously fucked up,' I say.

Diane nods slowly, not disagreeing. Eventually, she meets my eye again. 'You killed Marcus, didn't you?' she asks.

The question hits me like a sucker punch out of nowhere. It shouldn't have, though. She was bound to have suspected. She'd have been an idiot not to.

'Did he deserve it?' she asks.

My head snaps sharply in her direction. I can feel the response rising up my throat like bile, but I almost choke as I swallow it down.

'Don't worry,' Diane says, reaching into her pocket. She sets a small digital Dictaphone on the bed beside Isabelle's hand, then places two AA batteries beside it. 'I found your recorder. I turned it off.'

I'm tempted to play dumb and deny all knowledge of the device, but if she's smart enough to have suspected I'd hide it there, she's smart enough to see through my attempts to lie about it.

So much for capturing her confession.

'I told you one of my secrets,' Diane says. 'Only fair you share one of yours.'

I don't know why I say it. Even if I live to be a hundred, I'm not sure I'll ever really know. Maybe I think she's the only person who might actually understand.

'Yes. I killed him. Of course I killed him,' I admit. It feels good to get it off my chest.

I think of Marcus's raised voice, and his raised fist. His sneering, and his name-calling, and the tiny flecks of foam at the corners of his mouth.

'And yes,' I tell her. 'He very much deserved it.'

Diane nods slowly, processing this new information. 'Good. I'm glad. That he deserved it, I mean.'

'My parents didn't, though,' I say, and it takes everything I have to stop my voice from shaking. 'Isabelle didn't deserve what happened to her.'

'No,' she agrees. 'No, they didn't.' She taps her fingertips on the chair's wooden arms. 'I wanted to admit it. After it happened. I wanted to turn around and go back, and to sit with them until the paramedics and the police showed up.'

'But you didn't.'

Diane shakes her head, whispers a 'No' so quietly I can barely hear it.

'You drove on. You left them there.'

'Yes.'

I can hear the blood whooshing through the fine, narrow blood vessels in my ears. It's a crashing river. A raging torrent.

'You left them there to die.'

She nods, confirming it. Without the recorder, her confession is for me and me alone. But that's fine. That's enough. It's all I need.

'Even afterwards, I wanted to tell the truth, I think.' She rubs at her forehead. 'It's fuzzy. I don't remember the details. But they didn't want me to.'

'They? Who's they?' I ask.

She hesitates. Her eyes dart left and right, like she's searching for something, then she corrects herself. 'He. My dad. He thought it best if I kept my mouth shut. He got me to shove it all down. Bury it. Pretend like it didn't happen.'

'So, he knew? The whole time, he knew what you'd done?'

'Yes. From the start. From that day,' she admits, but there's something vague about the way she says it, as if she's not quite sure. She rubs at her jaw, like she's developed toothache or is nursing a bruise from a punishing right hook. 'I was hysterical. I went to him. He got me to calm down.'

Her eyes have been glassy, as though she's been watching something unfolding in the distant past, trying to make sense of it. Now, they snap into focus, fixing first on Isabelle and then on me.

'I told him today I wanted to talk to you about everything that happened. He told me not to. He told me I needed to take care of it,' she says, and there's a look of disgust in her eyes, like she's chewing on something unpleasant. 'He said I needed to end it. To sort it out, whatever it takes.'

I don't miss the meaning behind her words. It's impossible not to grasp what she's getting at.

'OK,' I say. She's sitting perched in the seat, tensed, upright, ready. I wish I still had that knife with me. I'd feel safer then. 'So, what happens now?'

'We could go to the police,' she suggests. 'But then we'd both go to jail, and I don't think that's what either of us wants.'

'I'd do it, if it meant putting you away,' I tell her. She dismisses that with a wave of a hand.

'But you haven't. You had all this evidence, you tell me, but you never took it to them. You came after me. You wanted to do this yourself.'

I don't offer up any arguments to that. They'd all sound hollow, if I tried.

'Even when that detective came round yesterday, you didn't say anything, did you?'

'Neither did you,' I point out.

'No,' she says, after a pause. 'Neither did I. But my dad's right. This needs to be over. For both our sakes. I can't keep living like this, and I don't think you can, either.'

Her head jerks like it's trying to look away again, but her eyes refuse to follow suit and stay on me.

'I'm sorry for what I did, Chloe, but I'm not going to just lie down and let you kill me. I wish I could do that, but I can't. I won't. But we both need to end this. One way or another. Tonight.'

I can feel my heart racing, but it's someone else's problem. Inside, the rest of me is calm. Collected. Steady as a rock.

'Where?' I ask. 'Back at the flat?'

She shakes her head. 'Too messy. Not fair on whoever's left.'

There's a faint jingle as she holds up a bunch of keys.

'The call centre. Eight o'clock,' she suggests. 'No one will be there by then except you and me.'

'And then we end it?' I ask.

She returns the keys to her pocket. She rises to her feet. She smiles. It's kind, and supportive, and genuine. The smile of a friend.

'And then, we end it,' she agrees. 'Once and for all.'

CHAPTER 37

Diane

It's Mum who answers the phone. I try not to cry at the sound of her voice and fight to keep a lightness to my own.

'Hey, Mum, how you doing?'

She's caught off guard. I rarely call out of the blue. Not recently, anyway. Not in the last few years. Add in the fact that I rocked up at the house unannounced and then left after the session with Dad, and it's no wonder she's a little thrown.

She doesn't know about the accident. Dad made me swear never to tell her. Not even when I begged him, when I told him how much I needed to talk to her, to feel her arms around me and hear her saying that it was going to be fine, it was going to be OK, and that she loved me, no matter what.

Mum would have made me turn myself in. No question. She's a good person, unlike the rest of us.

'Diane? Is everything alright?' she asks, and I can hear the worry sandwiched between each word.

The light above the doors comes on like a spotlight on the star of the show. Midges and bugs flock to it, swirling in a frenzy, their tiny bodies glinting in the dazzling glow.

'It's fine, Mum. I just… I just wanted to say…'

What did I want to say? Why did I call her? I can't tell her goodbye because she'll think I'm off to kill myself, and I'm not putting her through that. Not after how hard Dad had to work to keep it from her the first time.

She wouldn't understand, he told me. It'd only upset her.

I slide the key into the lock at the side of the doors, activating the automatic mechanism. Both doors glide open.

'I just wanted to say good luck with your jigsaw,' I tell her. 'It looks like a tricky one.'

'Oh, it is!' she says, and I get the sense of her tension easing.

The alarm beeps at me, reminding me I'm on a countdown. I punch in the code as Mum talks about the jigsaw puzzle. About making sure she built Jesus first. About how all the goblets look the same. About how she's thinking of leaving Judas Iscariot's face incomplete and tossing that piece in the bin.

I suggest she finishes the puzzle but maybe draws a moustache on Judas as a more subtle form of punishment. She laughs and says she likes that idea, then tuts when she remembers that he already has a full beard, so it'll be impossible for anyone to tell.

It's nice hearing her laugh. Making her laugh. It feels like a long time since I made anyone happy. I thought I was with Ronan, in our own messed-up way. But, turns out, that was all a lie, too.

I flick the switch that turns on the lights, and the reception area is bathed in a sterile white glow. It's strange seeing nobody sitting at the front desk. Even though I'm a keyholder, it's for emergencies only. Normally by the time I arrive, Lucy is already sitting there, smiling with all her perfect teeth.

Before that, it was Suzy, and then Julie before her.

Why can I remember all of them, and the tiny details of their lives, when so much of my own still feels lost to the mists of time?

Mum's still talking, telling me about the trials and tribulations she's faced while completing around two hundred and fifty pieces of a 1,000-piece jigsaw.

'But, of course, Jesus faced plenty of challenges of his own,' she says.

Were it anyone else, I'd think they were making a joke. Not Mum, though.

'I suppose he did, aye,' I agree, and I hope she can't hear the crack in my voice.

I cross to Lucy's desk, get the key to the stationery cupboard, and unlock it. Despite all the PCs, and all the expensive equipment in the server room, the only security in the place is the alarm system. There are no cameras. No way for anyone to watch or record what happens here.

That's what makes it perfect.

Headlights swoosh into the car park. A black cab, by the looks of it.

'Anyway, listen, Mum, I need to go. I just wanted to say good luck with it.'

'You sure you're OK, sweetheart?'

The concern in her voice almost breaks me. It takes me a moment to compose myself before I can reply.

'Fine. I'm fine,' I insist. 'But, eh, can you tell Dad something for me?'

'Of course. He's next door, if you want me to get him for you?'

'No, no, it's fine,' I say before she has a chance to call for him. 'Can you just tell him those tablets weren't helping?'

'Tablets?'

'He'll know what I mean,' I say.

Outside, a car door closes.

'Bye, Mum.'

I end the call just as the sensor above the front doors activates and they slide apart in opposite directions.

I was afraid that she might bring someone with her. Ronan, maybe. Or her friend, Sarah – assuming she even exists.

But she's come alone.

'Diane,' she says.

'Chloe,' I reply.

She removes her jacket and tosses it onto Lucy's desk. She's wearing a shirt beneath it, the sleeves rolled up like she means business.

'So,' she asks as I lock the doors behind us, 'how do you want to do this?'

Some part of me had been planning to jump her the moment she arrived. On the way over here, I'd thought about some of the ways I could do it. How I could sneak attack her and get the upper hand before she had a chance to respond.

But that wouldn't be fair. She deserves a chance. Far more than I do. That's why I'm here, after all. That's the whole reason for bringing her out here, for doing this. That's why I went to see Isabelle, so Chloe would be so afraid of what I might do next that she'd agree to it.

After speaking to her at the hospital, I think she'd have agreed anyway, but I had to be sure. One way or another, I need this to end. Tonight. And I think she does, too.

We can't get the police involved without our mutually assured destruction, so that only leaves us a couple of options. We can pretend none of it happened, that she doesn't know what I did and I don't know about her. There's no way that's going to happen, though. I don't give a shit about what she did to Marcus. She says he deserved it, and I believe her, I think.

But she loved her parents. She loves her sister. There's no way she's going to let that go. Which leaves us, then, with option two.

A duel, of sorts. To the death.

It sounds absurd when I think of it in those terms, but then why should that be? Neither of us is a stranger to killing, after all.

'I've been thinking, and I don't reckon we should just go at it,' I tell her, returning to the stationery cupboard and reaching inside. 'I'm bigger and stronger than you are. It wouldn't be very fair.'

She bristles at that, like I've insulted her honour. 'Remember, I've killed someone before,' she says.

'So have I. Twice,' I remind her, then I shrug. It's deliberately nonchalant, deliberately intended to rile her up. I feel guilty even as I say it. 'Well, two and a half, if you count your sister.'

She makes a run for me. I whip my hand out of the cupboard, and she skids to a stop with her throat just inches from the pointy end of a large pair of scissors.

She's angry. She hates me. That's good. If she's going to walk away from this, she deserves that satisfaction. I owe her that much, at least.

My phone rings. I wait until Chloe backs off, hands raised, before I take it from my pocket. It's Dad. I reject the call, then turn the phone off, still keeping the scissors raised.

I use them to point to a door on the right of reception. It leads through to the telesales team section. I've never liked going in there. The fabric of the place feels tainted by an odd mix of smug satisfaction and hollow desperation.

'You go that way,' I tell her, then I tilt my head towards the door behind me. Customer support. The training room. Carol's office. Places I'm more familiar with. 'I'll go through here.'

'Then what?' Chloe demands.

Still keeping the scissors held at shoulder level, I check the clock above the doors. It's eleven minutes until eight. There are clocks on the digital displays in both sections of the building, synchronised to the same second.

'We start at eight,' I tell her. 'That gives us ten minutes to get ready.'

She glances at the clock. At the door behind her. At the scissors, held steady in my hand.

'Fine,' she says, picking up her jacket from Lucy's desk. 'Eight o'clock it is.'

CHAPTER 38

Chloe

This is deranged.

Why did I come here? Why am I facing her like this? I want her to pay, yes, but I had a plan, or the majority of a plan, at least. Infiltrate her life, destroy it from within, get her to confess to what she did to Mum, Dad and Isabelle.

Then wave at her from the gallery as she was handed a jail sentence.

That was how this was supposed to end. Not like this. Not with me scrabbling for a weapon in a darkened call centre as a clock ticks down on the wall.

Can I really do this? Can I really kill her?

Marcus was one thing, with his threats, and his hands, and that horrible leering grin. Shoving me, holding me down, tearing at me, telling me how he was going to *teach me a lesson, teach me not to be so fucking stupid!*

But I taught him in the end.

This, though? An organised fight to the death?

This is insane.

And yet, I'm here. I came, even though I knew what I was getting into.

She was sitting in my sister's room, right beside her, right next to all the wires, and the tubes, and the switches, and the pumps.

She was right there, letting me know that she could get to her any time she wanted.

Seven years after almost wiping out my entire family, she could go back whenever she liked to finish the job.

I'm not going to allow that. I won't let her have that power. This ends tonight.

My phone pings. It's a text from Ronan, asking me – no, instructing me – to bring back a Chinese when I'm coming home. Salt and pepper chicken, fried rice. I'm not to forget the prawn crackers.

I turn the phone off and tuck it into a pocket of my jacket that hangs on the back of a chair. There's a phone headset on the desk beside it. I pick it up, wrap the wire around my hands and pull on it, checking the strength. It's thinner than a rope, but thicker than a garotte. It's a weapon of last resort, but better than nothing.

I yank the headset apparatus off the end, then roll the wire into a ball and stuff it in my trouser pocket.

The digital display on the wall ticks down. Eight minutes left.

What the hell am I doing?

My gaze falls on the paper guillotine over on the supervisor's desk.

On the long, razor-sharp blade with the handle on the end.

On the screw fixing it in place.

I check the clock. Seven minutes.

This is deranged.

But I've waited seven long years to have my revenge, and I'm damned if I'm missing my chance.

CHAPTER 39

Diane

I turn the lights on in the corridor but leave the main set off in the customer services department. Those ones are bleakly sterile fluorescent strips that are less a type of lighting than a form of corporate punishment.

Andy Baxter has left his chair wheeled out. Again. I roll it into place so the cleaners don't have to do it in the morning. The place immediately feels tidier. More organised.

I'm still carrying the scissors. There's another pair in the stationery holder on Andy's desk. I take them and hold a set in each hand, fingers looped through the holes so the blades become extensions of my fists.

I take slow, careful swings at the air, keeping my hands well away from my body, and imagine the pointed blade puncturing flesh. Striking bone.

Oh, God. What am I doing? I can't do this, can I?

I have to.

So, they'll do. The scissors. They're good enough.

Five minutes left. I wonder how she's getting on? Has she found a weapon yet? Does she already have her plan in place to kill me? Is she already plotting the details of my demise?

Four minutes.

I want to shout through to her. To wish her luck. But that would be mad, even compared to the current situation. Even for me.

I tiptoe to the tearoom. It's at the back of the building, joining the sales and customer services departments together, like reception does at the front. Two doors lead in and out, and as I step through the one on my side, I detect the faintest whiff of boiled egg.

'For God's sake, Colin,' I whisper, but nobody answers from the half-dark.

There's a streetlight outside the floor-to-ceiling window that takes up most of one wall. I see myself reflected in it and am surprised by how calm I appear. Looking at me, you wouldn't know what I was about to do. Or have done to me. Or however this ends up going.

Colin's newspaper lies abandoned on one of the tables, open to the sports pages. A long list of football scores from the midweek matches takes up a big chunk of the page.

I pick it up, roll it into a tight tube, then take it over to the recycling bin. It's jammed full. There's nowhere to put it.

Bugger.

I head back to my half of the building. Carol has a recycling bin in her office. I'll stick it in there.

I flick the light on in Carol's room, then flick it off again.

Too bright.

I leave the door ajar instead, letting just a sliver of corridor light sneak in. That's better. Softer. Less theatrical.

Not that this is a performance. Not really.

Carol's recycling bin is empty, so I toss the rolled-up newspaper into it, and take a seat behind her desk.

I can see the clock from here through the gap in the door.

Two minutes.

I remember sitting in here two or three years back, when I was still working on the call centre floor, explaining to Carol why my productivity had dropped. Explaining about the medication. About the insomnia. About the brain fog. She nodded along, then asked if I'd considered mindfulness.

Mindfulness.

I smile at the thought. I suppose I'm feeling pretty mindful right now. I don't think I've ever been more aware of my surroundings, in fact. Of the precise tick of the clock, of the weight of the scissors clutched together in one hand. They reflect the light from the corridor, the blades so shiny they look almost surgical.

One minute.

Here we go.

I sit behind Carol's desk and breathe.

In. Hold. Out.

Breathe, Diane. Just breathe.

I think of the faces of Chloe's parents, imagined or not, entombed in that tangle of metal.

I think of the rain, of the rhythmic *thum-thum* of the wipers, of her dad looking out at me, looking up at me through the driver's side window.

Next to me. Beside me. So close I could reach out and touch him as I pass him on the winding, narrow road.

The thought nags at me again through the haze, through the fog of half-remembered memory.

But there's no time to dwell on it. There's no time for anything.

Through the gap in the door, out on the call centre floor, the display ticks over to eight o'clock.

There's no gong, no fanfare, no bang of a starting pistol.

But it's time.

'Right, then,' I say, addressing the empty room.

I sound tired. Even my voice doesn't want me to go through with this.

Even it, I suspect, knows that I don't have a choice.

'Let's get this over with.'

CHAPTER 40

Chloe

It's eight o'clock, and I have no idea what I'm doing. Do we run? Do we charge at each other, shouting and waving our weapons, clashing in reception to swing, and hack, and slash at one another until one of us is dead, like we're two medieval knights settling an argument?

Feels reckless.

I've kept the lights off in this section. Peering through the little window in the door, I can see her side is mostly in darkness, too. The reception area is a brightly lit No Man's Land. Step out into there and I'll be instantly visible. An easy target.

For what, though? It's not like she's sitting through there with a sniper rifle, waiting to pick me off.

Unless she is?

She suggested this place, after all. She's had far more time to prepare.

Shit.

There's no lock on this door. Not even a handle I can jam something against to block it. The desks are too heavy for me to shift on my own, all bolted together in groups of four. The best I can do is to drag a filing cabinet in front of the door. It won't stop Diane pushing through, but it'll at least make a crash to warn me.

That done, I pick up the blade of the guillotine and give it a few experimental swishes. It's like a short sword, and the little whooshing noises it makes as it slices the air are quietly reassuring.

I'm just backing away from my filing cabinet blockade when the lights in reception go out, plunging it into darkness. I peer out through the window but can see nothing now besides my own reflected features picked out by the glow of the digital wall display.

Something shifts in the darkness behind me. I cry out, spin around, swishing frantically with the guillotine blade, my heart thumping in my throat.

There's nobody there. Just my imagination, triggered by the sudden rush of darkness.

Was that Diane? Did she turn the lights out? Or are they on some sort of timer or motion sensor? I don't suppose it matters. Not really.

I tighten my fingers around the plastic handle of my makeshift weapon. It's already slick with sweat. I need to be careful. I almost lost my grip on it. One big swing and it could fly out of my hand, leaving me defenceless.

With the filing cabinet propped against the door, there's only one clear path into this section of the building. If Diane wants to sneak up on me, she'll have to do it through the staff tearoom. I creep up to the door and tuck myself into the corner beside it, wrapping myself in the shadows, the guillotine blade held raised and ready.

If she sticks her head through, I've got her. One quick swing and she's done for. Dead.

I might not be able to get justice for Mum, Dad and Isabelle.

But revenge will be the next best thing.

I wait there in the dark, breathing as quietly as I can, listening for any sign of movement, expecting to hear her creeping across the tearoom, turning the handle, opening the door.

There's nothing.

If she's through there, she's not making a sound.

Is she waiting for me? Does she expect me to come for her?

It makes sense, I suppose. I'm supposed to be the hunter here. I'm the one who's meant to be out for blood.

The handle of the guillotine blade becomes more slippery in my hand as panic surges through me. My breath catches. My legs shake. I want to go. I want to get out of here. I don't want to do this.

But then I think of my mum and dad crushed in that wreckage.

I think of my sister trapped in that hospital bed.

I think of a fifteen-year-old girl, waiting forever outside a leisure centre, shivering in her shorts and T-shirt.

But that girl is long gone. There's only *this*, now. There's only me.

My grip tightens. My legs steady.

And I emerge, like a monster, from the shadows.

CHAPTER 41

Diane

There is a hatch that leads down into a space beneath the floor, where all the cables criss-cross around the building. I've seen Stewart, the IT guy, clambering around down there before. It would be the perfect way of infiltrating the other side of the building.

I just wish I could remember where it was.

Instead, I'm tucked away beneath a desk, the chair pulled in, my scissor-fists ready for whatever comes next.

I don't know why I chose to hide, exactly. It wasn't part of my plan. I thought I'd stride out to confront her at the stroke of eight, all noble and ready to face my fate.

But here I am, knees folded up to my chest, heart thrumming so fast it's like one constant modulating beat, rising and falling but never taking a break.

I'm a coward when it comes down to it. I was a coward back then, running from the terrible thing I'd done. And I'm a coward now, all these years later, no matter what lies I might try and tell myself.

I don't want to die.

But I deserve to.

I don't want to kill Chloe.

But I will, if I have to.

There's a creak. A door opening. The staff tearoom.

She leaves the lights off. The glow from the corridor doorway takes the edge off the darkness, but there are still plenty of shadows to hide in. She'll find me, but not for a while. Not yet.

'I know you're in here,' she says.

Her voice sounds small and far away, as though she's down at the end of a long tunnel. The room isn't big enough for how distant she sounds, though. My ears are playing tricks on me.

'Come on out, Diane. You said you wanted to do this. This was your idea.'

She shouldn't talk. It helps me pinpoint her. She's moving, passing in front of Carol's office now. I hear the door click as she nudges it open to peek inside.

Could I rush her now? Would I have time to get to her before she heard me and turned around?

I take too long to think about it. She's moving again, tiptoeing through the rows of desks. Past where Bibi sits. Past Colin's desk. Past Fraser's, and Gordon's, and Sophie's, and Ben's.

Closer, and closer, and closer to my hiding place.

She's stopped speaking now. She's no longer announcing herself. Did she somehow pick up on my thoughts? Is she somehow listening inside my head?

I tell myself not to be ridiculous. She's not magic. She's nothing supernatural. She's just a woman. She's probably more scared of me than I am of her.

Or is that bees?

I can see her now through the forest of furniture legs. Her trainers are scuffed and dirty, but still white enough to stand out in the gloom. I track her as she picks her way across the office, aisle by aisle, row by row.

Closer, and closer, and closer.

And then, one row over, she steps behind a small filing cabinet and vanishes from view. I hold my breath, waiting for her to reappear on the other side. But she doesn't.

I wait, counting the seconds in my head, not moving, not daring to. I wait for almost a minute, but her feet don't re-emerge.

Where is she? Is she just standing there, perfectly concealed from where I'm sitting?

She can't be. If she was, if she'd picked that exact spot to hide, then that would mean she knows precisely where I am.

I hear a creaking, but there's no sign of movement. A table leg clunks like the floor has shifted beneath it.

The hatch? Has she found the hatch? My eyes creep to the floor, just as the next desk along lets out a low, pained-sounding groan.

Above me. She's above me!

I look up through the cable hole in the desk, and she's there, looking down, looking right at me! A blade comes stabbing down, slicing through the wires, narrowly missing my head. I roll clear, throwing myself sideways, colliding with the chair and sending it spinning on its castors across the carpet tiles.

The roll is clumsy, and it's a miracle I don't impale myself on the scissors. One pair fold back beneath my fist. Pain explodes through my left hand as something goes *pop* between my knuckles.

It burns all the way up to my wrist, but I can't worry about it now because she's already pulling her weapon free.

It's a sword. Where the hell did she get a sword?!

From down here, she's a giant. Even when she jumps down from the desk, shaking the floor around me, she seems huge.

I expect her to say something. She doesn't.

I expect her to hesitate.

I'm wrong.

She swings with the sword, bringing it straight down, slicing through the air towards my leg. I manage to jerk it free, and she hisses when the blade strikes the floor. I kick out. Once. Twice. The first time finds air, the second hits something solid. Her leg. She stumbles, buying me time, giving me a moment to haul myself up on the desk.

My left hand is, not to put too fine a point on it, fucked. The scissors hang limply from my broken or dislocated fingers. I'm not sure which. It doesn't make much difference. The hand is no good. I'm down to one weapon.

I hear the whumming of the blade arcing through the air. I stagger away. I'm not quite fast enough, though. Pain draws a line through my ear, spattering blood across my cheek.

Off balance, I collide with a desk. Instinctively, I grab for it, but it's the useless left hand and there's no strength, no grip, only pain. The scissors slip from my swelling fingers and clatter to the floor.

I turn, throwing a wild swing with my right. The fine features of Chloe's face flare in sudden panic as the scissors scythe past just inches from her head. She grabs my wrist, pinning it, stopping me stabbing at her again. I try to wrench free, but she holds on, her nails digging bloody half-moons in my skin.

She's so fixed on the struggle that she's forgotten the weapon in her other hand. I need to do something before she remembers it.

My injured hand fumbles on the desk. I find the base unit of a phone. The plastic explodes against the side of her head, sending her stumbling away in a spray of jaggy grey shards.

She's bent double. Stunned. Half-blinded.

I tighten my fist, and the scissors the fingers are threaded through stand to attention, like they're ready to serve. Ready for me to finish her.

I kick her, instead. More a shove with my foot, really, pushing her away from me.

She roars. It's the sound of an animal. Her eye is flecked with red. Blood trickles from one nostril, painting her lips in shades of crimson.

I scuttle backwards, arching my whole body, trying to avoid the swing of her blade. The tip scrapes at my stomach through my clothes. It's not deep, but it could've been.

Idiot! Why didn't I finish her when I had the chance?

Because I'm not a killer.

But I am. *I am.* I need to remind myself of that.

Or maybe that's why I'm not fighting back all the way. Maybe I deserve this. Every cut, every broken bone, every laceration. A slow, painful, violent death. Maybe that's only fitting.

She stands there, her sword in hand, half her face smeared in her blood. She looks like a warrior. An Amazon. An agent of vengeance and an angel of death.

All of a sudden, the scissors I'm holding feel fragile, like they're the plastic safety kind meant for a child. They won't stop her. They can't hurt *this*.

She has been hunting me for years, closing in for months, closing the net for the past few days.

There's nothing I can do to stop her. I see that now.

She sees something in me, too. Maybe she really can read my mind.

'Don't,' she hisses. 'Don't you dare.'

But it's too late, I'm already turning, already running. Like I ran away last time.

Got to go! Got to go!

Don't look back!

I sprint for the tearoom, for the back door beyond it. I can get out there, get away.

The glass in the door explodes as Chloe's thrown sword smashes through it. The noise is immense. The air is filled with glittering diamonds that tear at my skin, driving me back.

She hits me from behind, around the middle, and we tumble into Carol's office. My legs hit the desk, but my top half carries on, bending forward, forehead cracking against the corner of the computer monitor.

It's even louder than the sound of the window smashing. There's a flash, a flicker of white, and I'm back on that road, in that car, watching the impact in my side-view mirror. Hearing the screams, even over the roaring of the engine and the shouting in my head.

Shit, shit, shit! Not my fault, that wasn't my fault!

I swing with an elbow, but hit nothing. A fist drives into my lower back. Pain bursts as a bubble on my lips.

She's still making animal sounds. Snorts. Shrieks. I can't tell if they're in my ear, or in my head, just like my own voice. That day. In the car.

Don't look back! Don't you fucking dare look back!

Something slips around my neck and pulls taut across my throat. She hauls me back, drags me up. We stumble together, me clawing at the cord around my neck, her hanging on and screeching in triumph.

My foot finds the bin and we go down hard together, sprawling across the room, her hanging on for dear life.

She's saying something, babbling wildly. My vision goes hazy, like it was that day, like it was back then. I see her face reflected in the window, scared and angry.

Not my fault! It wasn't my fault!

Stop crying! Stop fucking crying!

Get a grip, Diane. You can't do anything! You can't save everyone!

She's crying, I realise. Those noises she's making, they're sobs.

I watch her in the window. She reminds me, in that moment, of her father. I picture him through the glass of the car window. Looking back at me. Looking up.

Up.

Not across.

Colin's newspaper lies sprawled on the floor beside my head. I can barely see, and I could be imagining it, but the page swims into focus.

Two-one.

Four-two.

Three-nil.

Football scores.

Chloe's father is looking up at me through his window. Through my window. We're separated by seven years and sixteen inches.

My hands aren't gripping the wheel – they're on my knees, the nails digging in.

Headlights. A car rounds the corner, through the rain, through the dark.

Shit, shit, shit!

The words aren't in my head, they're spoken out loud. Bellowed. Screamed.

Seven years. Sixteen inches.

If I was driving, he'd be further away than that.

I try to cry out, but the cord across my throat is too tight. I force my fingers beneath it, prising it away with a newfound strength.

But she hangs on. She doesn't quit. She keeps sobbing as she hauls on the cable, pulling, pulling, pulling.

But I'm bigger than her. I'm stronger.

I heave myself onto my knees. She's on my back, pulling tighter, tighter, tighter.

Seven years and sixteen inches away, her father nods at me, granting his blessing. Urging me on.

Do it, he tells me. *Do what you have to do.*

She clings to me. A limpet. A parasite.

With the last of my breath, and the last of my strength, I heave myself, broken and bleeding, to my feet.

CHAPTER 42

Ronan

The front door opens and closes. About bloody time, too.

'I thought you'd got lost. I'm nearly chewing my arm off here!' I shout.

She doesn't answer, but I hear her stop to lock the door behind her.

'You'd better have remembered the prawn crackers,' I say as she comes shuffling along the hall towards the bedroom. 'Grab a plate, will you? I'll just have it in here, then we can get back to—'

I spring out of bed at the sight of her. At the state of her. At the blood, and the bruises, and the look on her face.

'What the fuck? What are you doing?' I say, looking her up and down. 'What are you doing here? Where's Chloe?'

Diane looms in the bedroom doorway. Her breathing is laboured. There's a deep red welt across her throat, blood on her ear, and her left hand looks like a bunch of bananas that are on the turn.

She looks like something from a nightmare. I mean, she has done for a few years now, since she lost her mind and let herself go, but she's really upped her game tonight on the horrifying front.

'It was you, wasn't it?' she says.

Her voice is hoarse and raw, like every word has to crawl through broken glass to reach me.

'What are you on about? What was me? Where's Chloe?'

I make a move towards her, clenching my fists. I used to settle for an open hand, but that was mostly to keep bruising to a minimum and avoid too many questions.

Given the state of her, a few more aren't going to be noticed.

She raises something sharp and metallic, like a short sword with a plastic handle, and points it between my eyes.

'Don't,' she says, and I stop a few feet from the door.

It's not that I'm scared of her. I could take her with my eyes shut. She'd be on her knees, begging me for mercy.

But there's something in her eyes. Something about the way the red line across her throat seems to curve upwards, like it's a smile. Like it knows something I don't.

'I thought it was me,' she says, lowering the blade again.

Her fingers flex, then tighten. I hear the plastic creaking in her grip. She's looking straight at me, but it feels like she isn't actually seeing me at all.

'You made me think it was me.'

'What are you talking about? Where's Chloe? What the fuck have you done with her, you mad cow?'

'Do you know why she did all this?' Diane rasps. 'Why she came here and tried to ruin my life?'

I shake my head and shrug. 'She never mentioned,' I say, and the look of hurt on her face makes my whole night.

'She didn't tell you?' Diane's brow furrows, like she's trying to process this. An egg-sized lump on her forehead seeps blood that trickles down over an eyebrow. 'You agreed to help her – you pretended to care about me – and you didn't even know why?'

I laugh at that. It's a sharp, sudden bark that makes her draw back in fright. The sword, or the knife, or whatever the hell it is, shakes in her hand.

I'm right not to be scared of her. She's right to be terrified of me.

'I never pretended to care about you, Diane. I shagged you, that was all. I gritted my teeth, and I shagged you.' I can tell that every word stings her. 'Because nobody else would go near you. I mean, look at you. Have you seen yourself? Not just tonight, I mean, which is a whole other level, but in general?'

I take a step forward.

She shuffles back.

'You're a mess, Diane. You used to be fit, but look at you now, you—'

'She's their daughter.'

It takes me a second. Just a second, maybe less, to understand what she's saying. Even so, my brain isn't ready to accept it.

'What? What you on about?'

'In the car. That day. She's their daughter.'

My throat makes a clicking sound as I swallow. It seems unnaturally loud in the silence of the basement flat.

'The car you hit?'

She shakes her head. This time when she looks at me, I'm fully in her focus.

'The car you hit,' she says. 'You were driving, Ronan.'

I sigh. Tut. Roll my eyes. Remind her that she's stupid, remind her that she can't be trusted to do anything right.

'That's not what happened, Diane.'

'I was too drunk. I'd never have driven.'

'You did.'

She turns her head a little to the left, like she's seeing something there. 'He was right there. On my left. I saw him, looking at me. Looking up. We were in your van.'

'No. No, that's wrong. Shut up. You're getting confused again, Diane.'

'I *was* confused,' she says. Her eyes blur, then tears cut shiny red through the dried blood on her face. 'But now I'm not.'

She looks to the left again, even though there's still nothing there. I shuffle closer, but she doesn't notice, doesn't react. The blade she's holding is still lowered.

'He was too close. His car was right beside me, right next to me on the road. So I had to be in the passenger seat. I had to be.'

'You weren't, Diane. Trust me. You're making this up.'

'Trust you?' It's her turn to laugh. More tears come. The blade shakes in her hand. She's unravelling before my eyes.

Silly cow.

'You had the radio on. Football scores,' she says. The dry rasp of her voice has become wet now, all snot and tears. 'I remember. I wanted to stop, but you wouldn't let me. You'd been drinking, too. You didn't want to lose your licence or end up in jail.'

'This is bollocks!' I bark the words at her, startling her again. Shocking her back from whatever imaginary la-la land she's been drifting off to. 'You were driving the car, Diane. You crashed into them. We've been over this a thousand times!'

'Did you beat it into me?' she asks. 'Is that what happened?'

Her face is puckered. The glistening snot on her lips turns my stomach. She's so pathetic that I don't even bother keeping up the pretence.

'Of course I fucking did!' I roar the words at her, savouring the fear it brings to her eyes. 'Because you couldn't get the story straight! We had to go over it, again and again, until you stopped fucking it up!'

She comes running at me then, raising the sword. I sidestep her easily, then catch her with a jab that sends her spiralling onto the bed.

The sword thing thumps to the floor. I consider picking it up, but just kick it out of her reach, instead. It's not like I'll need it. She's barely got the strength to stand.

And she's never really been much of a fighter when it comes to it.

My jeans lie crumpled on the floor, where I kicked them off earlier. I pick them up and slide the belt free from the loops.

'We agreed, Diane, that we'd say you were driving, if anyone found out,' I tell her. The leather belt creaks as I wrap it around my fist. 'We agreed that was better for everyone. It's not my fault you had to go and have a breakdown over it. It's not my fault that you were too weak and pathetic to just get your head down and get on with your life.'

She tries to get up, but I put a hand on her face, shoving her back, forcing her down.

'Now,' I tell her, bringing my face in close to hers. So close that she's forced to blink through my flecks of spittle. 'Where the fuck is Chloe?'

She looks to the window, to the door, like she's searching for a way out. An escape. There's no escape, though. She's not getting out of here until I'm done with her. Maybe not even then.

'No. No, look at me,' I say, slapping her on the cheek, focusing her attention. 'Where's Chloe?'

She tries to answer, but she chokes. 'She's…'

I slap her again. Harder this time. Then I press my forehead against hers, forcing her head back until we're face to face, eye to eye on the bed.

'Where. The fuck. Is Chloe?'

'She's—'

Diane swallows. This close up, she's out of focus. And yet, I see her face change. I see the crinkle lines appearing around her eyes, and the upturning corners of her mouth as she smiles.

Her voice is a rasp again, but it almost sounds like laughter.

'She's behind you.'

CHAPTER 43

Diane

There was a time when his scream would have terrified me. This loud, this close, this primal – it would have chilled me to the bone and sent me scurrying for cover.

He jumps back, thrashing wildly, grabbing for the source of his sudden, inexplicable pain. The handles of the scissors stick out of his shoulder blade, just beyond his reach. The blades are in too deep for me to see even the handles from this angle, but I know that's what's happened.

Chloe offers out a hand. I consider it for a moment, then let her help me to my feet. She nods, just once. I return it. Neither of us smiles. It's not that sort of moment.

We both turn to Ronan as he crashes into the chest of drawers, scattering deodorant cans and hair products, spilling make-up and perfume onto the floor.

He twists towards the mirror so he can see his back, and his enraged shouting becomes a high-pitched squeal of horror. Chloe has picked the perfect spot to embed the blades. Even if he could reach far enough to get a grip of them, there's no way he could pull the scissors free without doing way more damage.

There was a time when I would have hated to see him like this, flailing around, sobbing and blubbering, his body wracked with pain.

Aye, there was a time.

He collides with the wall by the window and stops, pulling himself together as best as he can. He considers us both, standing there, side by side, all blood and bruises.

'You psycho bitches. You total psycho bitches,' he rages. 'You're both mental. You're both as messed up as each other!'

'Yeah,' Chloe says.

She turns to me.

I nod.

'Yeah,' I agree. 'Seems that way.'

He unfurls the belt, letting it hang down like a whip. The sight of it dangling like that dislodges another memory that was pinned behind the others.

His leering face. The crack of leather on flesh.

The pain. The shame. The guilt. So many months of it. So many years.

I move without realising. Without thinking. He's too shocked to react, to move, to defend himself as I fly at him, driving my forehead forwards, finding my target between his eyes.

He drops like a puppet whose strings have been cut. He's already coughing and choking when he hits the floor, his hands over his face as blood burbles through the split in his broken nose.

Chloe is staring at me, slack-jawed. I feel my cheeks start to sting red, mortified by what I've done. Or maybe it's at the thought of her judging me for it.

A smile tugs at one corner of her mouth.

'Nice,' she says.

And I mumble out a sheepish, 'Thanks.'

'I'll fucking kill you! I'll fucking kill you both!' he chokes through the blood, and the snot, and the tears.

Chloe bends slowly and picks up the arm of the guillotine. She presses a finger to the blade, then whips it away when it draws blood.

'That's really quite sharp,' she declares, and though she's looking at me, I know the words are for Ronan's benefit.

He looks up at us from the floor, his face a mask of blood, his body twisted to stop the scissors pressing against the wall and digging deeper into his back.

'Look, listen. Listen,' he urges, looking up at Chloe. 'I was there, alright? But it wasn't my fault. I didn't do it! It was her. She was driving, alright? I told her to stop. I told her we should go back to help, but she—'

There's a swishing sound. It's so sudden – and over so quickly – that I'm just starting to think I imagined it when Ronan starts wailing again.

His big toe lies on the floor beside his foot. Chloe is staring down at it with an intense sort of fascination.

'See?' she says, shifting her gaze to meet his again. 'Really quite sharp.'

She turns to me and smiles. There's something almost dismissive about it, but polite, too. Like a party host suggesting I might want to call myself a taxi.

'I think I can take it from here,' she says. She glances up at the ceiling. 'You've got a cat to get home for.'

Something catches at the back of my throat. It's not a laugh. Laughing now, at this, really would make me a psychopath.

So, it's not a laugh. But it's not far off.

'I suppose I should get off,' I say.

Down on the floor, Ronan starts to blurt out a string of protests, begging me not to go, not to leave him with her, not to abandon him.

He looks so scared. So pathetic. My heart aches for him, or maybe it aches for the man I once thought he was.

I hear a voice in my head. It wasn't always in my head, though.

Get a grip, Diane. You can't do anything! You can't save everyone!

I turn to Chloe. I raise my uninjured hand and waggle the fingers in the air like they're claws.

'Meow,' I say.

And then I leave the flat, head upstairs and crank on some music.

And it's almost loud enough to cover the sound of the screams.

EPILOGUE

Diane

'So he looks at me – the doctor – he looks at me, right in the eye, and he says, "How's the dryness? Downstairs." And he points. At my, you know—'

Carol takes a draw on her cigarette for dramatic effect, keeping us all hanging.

'So, I says to him, I says, "Well, I wasn't dry until I stepped in here, you wrinkly old bastard, but I am now!"'

There's an eruption of laughter from the group gathered around the picnic table at the back of the call centre. Colin is the only one who doesn't join in, though even he seems to be struggling with a smirk.

'Dryness,' he mumbles, which leads to the laughter petering out again.

It's a cold, crisp day in December, and we're all wrapped up in jackets and coats. It's Carol's birthday, and we're sharing the cake that she brought in while she puffs her way through a succession of Lambert & Butler's.

Above the back door, the beady eye of the security camera watches on. Head office could be checking up, but Carol doesn't care.

'Let them bloody watch,' she said, as she dragged the picnic table directly into the camera's line of sight. 'See if they dare say a word.'

The cameras are a new addition. They were installed a week after the suspected break-in that happened a couple of months back, when a window was broken and a paper guillotine was partly disassembled. The police were called to investigate, but they were pretty much useless.

That, thankfully, seems to be the norm for the police around here. Nobody has ever followed up about what happened to Marcus. And, if Ronan's wife has reported him missing, nobody has come around asking questions. Then again, if I was her, I probably wouldn't say a word. Good riddance.

I still check the news, but it's a casual flick through once or twice a week now, not an obsessive daily doom scroll.

Maybe they're building a case against us. Maybe DS Brompton will appear at my door one day with an arrest warrant and a set of handcuffs.

Still, I'll cross that bridge when I come to it.

Most of my injuries have now healed, though there's a scar across my stomach, and my left hand aches in the cold.

Dad has given up trying to get me back on the medication.

Mum is still working her way through that jigsaw.

Things are… good. Calmer, certainly.

Sure, things were tense for a while after we got rid of Ronan's remains, but we managed between us, Chloe and me.

It wasn't like we hadn't been practising.

The back door opens, and Carol grins as she stubs out one cigarette while simultaneously lighting another. It's quite the party trick.

'Oh-ho! There she is! Employee of the month!'

Chloe tucks a strand of hair behind her ear and self-consciously dance-walks over to the picnic table. There's no space for her to sit, so I shuffle up, almost knocking Bibi off the other end.

Carol is already on the case, though.

'For God's sake, Colin, shift!' she barks, gesturing for him to make room with a jerk of a thumb. 'You not got work to do, anyway?'

'Uh, yeah. Yes. Sorry,' Colin mumbles, extracting his legs from beneath the table, leaving the spot across from me clear.

Chloe slides into the space he vacated. Her foot bumps against mine, and we both pretend not to notice. It was probably deliberate. It usually is.

'Cake. Here. Have a bit of that,' Carol says.

The cake is still mostly intact. Chloe glances across the table at me as she picks up the knife. For a moment, I see myself reflected in the blade, then she slides it down through the chocolate frosting and cuts herself a slice.

'Where's Emma?' Bibi asks.

Everyone else at the table, besides Carol, looks around. It hadn't really occurred to me that the HR manager wasn't here, but now that it's been mentioned, it does seem odd. It's not like her to miss a celebration.

'She's at home,' Carol says. She tucks her tongue in front of her bottom teeth and moves it around, like she's trying to stop herself saying something.

She fails.

'Called in this morning. Sounded quite upset,' she says, lowering her voice to a conspiratorial whisper. 'Says she'll be off a few days.'

'She sick?' I ask.

Carol raises her eyebrows and takes a draw on her cigarette. 'I don't think she's the sick one, if you know what I'm saying?'

Across the table, Chloe frowns. 'No. What do you mean?' she asks around a mouthful of cake.

There's a little blob of chocolate on her nose. I have to sit on my hands to stop myself reaching over and wiping it off with a 'Boop!'

'Well, you remember how she hurt her ribs a couple of weeks back?' Carol asks. 'Slipped on the stairs, she said. And then she had that bruise on her neck that she apparently got from falling in the shower.'

A hush falls over the table. Carol shoots a look up at the camera, then leans in closer, lowering her voice even further.

'All this started the same time she got herself that new man. That's all I'm saying.'

'Oh, God. That's awful,' Bibi says.

'Terrible,' Lucy agrees.

Across the table, Chloe is looking back at me. The knife is right there, right beside her hand. Between us.

Poor Emma.

The others are right. It is awful. It is terrible. That poor girl, suffering like that at the hands of a violent man.

Someone should really do something.

Someone like me.

I meet Chloe's eye.

My fingers throb with the cold.

'That's horrible,' she says.

'Just horrible,' I agree.

We both turn to Carol.

'You mind sneaking us her address?' Chloe asks.

Beneath the table, her foot brushes against mine. I pretend I don't notice. She knows that I do.

'And we can both pop round there,' I say. 'Just to make sure she's alright…'

A LETTER FROM JD KIRK

Dear reader,

I want to say a huge thank you for choosing to read *The Woman Downstairs*. If you want to keep up to date with all my latest releases, just sign up at the following link. Your email address will never be shared, and you can unsubscribe at any time.

www.bookouture.com/jd-kirk

I hope you had as much fun reading *The Woman Downstairs* as I did writing it. If you did I would be very grateful if you could write a review. I'd love to hear what you think, and reviews make such a difference helping new readers to discover my books for the first time. I love hearing from my readers, so if you want to drop me a line to let me know your thoughts on the book, you can get in touch through social media.

Thanks,

JD Kirk

jdkirkbooks

JDKirkBooks

jdkirkbooks

ACKNOWLEDGEMENTS

It's an interesting thing that, despite having written over two hundred books under a variety of different names over a fifteen-year period, it never fails to amaze me when I manage to stumble blindly through the process of writing another.

Each blank page one always feels like a frightening and insurmountable challenge. '*Who are you to think you can write a book?*' a nagging wee voice in my head always asks. For better or worse, depending on who you ask, I've always managed to ignore it.

Writing a book is both a lonely solo task and a collective group effort, and I'd like to take a moment to thank the people who helped make this particular book a reality. I will start, as is only fitting for a book about deranged women, with my wife, Fiona.

To be honest, she's not actually deranged at all, but you'll likely have noticed over the previous few hundred pages that I'm a sucker for a cheap gag. Fiona has supported me, encouraged me, kept me alive and ensured that I continue to function in the real world for a quarter of a century, despite me probably making all of those things quite difficult at points.

Without her, not only would this book not exist, nor would any of the others, as I'd likely have wandered into traffic, got myself locked in a shipping container or inadvertently angered the Yakuza years ago. So, for being my wife, best friend and partner through all life's craziness, thank you.

I would also like to thank my children, but I can't, because they've been nothing but a distraction from day one.

The actual pulling together of this book would not have been possible without my editor, Natasha Harding, and the rest of the brilliant team at Bookouture, who helped me sculpt a story from my often wild imaginings, and stopped me wandering too far off tangent.

Nor would any of it have happened without the hard work of my agent, Elizabeth Counsell, whose wise counsel (see what I did there?) is always welcome and appreciated, or the persistence of my assistant, Chrissie Parker, who takes care of all the other work stuff I'm supposed to be dealing with, freeing me up to write. She somehow makes it all look effortless, too.

Finally, to all the many thousands of readers who have followed me across the age ranges and genres, thank you. Without you, all of this would be pointless, and I almost certainly wouldn't have a house.

Best wishes,

JD Kirk

PUBLISHING TEAM

Turning a manuscript into a book requires the efforts of many people. The publishing team at Bookouture would like to acknowledge everyone who contributed to this publication.

Audio
Alba Proko
Melissa Tran
Sinead O'Connor

Commercial
Lauren Morrissette
Hannah Richmond
Imogen Allport

Contracts
Peta Nightingale

Cover Design
The Brewster Project

Data and analysis
Mark Alder
Mohamed Bussuri

Editorial
Natasha Harding
Nadia Michael

Copyeditor
Janette Currie

Proofreader
Lynne Walker

Marketing
Alex Crow
Melanie Price
Occy Carr
Cíara Rosney
Martyna Młynarska

Operations and distribution
Marina Valles
Stephanie Straub
Joe Morris

Production
Hannah Snetsinger
Mandy Kullar
Nadia Michael
Ria Clare

Publicity
Kim Nash
Noelle Holten
Jess Readett
Sarah Hardy

Sales
David Murphy
Jess Harvey

Typesetting
Ramesh Kumar Pitchai